Best Laid Plans:

A Hood Misfits Novel

Best Laid Plans:

A Hood Misfits Novel

Brick & Storm

www.urbanbooks.net

Urban Books, LLC
300 Farmingdale Road, NY-Route 109
Farmingdale, NY 11735

Best Laid Plans: A Hood Misfits Novel

ISBN 13: 978-1-945855-95-5
ISBN 10: 1-945855-95-9

First Mass Market Printing January 2019
First Trade Paperback Printing February 2018
Printed in the United States of America

10 9 8 7 6 5 4 3 2 1

Distributed by Kensington Publishing Corp.
Submit Orders to:
Customer Service
400 Hahn Road
Westminster, MD 21157-4627
Phone: 1-800-733-3000
Fax: 1-800-659-2436

Prologue

Jewel

Help Me . . .

I wish I were dead. Already, my body had become a husk, so why not the rest of me? *I wish I were dead.* My worth was now nothing but good enough to fuck, to sell, to cause chaos and death. I was nothing but an object now.

Bang, bang, clang. Cri-eeeeek, bang, bang, clang.

The springs of the dirty mattress pressed against my spine. I felt sick to my stomach and my body responded in kind. Vomit slipped from the corner of my cracked, swollen lips; piss soaked into the wet, already-dingy bed now that he was out of me. Forget the fact that I was soaking wet with a mixture of his sweat and mine from the heat, because there was no air conditioner in the house, and his sex. His anger was like the devil himself. He hated when I messed myself. That was why he threw over my body a bucket of scorching water that was sitting on a radiator.

Now he was back. His sinister hands were all over me. Now he was back to bring me nothing but pain. Tears falling so much that all I could see was the glossy haze of a nigga I wished I could kill with my bare hands. But I couldn't. He was too smart for that. Around my wrists this time were ropes that sliced against my flesh. He said it made it easier for me to give up the pussy that way.

I hated him. *Help me.*

I couldn't believe that I'd thought I loved him. Why was I so stupid? He was nothing but a liar and monster. He made me forget my own training by my daddy and mama not to fall for the games of a nigga coming for your excellence. By "excellence" they didn't mean my body by itself but all of me: my spirit, my mind, my soul. But, I didn't listen. Couldn't listen.

All I saw were his words on the computer screen:

You're beautiful.

Damn, why are you so pretty?

I bet you have all the niggas around you wanting you. I wish you were with me.

I wish I could kiss those lips and feel that waist.

I bet you taste like bubblegum.

Let me see you.

Let me near you.

We need each other.

I can give you everything you want and not what your daddy gives.

Tell me your address.

Leave me those digits.

We can go wherever you want.

This is me and you and we're one.

Be my ride or die.

Come live with me.

You're a sexy little mama. You don't need your daddy.

Your mother would want this.

She'd love the type of prince you have.

Leave with me.

I need you.

His touch, the gifts of money and whatever I wanted, and the way he looked at me as if I were his universe were all I needed to give myself to him. I felt right leaving with him and loving him, but I was fucking wrong. He claimed all of me, and made it into what he wanted: his fuck piece, whore, and bitch he hated because of some blood running through my veins. Orlando.

I despise him. Help me.

My body screamed at the weight on me, at the pain scissoring in and out of me due to the stupid choice I made by hooking up with the wrong nigga. I wished I were dead and I wished I had listened to Daddy and that he were here to protect me like he always did. But, above all, I wished I were home, back with my mama, eating her famous red velvet cupcakes and feeling her arms wrapped around me in love and protection.

God. I wish I were dead. God forgive me.

I figured God must have heard me. My captor stopped his assault on my body. I looked toward the nightstand. Saw the phone that I so desperately wanted to reach.

"Ugh. You stink," he spat at me. "That water didn't help nothing."

His cold gaze searched my body. I could barely make him out through the tears and my injured eyes. Everything that I'd thought was sexy about him repulsed me now.

"I'ma untie you just so I can wash your funky ass, but you bet' not try no shit this time," he warned.

I gave a nod. At least, I thought I did. I wasn't so sure my head could even move. My heart raced as I watched him grab a black hunting knife then walk over to cut the rope from my left hand. I felt my body shiver as he straddled me then freed my right hand. I could barely contain my desperate need to get to that phone as he freed my feet.

Without even thinking, I drew strength from somewhere and kicked him in his dick. He howled. The knife dropped to the floor as he grabbed his nuts. I made a mad dash from the bed to the nightstand. I needed that phone.

"You fucking bitch," he roared behind me.

I fell out of the bed scrambling across the floor. I'd no idea where my energy had come from, but I took advantage of it. My whole body ached. My private area screamed for reprieve. I yelled, kicked, and screamed as I raced on my knees to the nightstand. I could feel my captor closing in on me just as I made a leap for the phone.

He grabbed my left leg, nails digging into the skin. I drew back with my right and kicked him square in the nose. That sent him flailing on his back. I couldn't explain what came over me when I saw that it was my phone that had been on the nightstand. I pressed the emergency speed dial button and watched my daddy's face light up the screen.

While my captor tried to get his bearings about him, I yelled into the phone, "Daddy, Mommy, I'm so sorry—"

My words got cut off as a meaty fist to the face stunned me.

"Aahhhhhh!" I cried out.

Nothing but blackness and stars now. I should not have whispered that plea.

"Help me," was the last thing I remembered hearing.

Chapter 1

Antonio

July 2012 . . .

"I need your help."

The fragrant scent of various spices, rum, and tobacco flowed around me in a breeze. A crash of waves, warm rays from the sun soaked into my skin, which would have relaxed me any other time, but today wasn't that day. I was on the brink of madness and I had traveled out of the States just to get the help I wasn't finding back home in Miami.

"Tell me why I should help you," was nonchalantly thrown at me before the subtle sound of drinking started.

Squaring my shoulders, I stood like the proud man I had been raised to be and the warrior I had taken it upon myself to become. The moment I made the choice to fly to Cuba and breach every-thing my mother had worked hard to protect me from was the moment I had decided to shed my responsibilities as an average man, a doctor, and become whatever this man needed me to be. I had to.

I stood there without an ounce of fear in me and stated a saying my mother made sure I knew since I was an infant in her arms: "*La familia es la sangre. La sangre es vida y la vida es la familia.*" Essentially, I had said, "Blood is family, family is life, and life is family."

"Hmm. Pretty words, but do you understand what they truly mean? Or are you just regurgi-tating what you think I would like to hear?"

The man I vaguely recalled from my youth as a child playing on the island of Cuba watched me with no regard. His mannerisms were those of a man who didn't have a care in the world and who, at any second, could end my life if I bored him. Inwardly, a smile played in my mind. In my five years as a trauma surgeon, I had the privilege of patching up men like this as they lay bleeding from either bullet wounds or other injuries.

From my research on this man, who visited me occasionally as I grew up, I knew that he was nothing to trifle with. He was not the type of man you'd make the assumption of labeling like other criminals or kingpins. No. This man was an enigma on his own who deserved the respect to be labeled nothing less than what he was: King Caltrone Orlando. My father.

"I'm not the type of man who would waste your time on pretty words. I am an Orlando. The thirty-two-year-old son of Carmen Ortiz and Caltrone Orlando, and I am here before you because I live those words, nothing more," I explained, keeping hidden for the time being the urgency of the reason I had come.

My father sat back in his chair behind a small table full of various types of food and drinks. He was in casual wear: a white, breezy linen shirt that showed the white beater under it, and white pants. His feet were bare but the mat under them was clean. The sun soaked into his bronze skin.

In his features, I saw my own. We both had the same facial bone structure with firm, large lips. I also had a light beard along my chin. Though he had lighter eyes, and graying curly hair, I had longer, thick hair pulled back into a ponytail with a fade along the sides. It was a texture that was a mixture of my Afro-Cuban ancestry. My eyes were also a nutty light tone that contrasted against my cinnamon brown skin, and I had tattooed sleeves on my arms.

"Explain that to me, son. First, I am impressed with how you came through these doors unscathed. It shows that my blood does run through you. You were but a boy of eight years when your mother left the *familia* in order to fly like a bird and share the gift of her dancing with the world."

Caltrone paused and languidly leaned forward to grab a piece of fruit and take a bite, then continued to speak. "I attended almost every performance she had until she decided to live in Miami. But you know that, my son, for I visited you as often as I could. So, please, have a seat and share with me how, after all these years, you find yourself at my door speaking the family motto instead of being back home . . . Where is it now? And does my beautiful Carmen still dance?"

Licking my lips, I stayed where I was in thought. I came from this man who was King of the Underworld. A man who had as many wives and children as he had houses, cars, and guns. My mother became a part of that dynasty due to her best friend, my aunt Mariposa. When Mariposa returned to Cuba from New York then decided to leave for good to pursue her singing, my mother packed up our things and we left with her so that she could dance for Mariposa's band. After that, she became a dance teacher and she and I settled in Miami where, occasionally, I'd be visited by my father Caltrone.

Now, I was being asked to sit at this man's table as he dissected me. I was pretty sure he knew the answers to every question he shot my way. No, I was confident that he did. But since this was his world and I came to him in need, I decided to play the game. Stepping forward, I quietly pulled out a chair and took off my jacket, then sat down. I crossed my arms over my chest and began talking.

"Yes, Mama still dances. She has a club and restaurant now, where she teaches people to dance. It's named after my daughter, Jewel. As of now, yes, sir, we are still in Miami. I am an ER doctor as well as a father taking care of my daughter and *mi madre,* the feisty phoenix, as she likes to call herself."

Caltrone laughed loudly. Only his laughter wasn't that of a happy or cheerful man. His laughter always had a hidden meaning as he rarely laughed to begin with. He slapped a hand on a box then slid it my way. "Take one, my son, and enjoy it." Caltrone leaned back with an expression of pride on his face.

He gave me a nod with a wide smile. Wise lines hugged the corners of his lips as he spoke. "Carmen has always been my spicy phoenix since we were all children. When she was with Mariposa, she would always find a reason to dance. She was alluring, carefree, and passionate. It pleases me that she still dances after all these years."

I allowed myself to laugh with a man who used to make cherry lollipops appear in his hand with the slightest of moves, a man who I recall hearing say I would make an excellent prince for the family, and a man who used to train me in hand-to-hand combat until my mother felt that she had had enough of his unorthodox training. I reached in my jacket to pull out a picture and I handed it to him. I watched him study the image and I swore emotion flickered by his eyes.

My mother was in the picture with me and Jewel in Hawaii. At fifty-five years of age, Carmen was still a stunner. Her short, five-foot-four athletic but voluptuous body always reminded me of her obsession with health and keeping up an image that allowed her to continue to dance. Carmen stood with the same wide grin that matched my daughter's. Her feisty personality was on display as her sun-kissed, clay brown skin shined while she twirled in a bohemian dress. Her thick, kinky hair was in a crinkled freefall lifting in the wind as we all stood with her laughing in the photo.

It was a happy moment that we all cherished. Watching my father, I reached over to open the box. I pulled out a cigar, worked it between my fingers, and removed the tip, then lit it as I puffed in the smooth smoke. "Yes, she's still full of life. She stays with me in order to give me the blues," I said with love and respect in my voice for *mi madre*.

"I must see her again," he said locking eyes on me.

Understanding that his statement was not one of casual fluctuation but a subtle order, I gave a nod. "Before I came, we both knew that you would want to see her. I'll arrange it as soon as we are done here."

Caltrone reached over and, as he spoke, poured me a glass of the freshest-looking orange juice I had ever seen. "Good. From your words, I do see how you uphold the motto of this family. Now, tell me why you are here, my son. Your mother was insistent that she take you from the family and raise you her way. What of us do you still have in you?"

Pushing the glass away, I reached for a decanter full of a golden-brown liquid. Uncorking it, I poured it in his glass then my own. I sat back and took a sip, and allowed smoke to curl around my lips while I savored the cigar's smoky, bourbon-like flavor.

"My daughter—your granddaughter—is missing. She's seventeen. Jewel Carla Ortiz is a National Honor member, a gifted student, and a junior in high school. She's a wonderful runner, and a budding Orlando beauty, whose looks have caused too much attention in my opinion, as a protecting father," I explained.

"I've raised her to be mindful and smart, yet at seventeen she is gone. Lured away by some vulture on the Internet who coaxed her through texts and phone calls, convincing her that she can be free of my strict rules if she would be with him. For four months, I've been searching for her. I've used up all that I know how to do to find her myself. I've traced them to Tampa only to have them disappear on me. My resources have run thin."

Clenching my empty glass, I paused then set it down. "This is a situation that now requires me to stop being a doctor and practice the principles you taught me, Father. Your blood runs heavy through me. This is why I'm here. I will do whatever to protect my family. No man should be accepting of being robbed. My daughter was taken from me, and whoever has her will learn that she is of the wrong family to take from."

Ocean waves crashed behind my father. My gaze took in the tropical horizon while I kept my emotions locked down. I hoped that he'd help me. As an adult, I understood that I was gambling with the devil.

I had done my own investigation on this man; and when my mother learned that I planned to see him, she broke down, frantically trying to keep me home with the story of the corrupt power of the Orlandos. But, even with my mother's confession about the dangerous way my father chose to live, I couldn't stay away and not ask for his help. Jewel needed me, and though she had chosen to run away, there was no way that I would accept it. I had to get my daughter. I had to do this not only for myself but also for her mother, Kenya.

The Orlandos were a group of trained killers and criminals. It was deeper than just Caltrone. His power and reign flexed over the U.S. and internationally. It was what made my mother run with his sister Mariposa, when she ran from the start of the battle in Brooklyn to Cuba and elsewhere. The tale of a family battle with another family, the Kulu Kings, only added to the stress I was feeling about Jewel. Men bent on going after each other over . . . well, plainly put, pussy.

Shaking my head, I kept that knowledge on lockdown. Even while sitting in front of

Caltrone, my mind was still trying to process the truths that were shared that day. Like what my mother felt she had to do to protect me when I was a child, I was doing the same for Jewel.

"Carla," Caltrone quietly said finally breaking our silence. "After me?"

I gave a nod. Only a few knew his real name and that Caltrone was an extension of his middle name.

"Why haven't you gone the legal route? Gone to the police?" he asked.

I sighed and shook my head. "Humph. I did, but after they investigated and found she left on her own, they stopped treating it with priority. I mean, they claim to be looking into it but, as you can see, we haven't gotten anywhere with them yet."

He nodded once. "As I asked before, what will you do for me?" he asked.

"Two things: one, I will be your man, your weapon, whatever you need; and, two, you wanted to see *mi madre?*" Digging in my jacket, I pulled out my cell phone. "All I have to do is make a call."

A sly smile spread across his face. Tossing a grape in his mouth he chewed slowly and watched me in a calculating manner. "So she is not at the hotel with you?" he asked, which made me chuckle.

"Papa, my mother grew up around your family and loved you at one time. We know better," I said just as smoothly as he would.

He laughed, as he wiped his mouth and flicked his hand over the food. "Fix yourself a plate. Forgive me for doubting that you were an Orlando. The fact that you easily killed several of my bodyguards, including the two who were put on you the moment you landed, amused and irritated me. Now, it just pleases me because my prodigal son is back home. So eat up."

Doing as he said, I filled my plate and ate as I explained, "I have a gift for detecting patterns, remember, Father? I studied how they watched the land and house then I took them down with patience. Watch the wolf, then become the wolf."

My father gave a wide smile. I saw a flicker of pride in his eyes that I remembered his lessons; then he spoke.

"I will put the necessary people on it to help you find information on my namesake's whereabouts, but it will be I who will help you in the actual search. You are correct, Antonio: no man allows another to take from him. You remembered me telling you that and that makes me proud. See, a man who allows another to take from him is a weak bastard and a weak bastard can never be trusted or allowed to live," he stated. "That is my granddaughter; no man has the right to take her."

"Thank you," I started to say before he held a hand up.

"I have no need to explain to you that when you find this person, you will disembowel him or her, yes?"

Stabbing my fork into my eggs I took a bite, wiped my mouth, and then stared him in the eyes. "No, sir. No need to explain that at all."

"You still scared of dogs?"

I chuckled, recalling that the fear I had of them was long gone due to him. "No, sir."

"You still enjoy cutting up insects and studying them?" he asked after I answered him.

"Very much so. It is why I am a doctor."

He waved a hand, and several staff came from the house. He told them to bring out more food. "Then you have a plan?" he asked once they left.

"Yes, sir."

Silence was our friend again. Three of the people I vividly remembered as my niece and nephews strolled into the large gazebo where we sat in my father's gardens perched on a cliff that overlooked a beach and waves. A young woman with a long ponytail swaying over her breast stepped to Caltrone, gave him a kiss on his cheek, then sat by his side when he motioned for her to. Another, male and younger, sat by his side with a smile on his face; and the third, a male with a darkness in his eyes, stood at his back watching me. Maria-Rosa, Mark, and Freddie were younger than I but I remembered their faces.

"*Familia,*" I said sitting forward.

"Maria-Rosa, Mark, and Freddie, I want you three to do something for me. We have a delicate situation that needs rectifying. It would seem that your long-lost uncle is in need of help. His daughter has gone missing. Gather everything you can and give him the information. We do not allow family to go unaccounted for, understood?" Caltrone stated.

Everyone gave him their okays, then he continued, "In the meantime, we will be celebrating my son's return and you three will bring him into the fold. He is a doctor, which is something that we need in this family."

Tension began to dance over the back of my neck as I watched everyone's expressions. I wasn't disturbed by the distrust in their eyes; what I had a problem with was the calculating manner that was in Mark's eyes and Caltrone's. Shit was eerie but I made sure not to show I was shaken by it. If it was destiny to fall by their hands, so be it. I lived an honorable life and lived

it well. I had no regrets, yet, and I wasn't about
to let them plant any in me.

"Antonio, as they dig for information on your
daughter, after you debrief them on everything
you've already found, and after we conclude
our family welcoming, you and I will start our
training again. You're a doctor and I wish to see
if you can be a killer at the same time like your
elder brother Lu once was."

Keeping my cool, my stomach clenched. Lu.
I hated that motherfucker. Nigga had serious
issues as a child and, from what I had heard
on the national circuit, nigga was still bat shit
loco until the day he died. He even had his
son Damien tear up Atlanta while he rotted in
prison. The fact that Caltrone was sending me
that way annoyed me but I kept it to myself. In
this family, my mother explained, loyalty wasn't
formed just through dedication; it was formed
by what you could do for the family and how you
did it.

Turning into a killer wasn't going to be easy
but I had to show that I meant what I said. "I'll
do whatever to show my worth, Father."

"Good. Now that you're home, you will be
given the lessons and allowances you need to
be an heir," he laid out for me to understand.
"Do you have a wife?"

"No, sir. Jewel's mother, Kenya, and I co-parent," I explained.

"And she does what?"

Even though I was sure he already knew the answer to the question, my mother was right; Caltrone was about appearances and the purity of the family bloodline. If anyone lay with someone he felt wasn't worthy of an Orlando, then that person and their child would forever be deemed as nothing but a mutt to him. Though I was his son, the woman I chose to create life with also had to be worthy of my time and seed, which in turn would protect my daughter from my father's disdain.

"She owns her own bakery; however, she used to be a practicing prosecuting lawyer."

Caltrone's eyes lit up. "Ah, her brains and yours are the reason Jewel is so gifted. It is unfortunate that my granddaughter's youth got her in this situation."

"I agree," I said. The idea that my daughter was with some Internet lech and fell for such bullshit really fucked with my mental, but I wasn't about to show that. I rubbed the side of my neck then dropped my hand.

"Good. Everyone leave us," he said. One by one, my niece and nephews left me with my father. He sat in a haze of smoke, studying me before he said, "Now, on to the second part of our agreement."

Exhaling, I pulled out my cell, and dialed my mother who was in Jamaica waiting for me. I was now in with Caltrone. Whatever came with it, I had no choice but to deal with because I was willing to sacrifice my all for her. This was my battle. *No one fucks with my daughter*.

Chapter 2

Kenya

"It is nice to hear your voice again, Carmen. It's been too long, *sí?*" the man said into the phone.

I stood just inside the back door of the house. I watched as three of Caltrone's grandchildren strolled back. They passed me without a second thought, although the one they called Mark let his eyes linger on me a bit too long. Why I was in Caltrone's mansion would be a mystery to some. Not to me and not to that man. I'd stood there and listened to the whole exchange between him and Antonio. For as long as I'd known my child's father, not once had he mentioned he came from the dick of *the* Caltrone Orlando. Since Antonio carried his mother's last name, I never put two and two together.

My daughter was missing so I hoped Tone didn't think I would just continue to sit idly by.

It was in my blood to fight and fight hard. I knew
something was wrong. Knew it as soon as he
called me that day with the weight of the world
on his shoulders and angst in his voice. Jewel
was a good kid for the most part, but she and her
father often clashed because of his strict rules. I
made it my business to never go behind his back
when it came to disciplining her. If he told her
something then his word was law.

Tone had spoiled her but, at the same time, he
was stern. I knew why he was that way. He didn't
want our child to end up pregnant like I was as
a teenager. I respected that and I wanted the
same thing. Jewel often hated the fact that she
couldn't come to me and make me say yes when
her father had said no.

Tone told me he didn't want me to join him in
looking for her. He wanted me to keep watch at
home just in case she came back. He must have
forgotten who I was and what resources I had at
my disposal. Yes, I spent all my days baking now
but, before I knew pastry, I knew the law. All
those contacts I had before deciding to leave the
State as a prosecutor were still of use to me. And
none of them could get us any closer to finding
our daughter. So, I came to the one man who
owed me a favor.

Before all of that, allow me to introduce myself. My name is Kenya. At sixteen years old, I found myself pregnant and scared. Nine months later, Jewel came kicking and screaming into the world. Antonio and I had no business becoming parents that young, but it was what it was. We made the best of it. I didn't have a mother growing up. I was in and out of foster homes. I'd been to the juvenile detention hall way more than I cared to admit.

One day I met a boy who nobody knew much about. Tone was quiet. Didn't say too much to anybody. People thought he was crazy or something, but me? I thought he was unique. There was something about him that made me go against the grain and speak to him.

There I was, fifteen years old, with my first crush on a boy. His hair was curly, coarse, and unkempt; and anytime I looked into his eyes they reminded me of an endless pit. I never knew why that was.

"What do you want?" he asked me when I walked over to sit at the lunch table with him.

I shrugged. "I can't sit at this table?" I asked him.

He tilted his head up and looked at me. "Why? One of those niggas sent you over here to fuck with me? If so, don't do it. Girl or not, I'll handle you," he threatened me.

I knew what he was referring to. The boys at the school didn't know how to handle him. On one hand, they were afraid of him. On the other hand, they hated his good looks and the way he could handle a ball, so they wanted to fight him, hurt him. A few chicks had tried to get at him, but he wasn't falling for the hype knowing that there was sneaky shit afoot. Tone had always been too damn smart for his own good.

"Nobody sent me over here. I came on my own. So can I sit?"

He was quiet. He looked back down at his home-cooked meal then shrugged. "Free country, mami. You can sit where you want."

He had a bit of an accent that I couldn't place. I had to admit, I was kind of jealous of his lunch. I wanted to ask for some knowing that the shit they fed us at school wasn't all that. Still, I knew I had to eat it; otherwise, I would go hungry for the rest of the day and night. My foster mother had eight other children besides me and, although she tried hard to take care of us, sometimes the food stamps ran out before the month did.

So, I picked up my dry-ass sandwich and bit into it. Meanwhile, Tone had fried chicken, black-eyed peas, mac and cheese, and some cornbread that I was tempted to steal. We sat silently while we ate. All eyes were on us. I guessed the rest of the kids were wondering if some shit was going to pop off. I was considered a troublemaker. Where I went, trouble followed. I'd gotten kicked out of four high schools and I was only in the tenth grade.

I was always ready to fight. Always ready to take a broad down to prove that I was no punk. I'd gotten into fistfights with boys, too. Had the scars to prove it. I just didn't care.

"Is it true your mom is friends with that singer chick, Mariposa? True she's one of her dancers? The pretty one everybody's always fawning over?" I asked him.

"Yeah. What's it to you?"

"Just asking. If she's your mom, ain't you rich or some shit? Why you at this school and not over there with them crackers?"

"Crackers?"

"Yeah, them rich white folk over there at Pinewoods Academy?"

He shook his head in annoyance.

I opened my milk to take a drink, but the sour smell that assaulted my nose made me rethink it. "Damn, man," I fussed. "Assholes can't even give us fresh milk," I mumbled.

"Here," he said.

I looked up to see he had pushed a soda over to me along with a piece of chicken, some peas, and a piece of his cornbread.

I frowned. "Why you giving me this?" I asked. I didn't too much trust any male giving me stuff without me asking. I'd learned the hard way in the foster system that not everyone was as nice as they appeared to be.

"If you don't want it give it back," he said.

I swallowed hard, my mouth watering for the food I knew I wouldn't get later. "I ain't giving you nothing," I said, hoping he got my meaning.

He glanced over at me. "I didn't ask you for nothing."

Once I was sure he understood what I was saying, I tore into that food. Ate it like I hadn't eaten before and never would again.

I didn't know why I was attracted to him the way I was, but the next day, I was back at his table again. Yeah, with the hope he would share his food again, but also because I liked being near him. For two weeks, we ate lunch together, but barely held conversations. He would bring me food and, in turn, I would ask if I could do something for him. I didn't have any money and I had already learned how to use my body to pay for services or get what I wanted.

Most boys would have been mannish and asked for pussy, but Tone was different. He only wanted me to help him with his literature and history homework. Most people didn't know or recognize how smart I was, but he did. That was the way our weird friendship worked for a while.

He would feed me and I would help him with his work. It went on that way for a few months. We never really said we were girlfriend and boyfriend. It kind of just happened. He was walking me home one day and my hand ended up in his.

There was nothing special or romantic about our hookup. Not until the day I showed up on his doorstep, face bloody, as my foster mom's boyfriend had beaten me when I tried to protect her from him. I remember when his mother opened the door and found me there. Blood was dripping from my right eye and mouth. My shirt had been torn off, but I fought back. He was taller and stronger than I was, but I wasn't afraid of him.

Still, he had gotten the upper hand. My foster mom had put him out before, but he came back. She was genuinely trying to get away from him and he didn't like it. So he beat her then wouldn't let her leave her room. She had been the best foster mom I'd had. I had to protect her so they wouldn't take us from her. That night, after I'd run to Tone's home for help, I finally knew why I always thought of a bottomless pit when I looked in his eyes.

He'd caught Johnny coming out of Mama Sheila's house. Took his legs out from under him with a steel baseball bat. Beat him so badly I thought he had killed him. I watched as Tone took a knife and sliced the man open over and over again. Stomach, legs, sides, thighs, wherever his blade could reach. Then he put the unconscious man in his car and slammed the door shut.

I didn't question him. Just followed him as he walked back around the corner. In the back of the van Tone drove were three dogs. Their heads and upper bodies were so big they scared me, as they looked like they were on steroids. I moved to stand behind Antonio as he unhooked the chains on the dogs. They followed him like they had been trained to do so. Antonio opened the back of Johnny's Buick and let the dogs in. Two sat on the back seat while one took up residence on the passenger seat. They all sat that way, unmoving, staring at Johnny with their tongues hanging out of their mouths.

"You okay?" Tone asked me as we waited.

I nodded. "What are you going to do with him?" I asked.

"Don't worry about it. Just know he will never lay hands on you again."

It took another twenty minutes for Johnny to regain consciousness. When he did, Tone stood. The dogs started to growl. Johnny screamed and tried futilely to get out of the car, but Tone had blocked the door. He had pressed his body against it so Johnny couldn't get out.

"Eat," Tone said to the dogs.

At first, I was confused by why he would say that, until the dogs tore into Johnny. It was the cruelest shit I'd ever seen. Those dogs ripped Johnny apart. They started at the places Tone had cut open and ripped at Johnny like he was raw steak.

I'd never forget that man's screams as he was eaten alive by the meanest, most vicious pit bulls I'd ever laid eyes on. Just as I'd never forget the look in Tone's eyes as he watched on. That night I learned there was another side to the boy I'd come to love, a side that often scared me when someone pushed him to the point of no return.

Soon after that, I found myself pregnant, much to the chagrin of Mama Sheila and Carmen. Nine months later, Jewel was here. Tone and I were too young, our tempers too volatile. We fought about every little thing. We were two of those people who had a "fight then fuck" relationship. Tone and I had no business being parents. But we tried; honestly, we did. I went to school at night so he could go during the day. Both of us were smart in our own right. He worked after school and sometimes when I was at school. Carmen and Mama Sheila would watch Jewel from time to time. Sometimes Tone and I spent the night at the other's house, but most times the parents weren't having it.

We'd already gotten knocked up once; they weren't risking it again. Truth be told, neither were we. That didn't mean we stopped having sex, it just meant we got smarter about birth control. He got condoms and I got some pills. I stopped fighting in school so much and Tone stopped playing ball. We made it to high school graduation. We both chose careers that took up a lot of time when it came to the education aspects of them. Eventually jealousy and neglect crept into our relationship.

I was jealous of all the little future doctor chicks he always hung around and he started to neglect me as his girlfriend. I didn't think he could help it. It was just the nature of the beast. Both of us were students at the University of

Miami, but we were worlds apart. Eventually we both got tired of fighting. We were young, with a child, and very unhappy. As much as it hurt me, we decided the best thing to do for Jewel was to break up. That was one heartache I never got over. I would never tell Tone that, but yeah. Even though I'd eventually move on with someone else, I never got over seeing Antonio pack his bags and leave the apartment we shared near campus.

Even though Tone was a medical student, his time management was better than mine. Mama Sheila died when Jewel was five so I was truly on my own. Law school was demanding and, as hard as I tried, I was having a hard time managing mothering full time and school. Don't get me wrong, Tone was a great father, but Jewel was living with me. To make a long story short, Tone and I had a talk and we agreed that Jewel would be better suited to live with him since his mother would be able to look after her while he was at school. He had the help that I didn't. Since she was seven, she had been with her father. While my career took me from the gritty streets of Miami to the courtrooms of Atlanta, Tone laid his roots in Miami. Everything was going great.

I was the youngest assistant district attorney in the Dade County DA's office at twenty-five. I

came fresh out of law school having graduated
top of my class. I was the DA's pet, as people
used to say. I was taking cases, winning them left
and right. I got so good that ATL came calling.
They needed a new assistant district attorney. So
I threw in my hat.

At twenty-eight, I was an ADA for the City of
Atlanta, selected for one of the many special-
ized prosecution units maintained by the
district attorney's office. Head in the clouds, no
one could tell me a thing. And no one did. No one
told me that the old DA had lost his life because
he wouldn't play ball with the who's who of the
underworld. No one told me the new DA was a
puppet for the Orlandos. I had to find that out
the hard way. Lucifer Orlando was the defen-
dant. He had killed a woman, Sade Banks, in
Chicago in 2005, but we wanted him in Atlanta,
as he had been connected to the murders of
Fatima and Jamir Kweli in 2003.

According to the stories told, before the old
DA had been killed, he had convicted Lu on a
drug charge in which Jamir Kweli had convinced
witnesses to testify about what they saw. From a
prison cell, Lu ordered his sons to take out Jamir
and Fatima. It was all a mess. By the time Lu got
finished, and with all the people he had in his
pocket, the old DA was dead while Fatima and

Jamir were painted as the drug runners of the neighborhood. Lu was out on the streets again.

As soon as I had stepped foot in the DA's office, the Orlando name rang out heavily. We were trying to get Lu before the Feds tried to take over. I could feel it in my bones: they would come in and try to take the case over as soon as we came down on him.

I shook my head, remembering the way that man had watched me while I tried him for murder. I lost that first case. Couldn't get one damn witness to get on the stand. They would have rather gone to prison for perjury than testify against Lucifer Orlando. I assumed my boss, the DA, was just as amped about going after him as I was. I had been wrong. So very wrong.

A cold chill ran through me at the memories of what happened the first time I was alone in a room with Lu Orlando. I shook away the smell, and the look in his eyes.

Fast forward to 2008, Caltrone Orlando walked into my office and told me he would give me his son on a silver platter if I would play ball with him. I was so hell-bent on sending Lu Orlando to prison by then, I made a deal with the devil. It would be my undoing as, three years later, I decided to walk away from the job I loved and move back to Miami.

For some reason, I felt as if I had been played. Had Caltrone known who I was all this time? Did he seek me out because he knew the connection I had to his son, Tone?

"Caltrone, I would say it was good to hear from you as well, but that would be a lie," I heard Carmen's smooth voice say over the speakerphone.

The man chuckled. I could see now where Antonio got his looks from. Tone never spoke about his father, ever. A sinking feeling in the pit of my stomach settled over me. I knew Caltrone, way more than I should have. Had conversations with him that led me to leaving the life of a prosecutor behind. Antonio was a fucking Orlando. I swallowed hard. On one hand, I was borderline disgusted and somewhat amazed I'd survived a relationship with an Orlando. On the other, my flesh crawled with the knowledge that I'd lain with Lu Orlando's flesh and blood.

Caltrone chuckled. "Carmen, to still hold hostility for things of old is beneath you," he said.

"Which part? The part where you impregnated me and my sister at the same time?"

"I took care of that," he responded.

"Or the part that when you were angry enough you had no problems using your hands to get your point across?"

"I always told you to leave me alone when I was angry, but you never listened."

"Or was it the part where you knew your son was afraid of dogs but used them against him—"

Caltrone's smirk dissipated and his voice turned cold. "You can stop there now. I may have been unfair to you, but to my son, I wasn't. Fear weakens men. He was afraid of dogs; I made sure he got over it."

"Leaving a six-year-old in a room with a vicious pack of wild dogs was not the way to do it," Carmen belted out.

"I can't argue with your perception, Carmen. I long ago stopped explaining myself when I realized people only understand from their level of perception. You see things how you see them. I don't dabble in emotions. I deal with logic. As you can see, he is no longer afraid of dogs, *sí*."

"Kiss my ass, Caltrone. I'm only talking to you because Antonio needs help."

Caltrone chuckled. "*Sí,* I know. And I agreed to help. I have people on the job."

"I didn't allow him to come ask for help so you could put someone on the job. You want me back home? You want your granddaughter to be a part of your life? You don't send in the cavalry; you are the cavalry. I've always told myself that I would never have anything else to do with you or your harem of bitches. But someone has taken my grandchild. Most people think you're the devil, but I know better. I don't want to send the devil's imps after them. I don't even want the devil himself on the job. I want the God who tossed Satan out on his ass on the job."

If I didn't know anything else about the man on the phone with Carmen, I knew he was a manipulator and had a way with words. The first time he walked into my office when I was the ADA was my undoing. I knew that once I fell in with doing business with him, all morals I had were gone. But what could I do when the man who ran the underworld demanded a favor from me? I needed to see Lu Orlando in prison. So if his father was going to help me, I was all in.

I had no idea I was doing business with Tone's father then. The fact that I'd hopped on a plane then come right to his door for the sake of our daughter . . . I'd come to call in the favor Caltrone Orlando owed me without knowing he was my daughter's grandfather.

"I do this and you come back to Cuba, *sí?*" he asked Carmen.

There was a long pause on the other end of the phone. Caltrone did some kind of signal with his hand toward the house.

Antonio finally spoke up. "Mama—"

Carmen cut him off. "*Sí*. You get Jewel back and I come back to Cuba."

"You don't have to do that, Mama," Tone said then looked at his father. "That wasn't part of the deal."

Caltrone smiled coolly. "That wasn't part of our deal, no," he said pointing between himself and Tone. "But, your mother knows the price of asking me for favors. I scratch your back and you have to scratch mine."

My fists clenched at my sides while I watched on. I turned to find right behind me the young man I'd come to know as Mark. I hadn't even heard him walk up. There was a slick smirk on his face.

"Papa wants to see you," he said.

While a woman who didn't know him may have been turned on by the slight Spanish accent in his deep voice, I knew better. "Get away from me," I demanded.

"I've been watching you since you've been here," he said. "You're pretty, very pretty. Bet you taste like licorice," he said then flicked his tongue out at me.

"Leave her alone, Marco. Papa said not to touch her," Mark's older brother, Frederick, said. He came from the back room. He was dressed all in black, with a gun holstered on his left side. I liked him better than I did the one named Mark. Mark was evil personified. At least there was a little light in Frederick's eyes.

Frederick looked at me. "Papa would like to see you now." He took my arm in a firm hold and ushered me outside.

By then, Caltrone was off the phone. He smiled lazily when he saw me. When Tone turned around, I saw shock then anger register in his eyes.

"What the fuck are you doing here?" he asked as he abruptly stood.

"Is this your Kenya?" Caltrone asked. "Assistant District Attorney Kenya Gates?"

"I'm no longer an ADA," I said snidely then snatched my arm away from Frederick.

Tone's brows furrowed as he stormed over to me. "What are you doing? Did you follow me?"

"No," I answered.

"No, son, she didn't follow you. In fact, she got here hours before you did. I'd say it was fate that brought us all together, *sí?*"

Tone's face was stuck between confusion and anger. "Somebody needs to tell me what the fuck is going on, now!"

"Can I talk to you alone?" I asked Tone.

"Please do," Caltrone said as he prepared to leave. "Make it quick. My grandchild is missing. I'd like to get her back as soon as possible."

I waited until after he and his grandsons had walked off before looking back up at Antonio. "I can explain," I started.

"I'm listening," he all but growled out.

I started with my move from Miami to Atlanta. I told him everything, from my first trial that I lost when trying to convict Lu Orlando to the second trial when I had all the evidence possible in the world. So much so that I didn't worry about witnesses who wouldn't testify. Caltrone had made good on his promise. Chicago's DA had received an anonymous tip about the murder of Sade Banks. Lu was convicted in Chicago and sent to prison there. Working in tandem with them, I got Lu charged with first-degree murder in Atlanta. I got primary jurisdiction for the City of Atlanta. I knew for a fact he didn't kill Fatima and Jamir Kweli, but he for damn sure ordered it.

Still, I lied in the courtroom. Used every underhanded tactic I could find, with the help of Caltrone Orlando. The day Lu was sentenced to life in prison the darkness over my life lifted, partially.

By the time I was finished, Tone had no emotion on his face.

Chapter 3

Antonio

I wasn't the type of man who was prone to outbursts of anger. Pause, let me restate that. I wasn't the type of Orlando who was prone to bouts of anger. But as I stood in front of the mother of my child, all I saw was red. The anger management lessons my mother had taught me at a young age—something I later learned was a tactic of hers to make me less Orlando, more humane, as a means to undo my father's lessons in Cuba—weren't working. Heat blazed in my body. My mind was thumping, my eyes tight, as one occasionally twitched. The way my fists were balled up, I knew that if I didn't hit something, the desire to hit an actual human being would take over and I'd find myself going after one of the many men roaming the lands. All because of Kenya.

As I stood there breathing in and out, my thick lips turned down into a tight scowl. My gaze locked on Kenya's beautiful face. At one point, I loved her to the core of me, after the high of lust went away. Now, I felt like she was another fucking obstacle in my way and, for a second, I wanted to hate her for coming here.

While she spoke with her hands, following me as I walked away from the ears that tried to listen to us, we moved to where I could look out at the sea and allow the crashing waves to drown out our conversation. Once we were in a good spot, I turned to look at her with a blank stare and I slid my hands in my pockets. Kenya's brown eyes were wide as she waited for my reaction.

Her dark caramel skin was flushed red. All I heard was the blood rushing in my ears and the pounding of my heart. I wanted to wrap my hands around her throat for this, something I'd never wanted to do before. I wanted to snatch her by the nape of her neck and force her off the land and throw her on a plane. But as I stared at the woman who had disrupted everything I had planned, and had me recalculating my plans, all I could do was seethe with anger. I wasn't feeling her right now. I truly wasn't.

I finally made out what she was saying. "Tone, you're not listening to me. I had to use my resources too. This is our daughter. You can't really expect me to just sit back and twiddle my thumbs! You know me better than that."

Again, the Orlando blood in me began to rise to the surface and fuck with my mental. All I heard in my mind was, *is this bitch really that stupid?* But instead, I said, "You don't know what you just did."

"I did what I had to for our daughter," Kenya rushed out again, keeping her distance.

"You don't fucking make deals with my father! You don't do that and expect not to lose out on your end," I shouted then clamped my mouth shut trying to chill the lion within.

Kenya stared up at me, then tilted her head to the side as if I had said something ridiculous. "He owes me. I'm not making a deal. So this is different."

I settled into a quiet anger, and my voice came out in low, even tones. "Nothing about this is different, Kenya. You saw what he did to me with regard to my mother. He twisted everything to his favor and now my mother has lost her freedom because of this. Because she asked me to use her as a bargaining chip, or additional icing on the fact that I was coming back home to be an Orlando."

"I know him. He's a man of his—"

Cutting her off, I sliced my hand in the air. "You don't know him!" I shouted. "I do. I am his son. You know only what he wants you to believe. He is an ominous actor who wears many faces and holds many cards. You just played in it. You just allowed him to play you. Do you not see it?"

Kenya gave a quick jerk of her head, turned her lips down, then rolled her eyes as she spoke. "Whatever. I'm going to do and risk all for my daughter, regardless of what you think, Antonio," she said heatedly as if she knew better than I.

Because of that familiar attitude of hers, I laughed. She used to be a sweet woman who was laidback in life. When she became a lawyer all that changed. She became hard-edged, and the woman I used to know became a stranger who I didn't really like dealing with all the time. Those were the tough years with Kenya, when our daughter was young. Kenya became a subtle manipulator in her work. Once her job broke her down, and she quit law to open up a bakery, the softness in her started to come back. Though, even opening that bakery, I felt, was a front.

It was when Kenya came out in front of my father and told me about how she knew him that everything from our past, and our fights, made sense. She had been trying to hide her dirty deeds and it had started to weigh on her. So what she didn't know until today that I was an Orlando? My mother had intentionally made sure I always used her last name so the taint of being an Orlando wouldn't hinder me. I didn't make it my business to tell anyone who my father was. But he for damn sure went after her with specific reason. Because she was linked to me.

"You should have been doing whatever you could back home and not with my father, because now you are going to be whatever you can to keep him at his word, and I can't save you from that shit because you laid your fucking ass in that bed. And, in the process, you fucked up what I had going on." Running a hand through my hair, I walked to the side. "He's been playing you since day one of you meeting him, Kenya. Do you not understand that? Why would he come to you of all fucking people about Lu? Huh? Let me tell you why."

In my anger, all English melted away and I was speaking the tongue of my mother: Spanish. I knew Kenya understood me because I'd taught her well, back when we were kids.

"Because my father invests himself in all his children and what they do. You were tied to me. So because he watches me, he watches you. He knew about Jewel the day you birthed her!" My hands smacked together as I spoke. Heat rose around the collar of my shirt and I tried to ignore it as the blood rushed in my ears. "He has pictures of both of our graduations. He came to you because it was his way to introduce himself to you and keep tabs on me at the same time. He is why I broke us up, to keep you safe and make sure that you and Jewel had a normal life, and here you fucking go! You never listen to what the hell I have to say. Never!"

Kenya stood speechless in front of me. She tucked behind her ear her crinkled, long hair that lifted behind her due to the breeze, and she kept her mouth shut. Though, I saw her jaw ticking in anger like my own. I knew she hadn't seen me this angry in a long time. Not since we were kids and I was protecting her. As I paced back and forth like an animal in the wild, my mind was already thinking of how to make the best of this while trying to school my ex on what she was dealing with.

"Now you're his pawn and I can't do shit about it. So if he wants to fuck you, guess what's going to happen? If he wants to tear you apart in front of me, to teach me a lesson because I've been gone for so long, Kenya, he will strip you, and take pieces of your flesh little by little." By this time I was back in her face. I thumbed my nose. I kept my voice low hoping this shit was sinking in because, by the fact that she was here, I knew that she didn't give a damn about her life.

"You think Lu was a sick motherfucker? Think about who created him, Kenya. And now you fucked it up! You could have stayed home and continued searching for our daughter there. You could have put out flyers, taken to the news, taken to the streets there while keeping in the area just in case she came home; but no. You gotta fucking meet with my pops? Fuck your life right now, Kenya. Fuck you! No matter how much I got love for you, fuck you right now."

"I'm going to do whatever I have to. I don't care how angry you are. I'm her mother. I carried her. I birthed her. I—"

"Fuck your 'I,' Kenya," I barked out. "If both of us are dead, then what? Huh? Jewel has no one but this family then."

"If he keeps his end of the bargain, she'll be safe with me," she yelled at me with tears rimming her eyes.

"No, you just think that's how it's going to go. But I know the reality of this bullshit. How it's going to go is you get her back by his help, then he flips that shit to his favor and takes her. That's it. You have no power here, Kenya."

Shaking my head in disappointment and fury I turned my back on her. "You screwed everything up. I was to take this on, not you. Not you dealing with him. Why? Because in the end if I had to go away because he ordered it, I'd readily do that for our daughter and you," I said with my hand slapping against my chest. "Jewel needs one of us and I was not about to allow you to risk all with my father. She needs her mother. If I have to die to save her, I was good with that. I know what being an Orlando entails and you did not have to get involved in it. Fuck!"

"I was already involved! Did you not hear anything I just said to you? Jewel is my responsibility too. I'm not going anywhere. I understand your point of view and your anger, but it's too late. I came and now we have to work together in this," she said. "I didn't know Caltrone was your father. I was involved with Caltrone long before you knew. Regardless of what you say, Caltrone has always kept his word as long as I kept mine. I didn't know anything about this man when he walked into my office and I still don't. All I knew was he . . . he was dangerous and he had a lot of power. Power that I was able to use to get Lu locked away."

I wasn't here for what she was doing. Wasn't here for the old memories, of us falling in and

out of love. Of our many exhausting fights growing up as young kids in love raising a child.
Then, after, when the load of her work started to
change her and me. I didn't want to hear it.

Kenya was defiant. It was what made her a
powerful ADA but, at the same time, that defiant
personality wasn't going to work here. "Yet, you
are here dealing with the devil again. You just
lost your soul and you don't even realize it," I
said deflated as I sarcastically laughed at the
whole situation.

We stood in silence for what felt like an eter-
nity. I wasn't so angry not to recognize that
Kenya and I were fighting for our daughter. I
wasn't upset about that at all. I was upset in
principle over the fact that she just went about it
in the wrong way.

"Again, Tone, I'm not going anywhere," Kenya
quietly repeated. "She's my daughter and I don't
feel bad about my choice. You won't make me feel
bad about my decision and my view on this, not
when this is about our daughter."

The palm of my hand ran up and down my
face. I moved away from the elaborate stone
wall we stood near. As a little kid, I spent hours
here sitting on it, watching the water, wondering
what was on the other side of the ocean. It was
also where remnants of my blood were soaked

into the mossy ground and stone, due to my father realizing that I loved this spot. Instead of nurturing that, he twisted it into a lesson about power. Using the old-school idea of kneeling on rice, or frozen peas, he'd make me kneel on pebbles as the salty sea air blew over my bleeding cuts.

Settling my gaze on my hands, I had a flashing image of them covered in blood, the memory of several dead dogs around me, and the sound of my younger voice crying, before shaking it off. I was a doctor, a surgeon. These hands healed and now they were going to bring death, yet again.

"I can handle myself," I heard Kenya say behind me. "I won't be a burden and you don't have to worry about me at all. I'm a grown woman and a mother who is very clear on her choice here. I'm not taking it back, so move on and get over it."

"There goes the lawyer I know. When bullets start flying, make sure you duck then; and, while you're at it, record yourself for our daughter about your choices here. So if you die, she knows why; and let her also know why you didn't listen to me so you could stay alive." Thumbing my nose, I walked away.

"You're so indignant over me not listening to you? Get over yourself, Tone."

"Damn right, because I know the consequences. Where is your fiancé? Nigga just let you bounce and he's doing what?" I asked out of spite.

"That pussy shit you said that I needed to do, just to keep me in my place? You know, when you told me I needed to stay home? He's doing that. He's staying back home so if our daughter shows up, someone she knows will be there. We work in tandem, as a unit, unlike you and me. He and I are on the same page to save my daughter," Kenya said with a hand on her hip.

I laughed hard because the shit was ludicrous. *They work in tandem? Bet.*

"I'm happy for you, but the pussy shit makes sense and you need to go do it with your bitch-ass fiancé. Because, you're right, you can't even listen to me on this to let me save our daughter. You have to move your self-righteous ass in the middle because you think you know better, just to spite me at this point."

Kenya gave a roll of her eyes, sucked her teeth, and then crossed her arms. "Yeah, that's what it is. That just makes all types of sense, doesn't it? I didn't even know you'd be here."

"It's true. You being here is fucking stupid and a death wish."

"No, it's not! You're being petty as fuck," she spat back.

Fists clenched, I growled, "You need to keep your eyes open and recognize when shit isn't what it appears. Can you do that? Huh? Can you? Nah, you can't."

We stood glaring at each other, breathing hard. There was a moment when we used to get each other. There used to be a time when all either of us had to do was blink and we knew what the other was thinking. Over the years of our on-and-off relationship, that changed, especially when she got deep into her career. I was all for it until she started taking out her stress on me. Like I said, I now understood it. Her stress, I believed, was her subconscious way of recognizing my lineage. Her fear and anger were about my pops, along with her work back then, and I couldn't blame her for it.

In my mind, I knew that logic. However, my anger wouldn't let me register it. Whenever it came to her, like now, all I felt was myself back when we were breaking up. She never held me down like she used to back then. Now here we were again, with her not trusting in my integrity and thoughts. She just had to do shit her way.

Trying to get her to back away with my words wasn't helping, so I said fuck it. "Do you, Kenya, and don't get in my face or way." Muttering several curse words in Spanish, I threw my hand up and walked to the mansion.

I had a deep headache. I came here for my daughter. She was my priority and worry. However, my mother and Kenya were now in the mix of this and it had my mental fucked up even more. If I was going to become what my father wanted, I needed to keep my mind focused on who had my child, but that had changed.

As I walked inside, I was unimpressed by the glamor around me. Paintings from the sixteenth to nineteenth centuries that adorned the walls, the gilded antique furniture, the mixture of contemporary art, and the sparkling hanging chandeliers were nothing but reminders of the evil that helped build this empire.

Several relatives moved around the manor. I saw Mark and felt his sinister gaze on me. No matter how *Children of the Corn* he got on me, it was in me to remind him that I came from the same stock. That, in the past, I had gone *The Omen* on him and I would flip that switch again if I had to.

Throwing open the doors to my father's office, I walked in noticing him leaning with a cigar between his fingers, his gaze locked on a screen, and a woman in a suit behind him.

"Your affairs in line now, son?" he asked in that asinine way he did.

"Yes, sir," was all I said, keeping my temper in check.

Caltrone chuckled as he leaned in his chair. "You lie. You look like me so I know . . . Ah, ADA Gates, it's lovely to see that you are still here. Have a seat. You too, my son."

My father stood and waved a hand in front of the two chairs near his desk. I gave a quick glance toward Kenya and waited for her to sit first; then I followed.

"Great. Let us now convene in here and talk about getting your daughter, my grandchild, back," he said calmly, sitting down.

It was time and I was ready for it. Wherever my little girl was, I planned upon finding her. Come hell or high water, I'd scorch the earth in pursuit of her and take down anyone who got in my way. Standing, I reached in my pocket, pulled out my keys, and unclipped a black flash drive stick and set it in front of my father.

"Everything I have is on that flash drive. I have another as backup, but there're files, places I already searched, including hospitals, people who were interviewed by my private PI, and people I interviewed myself."

Handing that drive over felt as if an extension of my life were leaving me. I had spent countless hours exhausting every resource I had and every outlet in looking for my child. The energy of that was latched on that drive and now my father had it. From the emotionless expression on his face, I knew my father was in his mode. When he handed the drive to the woman behind him, and she bent over to plug it in, his subtle grunt let me know that he approved of what I had done.

When Kenya quietly lifted folders from her purse I was just noticing, I realized that she still hadn't said anything. I watched her as she set them in front of my father in a timid manner then gave me a look that said she could handle herself. The glint of anger in her eyes made me want to chuckle to myself. She was playing the game well in front of my father, while silently letting me know that she was still very much pissed at me. I liked that, but I wasn't going to tell her so. I also didn't give a damn if she was pissed at me. I wasn't sorry about anything I said to her because that was my truth in it.

Scratching the side of my nose, I watched my father give a similar grunt; then he reached out for his phone. "Go eat. Go rest. When I'm ready to speak to you both, I'll send for you. We're done here."

Like that he dismissed us without another
word. Both Kenya and I walked out and found
ourselves led to adjoining rooms. Annoyance
had me keeping my focus off of Kenya and on the
room before me. I wanted to call my mother to
beg her not to come to Cuba, but I knew that it
wouldn't stop her.

My mother was sacrificing herself for the
same cause we all were. It was all fucked up.
So, in my thoughts, I dropped on the bed. I
clutched my fisted hands between my legs then
stared off into the distance thinking about
my daughter, wherever she was. My daughter Jewel's actions had effectively affected this
family in the worst way but, in the end, I didn't
care. I just wanted my baby girl back, safe,
untouched, and unharmed.

Chapter 4

Kenya

"You used me," I said.

Caltrone turned to look at me with a frown etched across his handsome face. I searched his features, finally seeing signs of Antonio there. Since Tone looked more like his mother, I hadn't picked up on the similarities before. I felt stupid. So fucking stupid for not seeing it before. How could I have missed that shit? It was staring me right in the fucking face.

Two hours after Caltrone had dismissed me and Antonio, I decided that I just couldn't sit still anymore. Being laid up in a sprawling villa in Cuba didn't sit too well with me. Not when my daughter was somewhere out there. I had no idea where and that ate away at me. She had been gone for four whole months. I'd started to suspect the worst, but couldn't bring myself to actually voice my worry.

Where was my baby? Was she okay? Did she cry at night? Had her body been violated? Was she fighting back? If she was anything like me and her father, she was giving whoever had her hell, I was sure. At least, that was what I liked to tell myself. Truth of the matter was, Jewel had run off on her own volition. More than likely, she'd done it just to spite her father. Yes, Antonio could be an asshole, but our daughter had to know he was looking out for her best interest.

"I no more used you than you did me," Caltrone finally answered, jarring me from my thoughts. "Fair exchange is no robbery."

He was fresh from the shower, a large white towel wrapped around his golden waist. Caltrone was really a conundrum. I knew the man was older, much older than I was, but he didn't look a day over thirty. It seemed as if the man aged so slowly that he didn't actually age at all. The only telltale sign of his age was the salt-and-pepper hair on his head. His skin was so smooth it made me envious. I couldn't really explain what colors his eyes were. Sometimes they were hazel, other times just light brown. When he was angry, I'd seen them darken and turn to slits.

His lips were plush and made a woman want to know what it was like to have them somewhere on her body. He stood well over six feet with a body that put younger males to shame.

Caltrone had been sculpted and carved into perfection by God, or some evil force that sent him to earth to wreak havoc on the female persuasion. It was as clear as the night was long why he had a harem of women at his beck and call.

Caltrone's butterscotch skin had been kissed just right by the sun. As he moved around his room, I watched the muscles in his back coil and move around like steel cables. His slow strides were powerful. He moved like each step meant something.

"You knew who I was when you sought after me," I said.

He didn't answer right away. He took his time putting on oils and cologne. That smell could be mesmerizing to any woman. Airy, musky, and spicy. The shit tickled my senses and made me shift my weight from one foot to the other. Clearly, Caltrone didn't care I was in the room with him. He snatched the towel from around his waist and my eyes widened at the sight. The round globes of his ass sat perfectly as he took the time to neatly fold the towel and lay it where his housemaids could get to it easily.

Thighs thick with muscle and the patch of black silky hair around his dick drew my atten-

tion where it shouldn't have been. That was the
only place other than his head there was hair. I
quickly cast my gaze on other things in the room.
The big four-poster California king–sized bed
was made up with white down comforters and
pillows that looked inviting. There was a photo
of a dark-skinned woman on his wall. Chick
looked as if she could be a warrior as she was
posed regally dressed in a leather catsuit with a
spear in one hand and a gun in the other.

The hardwood floor was spotless and shined
so smoothly I could see my reflection. A throne-
like chair sat next to the floor-to-ceiling window
on the left side of the room. Right across from
the bed was a double door that led out to a
balcony. I could see the waves crashing against
the shore of the beach below.

"Of course I did, Kenya. What kind of businessman would I be if I didn't know everything
needed about the person I was doing business
with?" he asked casually.

I wasn't looking at him, but I could hear him
moving around the room. I could only assume
he was getting dressed, probably putting on
pajamas since it was late at night. That was, until
I heard shoes thumping on the floor. I turned to
find Caltrone dressed in all black. Black turtle-
neck. Black jeans that fit his tall, athletic frame
perfectly and black combat boots.

"I thought . . . I thought you only sought me out so you could put Lu away," I said.

"Foolish of you to think that, although that was one of the reasons. The other reason was because I always wanted to have a lifeline to my son. I knew I could get that through you. Lu was collateral damage. He was too far gone, and had done too much wrong without balancing it out with good. My oldest son had to be put down. I knew he needed to be locked away. The fact that you were an ADA was icing on the cake," he said.

"You played me."

"No, I didn't. I offered you a deal; you took it. Fair exchange is no robbery."

"When you found me in my office, after Lu . . ." I stopped talking abruptly because I didn't want to relive the memory. The only other person who knew what Lu had done to me was Caltrone. I swallowed the bile down as memories assaulted me.

"I'm sorry for what he did to you. Believe it or not, no matter what people say, I did not approve of the monster Lu became, just as I don't approve of his sons."

I cringed at the mention of his grandsons. Lu's son, Damien Orlando, was raising hell in Atlanta. He ran the underground world of drugs, sex, gambling, and guns, and he even had his hand in politics. Damien's reign was so legendary, not even the governor wanted to tangle with him. Shit had gotten progressively worse once his father was locked away. Damien made it his business to stalk me any chance he could. The threat was clear: I was going to pay for sending his father away.

For a while, nothing Damien had done could scare me. At least, that was what I'd told myself.

The men watching me outside my office, people breaking into my home, I still kept my head high and went into work every day. One day a kid in a hoodie with short locs gave me a message from Dame. The kid walked into the DA's office and simply laid on my desk a bullet that had my name carved into it. While I wouldn't lie and say it didn't rattle me, there was something familiar about the kid I couldn't place. I could have sworn he looked just like Jamir and Fatima Kweli, but I thought maybe my eyes had been playing tricks on me.

"You probably shouldn't be here after hours," the kid had said to me. He said it in a sense that he was warning me but not threateningly so. That night, it was reported that the DA's office had been burned to the ground. Although I'd put the biggest criminal in Atlanta behind bars, people at the DA's office treated me as if I had the black plague from that day forward.

When word got around that Lu Orlando had been murdered in prison, Damien made his presence in my life more prevalent. My car was blown up, my house was burned down, and I was stalked mercilessly. It had gotten so bad that I holed myself up in a hotel room under a fake name. I couldn't trust anybody. I thought for sure Lu would have me killed from beyond the grave. That was, until Caltrone called me and told me his grandson would no longer be an issue for me.

I didn't know what he had said to the man, but Damien stopped his tyranny. He was still causing hell in Atlanta, but he left me alone. During that brief phone call, Caltrone insisted I continue to live my life as I did before.

"So why not help take Damien down same as his father?"

"Damien will meet his end soon enough. That isn't my concern at the moment," Caltrone said in a tone that told me that part of our discussion was over. "You should get dressed and grab everything you need. Based on the information you and Antonio have given me, my leads tell me Mexico is our next destination."

My eyes widened. The man moved fast, but I
was so damn happy he'd found something. I'd
run into a brick wall, but Mexico? How the hell
had she gotten into Mexico? My heart raced as
I rushed to my room to grab my bags. I hadn't
brought much with me, just a purse and a small
duffle bag with the necessary toiletries and a
change of clothes. Packing hadn't really been on
my mind when I'd flown out here. It was easy
to get a private flight into Cuba when you threw
Caltrone's name around.

Mexico? My baby had been taken to Mexico. I
prayed to every god I knew in that moment.

I was just about to knock on Antonio's door
when I saw Caltrone already there. To see him
and Antonio standing next to one another, the
similarities in looks smacked me dead in the face.

I'd never understand how I didn't put two
and two together before now. But I didn't have
time to beat myself up over it. Dressed simply
in denim jeans and a red tank top with calf-high
combat boots, I was ready to go.

I didn't have much else to say to Antonio. He
didn't want me here. He'd made that painfully
clear. He swore I'd come only to defy him. I
didn't know how he felt that way when I had no
idea he was coming in the first place. My only

goal was to find Jewel. I needed my baby back home. She had barely lived life. She had so much more life ahead of her. To think some asshole could convince her to run away was baffling.

Jewel was an otherwise smart child. What in hell could Antonio have done to make her run off like that? No, I wasn't blaming him. I simply wanted to know the straw that broke the camel's back.

Caltrone had a black SUV drive us to a private airstrip. The jet we were getting on was a magnificent beauty. The cream-colored aircraft may have looked plain on the outside but once inside, I could see Caltrone was indeed a man who liked the finer things in life. The forward cabin consisted of four single cream-colored leather seats in club configuration. The seats had telescoping headrests, electric recline, electric leg rests, electric seat bottom cushion tilting, and swivel capabilities.

The place was spotless. Everything sparkled and shined like the jet had just been purchased fresh from the showroom floor. I didn't want to be near Antonio's rage and anger so I opted to grab a seat across from Caltrone, and I hoped Antonio would sit next to his father. My wish was granted a short time later.

"We're ready for takeoff, Señor Orlando," a woman's voice said over the speaker system. She sounded like a sex operator her voice was so pleasant. "Will there be anything else you need before we reach our destination?"

"No, thank you, Benita," Caltrone answered.

It took us less than thirty minutes to get up in the air. Three hours later, we landed in Mexico City, Mexico. While nightfall was upon us, we'd gained an hour since Mexico was one hour behind Cuba. A fleet of black SUVs were waiting for us as we exited the jet. I wasn't sure what was going on, but I decided to follow Caltrone's lead.

The women who had been flying the jet stepped out and placed themselves in front of Caltrone. My heart just about jumped in my throat when the doors to the SUVs opened and out stepped men armed to the nines. They all stood silently watching us until a fat, older, brown-skinned Mexican man stepped out of the last SUV with a cigar in his mouth. The potbellied man frowned as the sun was directly in his eyes.

"Ay, Señor Caltrone, it is very nice of you to join me here at home," the man greeted him, his accent so thick that, every time he spoke, the Rs in his words rolled more than once.

Caltrone nodded once. "*El Capitán* José Luis, thank you for hosting us."

"Eh," he responded. "I can assure you if I had a choice, I wouldn't let you set foot in my towns, *sí?* But I do understand the nature of the visit. This is your granddaughter, *sí?* She who is missing, yes?"

When José Luis said yes, it sounded more like "chess." Caltrone nodded. José Luis looked at me then to Antonio.

"And she is? No need for me to ask who he is. All you Orlando males seem to have tricky shit going on with the eye colors, *sí?*" he said then laughed.

"She's my son's wife," Caltrone answered, unamused.

I was tempted to look at the man like he had lost his mind. *Wife? Antonio's wife? I'd rather jump in a pit of vipers.* With how angry Antonio was with me being here, the pit of vipers was safer. But I knew there was a method to Caltrone's madness so I kept my mouth shut and eyes forward.

"Ahhh, the mother of the girl, I assume. Well now, let's get down to business, shall we? While I don't mind you searching for your precious grandchild, I have to insist that you leave all guns and other weapons with me, eh?"

I saw Caltrone's jaw set. Antonio frowned so hard, his forehead bunched like he smelled something foul.

"That wasn't a part of the deal," Caltrone uttered in a low growl.

"*Sí,* correct, but I know you and I don't trust you, Caltrone. You're an evil motherfucker and I can't have you shooting up my home. Bad enough that I'm sure you will leave dead bodies behind, yes. But you will not be using guns to do it. The Cartel needs no more bad press than it already has. I'm sure you can understand, *mi amigo.* This is my turf and you must respect it same as I would have to respect your turf, *sí?*"

"This is bullshit," Antonio told his father.

"Curb your tongue, *mijo,*" Caltrone responded. "Benita, leave the guns," he told one of the women who had been flying the plane.

I didn't understand why or how we were going to get anything done if we had nothing to fight with. People tended to be a lot more accommodating when they had a gun to their head.

Benita returned from the jet with a black bag and dropped it at the captain's feet. He snapped his hand and a few of his men stepped forward to rid the women and Antonio and Caltrone of their guns. When they went to touch me, I flinched away.

Caltrone laid a hand on my shoulder and I stood still. I felt as if I was being violated. The man who searched me was too free with his damn hands. So much so that, when he was done, I kneed him in his dick. I got satisfaction when he fell to the ground clenching his dick. The captain found it comical as he spoke in Spanish to the other men, telling them I was feisty and he liked that.

"Now, I'll leave you to your own recognizance, Caltrone, but please try not to tear up the city, *sí?*" the captain said with a smile that told me something sinister lived within him.

Once they drove off and we were alone, I looked at Caltrone. I didn't think he was a man who had ever asked nicely for anything. The fact that I felt like the captain had all but punked us didn't sit too well with me.

"Why did you do that?" I asked Caltrone.

"Do what?" he asked.

"Give away all your weapons."

"I could have easily come through here and done whatever the hell I wish. But I believe in order and balance, especially with a situation as delicate as this. If I'd come through here without going through the proper channels, we'd get nowhere. Besides, a man who relies only on guns is a man sure to meet his death by another's gun. We have work to do."

With that, Caltrone turned and briskly walked to a black van that had been sitting in the distance. The woman I knew as Benita got into the van first. She thoroughly checked it before cranking it and driving it around in circles a few times. She even sped up then stopped quickly, pumping the breaks several times. If I had to guess, I would have said she was checking to make sure nothing was wrong with it, or no one had booby-trapped it to kill Caltrone.

Once she was sure it was safe, we all hopped in with Caltrone taking the passenger seat. I slid into the far back seat, hoping Antonio would take a seat in the middle row. He didn't. He climbed into the back seat with me, which told me he was intentionally fucking with me.

"You missed a whole damn seat," I said. "That whole front seat and you had to come park your ass back here next to me."

Antonio paid me no mind. I shook my head and slid over next to the window. Shit reminded me of when we were young and trying to play house. I didn't know why he did it, but anytime I was pissed at him, he would find some way to get next to me.

"Your name etched on the seats now? I can't sit where I want to? For the record, I was going to take the back seat anyway. I think you knew that, which is why you went for it first," he said after a while.

I sighed and shook my head. "Why do you always feel I'm doing something to intentionally mess with you in some way, huh?"

"Because it's what you do, Kenyetta," he answered solemnly.

"Don't call me that," I snapped at him.

"Whatever."

"Now who's doing shit to intentionally annoy the other one?" I asked, not because he would answer, but to make a point.

Antonio said nothing. For as much as we'd grown in our careers and as parents, sometimes we fell back into our youth and immaturity.

I took in the city as we drove. The place was alive with festivities. Clearly it was a tourist attraction. People of all races and ethnicities milled about taking photos, trying new foods, laughing and dancing, with some tourists being oddly out of place. I'd been to Mexico City once before and the place was as vibrant as I'd remembered.

As we passed through the main square, known as Zocalo, I took in the pre-Hispanic ruins and majestic colonial buildings. In the surrounding streets was a cross section of Mexico City's population. Business executives, workers, and fashionistas, as well as vendors, buskers, and Aztec dancers along with tourists and locals wandered the streets.

The van stopped just outside of a local market. I noticed that Caltrone pulled on latex gloves and a surgical face mask before he exited the van. The man had OCD and didn't like for people to breathe on him or touch him without his consent. It wasn't unusual to see people walking around with face masks on as some areas could be a bit dusty. Antonio helped me down after he got out of the van. I looked around, kind of anxious and nervous, hoping to see if I could spot Jewel in the crowd somewhere. I knew I was setting myself up for disappointment, but since we had touched down, nothing else had mattered to me.

I quickly caught up to Caltrone, wondering what the hell we were doing at a store. "Why are we here? At the market, I mean?" I asked him.

He spoke to Benita in Spanish before answering me. He told her to look for something that I didn't make out since noise drowned out the tail end of his order. Caltrone glanced down at me before answering. "We need weapons," was all he said.

I frowned a bit then looked around. The place we were in looked like a home goods store. I had no idea what kind of weapons, besides knives, we would get in a place like this one. I looked behind me and saw Antonio picking up vases, glasses, and crystals. Caltrone walked over to the bedding aisle and picked up every set of pillowcases he could find. Benita came back with a hand basket full of toothpicks, salt shakers, and bars of soap.

We bypassed about three cashiers until we got to the one with the longest line. Why we passed all the other ones until we got to this one was a mystery. The man cashing people out had a generic smile on his face, the kind that said he was only being nice to you because you were spending money.

"Gracias," he said cheerily. "Please come back to visit us before you leave," he told a white American couple, his Spanish accent thick.

Caltrone handed Benita all the items he had in his hands. Antonio had already gone through another line and had exited the store. For some reason, the hairs on the back of my neck stood up. Once we got up to the counter, the man looked at Benita and spoke to her with the same generic smile. He was about to say the same to Caltrone until he looked into his eyes. The man gasped and backed up like he had run into a wall. His eyes darted around wildly like he was looking for a way out. I didn't know who he was, but the fact that Caltrone had rattled him told me he knew something about my child.

Caltrone didn't say a word, but his eyes told
of his intent. As soon as the thought crossed
my mind, the cashier bolted toward the exit. No
words needed to be said to me. I took off after
him like a bat out of hell. As I bumped into people, I pushed and shoved them out of the way.

"Excuse me," I yelled at some. "Move!" I
yelled at others.

The man had a good lead ahead of me. He
made it out of the store before I did, but that
didn't stop me. The heat blasted me in the face
as soon as I stepped foot outside. Nothing else
mattered to me in the moment. All I heard was
my heart in my ears; and the thought that this
man knew where my child was made me run
after him like my life depended on it.

As he ran, he shoved people down and knocked
over carts. The fool jumped over a table like it
was a hurdle and I did the same once I came
upon it. We ran past a wall that had been painted
with different murals, past street vendors selling
clothing, food, and other trinkets. He was running toward the Metropolitan Cathedral. I knew
if he got there he could disappear inside and I
would never find him. I was gaining on him as he
turned down a side street. My mind was telling
me I had to be careful since this was his turf.
He could very well be leading me somewhere

he could ambush me, but I seriously doubted it since he was running erratically. He seemed to be going nowhere. He just wanted to get away.

I was so close upon him now, I could feel his fear. I ran and leapt onto a table, then jumped off to tackle the man to the ground. We both rolled and tumbled until we bumped into the brick wall of a building behind us.

"I don't know nothing. I don't know nothing. I swear."

For a moment, I looked on in confusion. That deep Spanish accent he had was gone and he sounded more American than I did.

I quickly got to my feet, breathing hard and annoyed that he made me chase him. He had fear in his eyes as he held his hands out in front of him.

"Know nothing about what? And why are you running if you know nothing?" I yelled at him.

The man was breathing so hard, it seemed as if it hurt him to do so. "Tell Caltrone I don't know nothing, please! I don't want to be involved."

The man was talking in riddles, aggravating me further. All I could think about was that he might know something about the whereabouts of my daughter. I also wanted to know how he knew Caltrone, but I didn't bother asking. When your name rang internationally like Caltrone's did, people were bound to know you in some capacity.

I kicked the man in his dick then slapped him for good measure. He groaned out while holding his dick. "I didn't take her. I had nothing to do with it, I swear," he cried.

Tears blurred my eyes. How the fuck did he know a "her" had been taken in the first place? My adrenaline spiked. Rage had taken a hold of me. I punched the man in the nose then kneed him in the face for good measure.

"Where is she?" I yelled. "Where the fuck is my daughter?"

All the man did was yell gibberish in Spanish. Some of it I could make out; some of it I couldn't.

"Speak English or slow the fuck down so I can understand your Spanish! Either way, you better give me something concrete or you're dead," I threatened.

I gave a quick glance around to make sure no police or anyone else were coming. That quick diversion of my attention gave him an opening. The man grabbed my left breast and squeezed for dear life. I yelled out as he shoved me back, and I stumbled into the wall behind me. Before I could get my footing, he was running away.

I cursed myself as I got up with haste. I started after him but stopped abruptly when, out of nowhere, Tone stepped from another building and clotheslined the man. The man's neck snapped back so hard, I thought it was broken. He was out cold on the cobblestone walkway. Tone rolled his shoulders as he stared down at the man. There was a look on his face that I remembered all too well. I found myself happy there weren't any dogs around.

It was cold in the damp warehouse. Caltrone was upset because the place was filthy. He had taken off his shirt and the golden glow of his skin shined underneath the low-hanging lights in the space. We were back at the airstrip in one of the old warehouse buildings off in the distance. I could hear water dripping from somewhere. Benita and the other female guards stood stoic at different entrances and exit points in the building.

In front of me was the Mexican man who had run from the store. His arms were strung up above his head, his feet dangled off the floor, and tears ran down his cheeks. Blood slid down his back, chest, and abdomen. His whimpers and pleas fell on deaf ears.

"I'm going to ask you again," Tone said. "What do you know about who has my daughter?"

"I don't . . . I don't know nothing. I swear on *mi madre,* amigo," the man cried. "*Por favor,* I know nothing," he cried. "*No mas, por favor, no mas. . . .*"

Tone twiddled with the toothpicks in his hand. He stalked up to the man. Found a soft spot between his neck and shoulder blades, then jabbed the toothpick down into the man's flesh. To most people that probably didn't sound as if it was enough pain to have the man squealing and jerking against the chains as he was. But I knew better and so did the cashier. In his back were about fifty more of those toothpicks. In his chest and stomach were more. Tone and Caltrone had placed them there. Stabbing him with the toothpicks each time they felt he was lying to them. Torture of the worst kind.

Caltrone shook his head. "You're lying," he barked at the man. "Why did you run, Jesus, huh? If you know nothing, why run?"

"Because word got out a few hours ago that you were coming," the man wailed.

"But what's that gotta do with you?" Tone asked.

"My brother . . . My brother is friends with Hector and Hector knows something."

"Ah, *sí.* Now we're getting somewhere," Caltrone said with a smile so cold, it chilled me.

I watched as Caltrone opened up a set of white pillowcases. He took his time, making a show of whatever it was he was about to do. He grabbed some of the crystals and vases Tone had bought in the store and dropped some in each pillowcase. He then placed the ends of the pillowcases on the floor and crushed the glass with his combat boots. I frowned as he wrapped the ends around each of his big fists.

"Who is Hector and where can we find him?" Caltrone asked.

"I don't know," Jesus stammered. "He left town last night, *sí*."

Caltrone's lips turned down and then he grunted. "Where did he go? What does he know?" He slowly stalked Jesus. I looked at the front of the man's pants to see he had pissed himself.

"*Madre di'Dios, por favor*. I don't know," Jesus said, eyes widened with fear.

Caltrone stood behind the man. "You keep lying to me and I am out of fucking"—Caltrone drew back and swung one pillowcase—"patience."

When it came crashing down on Jesus's back, I yelled out. The crushed, broken glass ripped toothpicks and flesh from the man's back. Jesus's yells and screams made my flesh crawl. The man howled out in pain so loudly that it made me grit my teeth. Caltrone swung the other pillowcase just as hard as he had done the first one. Each time he swung the muscles in his chest and arms flexed, coiling underneath his skin. Sweat drenched his body and anger masked his face.

"Ahhhhh! Ahhhhh! *Dios!* He said he was leaving to meet a connect in Texas! Ahhhhh, ahhhhh, God," Jesus wept. His body violently jerked against the chains each time the force of the glass-filled pillowcases made contact with his back.

Enough! I wanted to yell, but didn't.

By the time Caltrone was done, Jesus was barely alive . . . if he was alive. Caltrone stopped his cruel punishment then turned to his son. "We leave for Texas in the morning," was all he said as he rushed from the building.

Benita exited behind him yelling at the other ladies to hurry so they could clean him up.

I looked at Tone and licked my dry lips. The look in his eyes as he gazed at Jesus's limp body told me he had no qualms about what he had just done. There was no doubt in my mind that he was indeed his father's son. Since Texas was our next stop, I felt good knowing we were one step closer to finding our daughter.

Chapter 5

Antonio

Sun reflected off the dark shades of my sunglasses as I walked out from where we left Jesus to hang in the secluded warehouse for his crimes. Taking in the dry, arid terrain, I slipped a toothpick in my mouth in thought. Never would I truly understand why my daughter ran off with some stranger she met online, to Mexico of all places. Maybe it was easier for them to come here and disrupt their footsteps. I wasn't sure, but I planned to find out. Who was the nigga who took my daughter? The only thing I knew from my own information was that he went by the online name of Eric, but further digging let me know that wasn't his real name.

"What are you thinking, son?" I heard next to me.

I stood akimbo with my hands in my pockets. Keeping my gaze locked on the distance, I studied the way the wind would pick up dust

and swirl it around. "We need to find out what's
Jesus's connection to who took my daughter
before we leave," I explained.

"We know what his connection is, son. His
brother is friends with Hector."

"Yeah, but that didn't really tell us anything
other than a name and that this person knows
something." My mind was having a hard time
accepting what I had just helped to do to that
man in the warehouse, although a larger part of
me felt that he had it coming. Jesus's screams
and pleas battled with my psyche as I kept my
face stoic while I felt my father's gaze on me.

"And what do you intend to do to find that
out?" Caltrone asked, the scent of his freshly lit
cigar curling under my nose.

"Go check out his apartment. Heard he had a
little shop underneath where he sold shit. Like
you taught me," I said, turning to look at my old
man, "there's always more to the painting than
the image."

"Yes, I did. Then that's what we'll do," my
father said, walking with me as we headed to the
car where Kenya stood pacing back and forth.

I wasn't sure if Caltrone could see it, but I
knew that I could. Kenya's hands slightly shook.
Though she had a strong poker face, my years
of knowing her allowed me to pick up on the

small giveaways of her emotions. With my gaze running over her curvy, petite frame, I saw that Kenya stopped to briefly glance at me then lock her eyes on my father. We were still at battle with each other and we didn't give a fuck how that translated to others.

"Can we go?" she asked. There was annoyance in her tone.

Behind us smoke blazed from the fire my father had her set. "Did you do as I said and saturate everything in the warehouse with bleach and gas?" Caltrone asked with a bored expression.

Screams could be heard from within the warehouse. It made me scowl and had me walking past her as I muttered, "Should have listened to me." I watched her from the corner of my eye.

She cut her eyes at me, gritted her teeth, then ignored me. "Yes, Caltrone, I did," she said.

I knew what I had said would piss her off. All I could do was chuckle and climb back in the car while I watched her seethe in her anger from my window.

"Good girl. Let us go. You and my son will be looking through Jesus's shop and apartment while I conduct a little meeting."

Helping her into the car, Caltrone also got in and we headed back to town in silence. It didn't take long to handle business once we made it to Jesus's shop and my father left. Though Kenya's and my conversation was strained, I had her handle the shop and look around while I went up top to Jesus's apartment. After a while, we both turned up empty in our search. I had Kenya check the computer, as I rummaged through papers, finding Jesus's cell phone.

Paper rained over me as I stood in the middle of an adobo-style loft apartment. Several lamps lay haphazardly on the floor and flickered off and on as I stared down at a cell phone that had images of my daughter with a tall nigga. I could only see his back and her huge, laughing smile. Various thoughts were going through me as I stood there paralyzed in my angst.

"There was nothing downstairs and now I'm not seeing a damn thing on this asshole's computer. Nothing," I heard Kenya say as she forcefully clicked the keys of an old 2003 Intel computer. A harsh, tired sigh escaped her lips. She pushed back from the long banister computer desk that held the computer and other random crap, including various pictures. Papers shifted while she moved; then she paused to look through them. "Did you find anything on his phone?" she asked.

We switched what we held between us. I made note of several receipts, noticing money payments that coincided with the date of the pictures on the phone.

"Yeah," I sullenly said, taking two strides her way. "Several pictures of Jewel."

From what I was looking at, it seemed that Jesus had a side job as a driver. Though the transactions on that day were done in cash, he still made notes, which was smart and helpful on our end. Nigga was dead but he still had secrets.

"She looks so happy. I don't understand," Kenya whispered, her voice cracking with emotion.

Dropping to sit on a couch I passed, I folded my hands in front of me, thinking. "She thinks she's in love. Shit's not hard to understand. Baby girl got her a whiff, and like all girls that age who get their mind blown and twisted by the wrong nigga, or the right one, she let herself get played in thinking she had a good dude, even though he's too old for her. Same game, different generation."

"Jewel was smarter than that. We both taught her better," Kenya tried to reason.

I knew her words were hollow and that she was just trying to rationalize how this fucked-up situation even happened.

"We knew better and we still had that pull to be with each other at her age, damn the consequences. Like I said, same shit, different toilet. Once a teen gets that whiff of sex, baby, it's outta there. Can't tell them shit. They think they know all, are all, and are grown, regardless of the stupid-ass waving flag that's in front of them. No grown-ass nigga need to be chasing young cunt when it's some around his age or older who might want his lame ass."

"Tone," Kenya started in that way that always commanded my attention to make me check my language.

"Fuck it, you know the shit is truth. Our daughter fell in that same youthful bullshit and now we, the parents, are paying the cost for her fuckup. I want to just . . ." Hands forming into fists, my eyes narrowed as I shook my head.

Heated, Kenya abruptly stood up and pointed at me with the phone in her hand. "And what is that going to help, huh? You stayed strict on her and look where we're at. Besides, how you and I were as teens was different. We were friends and . . . it was just different."

There was something more behind her trailing off. It was the thing we both chose to ignore. Brushing off that whisper of my conscience, an amused but pissed-off laugh rumbled low in my chest and I focused on the bullshit she tried to slickly shade me with. So, we were here finally and going to play this game. *A'ight*.

"So, telling our daughter to be responsible in how she picks a nigga—because I knew, considering the fact that she is my child, she is intelligent, and beautiful, and could handle herself better than some of these other kids—was wrong?" I slowly rose off the couch and glared at my ex. "Being stern and telling her to keep her grades right so that she could earn the fucking luxuries she had, like that computer she loved, is my fucking fault? Giving her a gotdamn curfew so she couldn't run around Miami with a wet pussy and dulled-out mind because some wack-ass punk knew how to say the right thing, was wrong? Shit was at midnight and she seventeen, but I was wrong in that?"

I felt myself pace around the room as I kept a level voice. "Teaching her to value her body, not by shaming her but educating her about having a responsible, healthy, budding sexual ownership. I mean, you and I were both there for that, but you like to think I'm a fucking asshole and tyrant with our daughter? Oh, a'ight then. Fuck outta here, Kenya. I'm not even going to waste my anger on you. Back to business."

Kenya snapped, "Screw that. Yes. Because, in all of it, you were an asshole and you know it. I give you respect that you're a damn good father to Jewel. But, you're right: we don't get along. Let me cross you and—"

Jumping in, I shook my head. "Right, to you I may have been an asshole! I never raised my voice to Jewel. Fuck, I never raised my voice to you. I stayed cool. We both did. You and I argued like normal people, Kenya, but I'm the asshole. You are just as much an asshole as me. Own ya shit, mama. I still made sure that you had all you need for Jewel and even yourself. Yeah, we can't get along, but I respected you even with how you distanced yourself when we were together. So, don't play me like that. I sucked as your man because I was keeping you from this half of me; and, no matter what the hell I did, it was wrong according to you. That's all. I did everything right by Jewel. Everything. You still can't trust in me to believe that I can lead us."

"Because you can't. Look where your leadership led us now. Look where our child is at now. Gone," Kenya spat out. "What's your plan, huh?"

My lips turned up as if something stank in the room and I found that Orlando part of me wanting to abuse her verbally. Instead, I turned my back on her, frustrated at everything, even though I knew that this was our grief and anger at losing our daughter.

After a while, a long moment of silence followed until I heard sniffles. Gripping my fists, I saw Kenya staring at the phone holding herself. I still hated to hear or see her crying. Even throughout all our fights and battles and close blows, where I found myself ready to choke out her fiancé, I hated her crying. We didn't work, so I thought, but we did; and, like I said, I knew all her triggers and she knew mine. Right now, we were in a psychological and emotional war and being near each other wasn't working.

"Look—"

"Shut the hell up, Tone," Kenya quickly cut me off. Her honey brown eyes narrowed in her quiet angst as she spoke. "Somewhere in both of our parenting we messed up with Jewel. I mean, that's apparent with the fact that she ran away with a damn stranger. I was wrong in what I just said, because it wasn't all you. It was me too. I did the same thing. I thought being lax with her would help and it didn't."

Sulking, I stayed where I was watching her. "Why do you say that?"

Kenya was walking back and forth in the room. Her boots scraped the wood floor. She fiddled with the side of her jacket until she settled upon resting her hand on her ample hip, clad in blue jean leggings.

Inwardly cursing, she glanced at me. "Because, I recognize this number," she said holding the cell up. "It's the same one that used to call the house. I remember talking to the voice on the other end. My gullible ass thought he was a kid her age."

"Call it. Fuck, give it here," I shouted thrusting my hand out. I found myself shouting in Spanish about this being why I hated Jewel having a cell, and why I never allowed Jewel to have niggas call my home at all hours of the night. A slight red haze was sliding over my eyes. I wanted to kill. I wanted to punch a wall in but, above all, I wanted my daughter back alive and healthy.

Holding the phone away from me Kenya shook her head. "Can't we trace it?"

Several deep, meditative breaths kept me from being pissed at Kenya as I tried to listen to her like a civilized man. "That's what I am trying to see. If it's the same number that I found when I was doing my own search, then we can cross that shit off the list because it's long been disconnected," I explained.

Kenya spat out the numbers then cradled the phone. A part of me realized in the moment that she was doing that because it was the only tangible link we had to Jewel. Pictures were worth a thousand words and I guessed Kenya needed them close to her, so I dropped my hand and let it be.

Digging in my pocket, I pulled out my cell, which held some of my personal notes and leads; then I nodded in disappointment. "Yeah. Same number. It went dead about a couple of weeks ago after I traced it and had a private investigator call it."

"The time and date of the call matches that window. I guess they were down here then," she quietly said.

"Anything else in the pictures? From the receipts, they were dropped off at some restaurant. Is that matching up?" I asked, moving around to head to the computer desk where I noticed a lot of pictures resting. "Seems he took tourist pictures when he dropped them off or when they came into his store."

"I see a corner of something, but look." Moving by my side, Kenya pointed to a smiling blonde and a sunburned fat boy.

Behind the tipsy couple was a pink adobo-style building with a wall of Mexican tchotchkes. In the picture of Jewel and her kidnapper, I saw the corner of the same wall. Quickly going through all the pictures, I stepped back. "Let's go."

Storming out, we left Jesus's place from the back. A large, blaring horn drew our attention, and I saw that it was the same female driver who chauffeured my father around. Jogging, we made it to the ride. I opened the door for Kenya to get in, and then I followed her.

"I'm doing a search." She silently clicked on the phone then glanced my way with a determined expression. "It looks like it's Teresa's Hotel and Cantina. What's the plan? We need to be on the same page."

Adjusting my gloves, I stared at the winding road. "You're right. A'ight, the plan is to gather any witnesses. We'll need them as legal backup just in case this whole thing goes south; and we find out names, aliases used, and if they have a rental car. We probably can trace them exactly to where they went in Texas. Then we leave in the morning like Pops said."

"Do you think he's doing some of that already?" she asked as she shifted to the side watching me.

"Yeah, I have no doubt that he is. Father is always a step ahead of everyone. It's how he's successful in being who and what he is."

Slightly laughing, Kenya scoffed. "Yeah, don't I know."

Immediately I stepped right into old shit, remembering the connection between her and my father. I had so many damn questions I wanted to ask, but now wasn't the time, I knew. Still, I had to at least get it off my chest in some way.

"And how do you know again? Why do you know again?" I got ready to go deep with it again, but I stopped myself. I was emotionally drained and didn't feel like it, just like I knew she felt the same way. "Never mind."

We pulled up in front of the cantina. Funny enough, music blazed and the place looked like the stereotypical tourist trap. Townspeople paraded around singing and dancing, tourists did the same drunk and "lost in the sauce" dances. In the midst of it all, my father stood at the door of the establishment, waiting. He watched us both with an unreadable expression as Kenya and I climbed out of the car.

"I assumed you knew to come here, because?" I asked needing to know.

"Jesus was known for frequenting Teresa's and when he chose to speak to us, even though he was at work, his breath smelled of liquor. There's details in the smallest inkling, son, remember that, because it is a lesson I taught you." Turning on his heels, he walked back into the cantina.

Looking down at Kenya, I shook my head. "Like I said, he's always a step ahead of everyone."

Once inside, we questioned everyone on whether they had seen my daughter. Surveillance cameras were confiscated and people were shaken down. Of course, people played stupid and said they knew nothing, and that was a shame, because they were cantina regulars and townies. This was verified by my father, who sat drinking tequila with the town's mayor in the back of the cantina. After not getting the answers I needed and wanted, I noticed Kenya had disappeared, so I searched the place for her.

It was when I entered the cantina billiards room that things changed for the better. As she fed her fist into the side of a voluptuous and beautiful lounge singer, I stood observing Kenya show her dark side. She slammed the screeching woman's dark, curly mane into the floor.

"Tell me the name of the bastard who took my daughter. I saw your funky-ass expression change when I showed you the picture. Who is he to you?" she yelled out, her teeth clenched together in anger. "Do I need to ask you in Spanish?" Kenya spat out in anger.

When the woman tried to pull at Kenya's lush, natural mane, I chuckled knowing that was a huge mistake. Kenya went livid. She slammed her elbow into the woman's eye then repeated her question in Spanish as they battled.

Part of me was about to break it up, but considering that Kenya sat on the woman's chest and was effectively handling things, I left her to it. I walked to where my father sat, as he too watched on. It was Kenya's turn to learn some lessons and I planned on watching as a means to pass the time before morning came. There's nothing like a woman scorned. Turn that woman into a mother and the gates of hell always opened on earth.

Chapter 6

Kenya

I grabbed the woman by her hair up from the floor then slung her into a nearby wall. The pictures and plaques attached to it came tumbling down onto her head. I didn't care who was in the place or what they saw. The woman I was assaulting knew something about the whereabouts of my child and I intended to make her tell me one way or the other. People, men and women, scurried out of my way. They already walked on eggshells as they knew Caltrone Orlando was in the building. I was sure many of them assumed I was of some relation, being that no one moved in to stop me.

Bella, the woman in question, whimpered as her body hit the floor in a hard splat. She was about sixty pounds heavier than I was, but I didn't care. Somebody had my child and nothing could topple the rage I felt inside as a mother. I slung a chair out of the way as I stalked over to her. She had fallen onto her stomach, so I straddled her back, lifted her head by the back of her hair, and slammed it into the red-painted concrete floor over and over and over again.

Moments before, I'd shown her the picture on the cell phone same as I had done with other people in the establishment. But, unlike others, Bella's face told the story that her mouth wouldn't. It was like looking at the picture triggered some kind of memory for her. While she lied about seeing or knowing them, her eyes held a glint of something that caught my attention. It was miniscule, but being that I paid attention to detail, I caught it. It was a skill I'd picked up while being an ADA. Paying attention to the smallest details could make or break a witness on the stand. The bitch, Bella, knew something and I intended to make her tell me even if I had to beat it out of her.

"*Bueno!* Okay," Bella managed to squeak out. "Okay, *sí. Sí,* I know something of him," she cried.

I stood up then pulled her heavy body behind me. I grabbed a chair then shoved her into it. "Talk," I barked out at her.

Before she said anything, her eyes roamed around the small cantina, trying to see if anyone would help her. I kicked her in the knee, which caused her to yelp out like I'd just tried to rip her heart through her ribcage.

"I said talk," I demanded again.

"Jesus's brother, Hector, brought them here. The girl looked happy. Her and the guy."

"What guy?" I asked.

"I don't know his name," Bella said with a pained expression on her face, her accent becoming thicker with each word spoken. "He was tall and black with muscles and he had some kind of chess piece tattoo on his arm."

I glanced over my shoulder at Tone. We had something else to go on now. The description of the man she was with was vague at best, but the fact that Bella gave us a specific tattoo to look for made it better. Still, I was angry. I was beyond reason. I needed to hurt someone, anybody, because my child was gone. So I threw a punch to Bella's face that knocked her head back. Blood shot out of her nostrils and pooled from her bottom lip. I hit her again and this time so hard the chair she had been sitting in rocked back, tilted over like it wanted to fall, and then clanged back down on the floor.

"Kenya," Caltrone's booming voice called out to me. The man's voice demanded attention, even when he was being gentle in his tone.

I whipped my head around at him. "Yes," I answered.

"That's enough. She can tell us nothing more. She's of no use. We don't want to waste precious time now," he said plainly as he made his way from the building.

The fact that the man had changed clothes and cleaned himself up after the happenings at the warehouse told me his OCD was kicking into overdrive. I knew being in this place was nerve-racking for the man, but the fact that he was willing to do it in order to find my child made me appreciate him.

Tone walked over to me and placed his hand on my shoulder. "Calm down," he said to me.

I almost wanted to ask why I had to calm down, but something in his eyes made me hold my tongue. There were times when I gave Tone a hard time and there were other times when I knew not to test his patience. I looked around at the other people who, I'd forgotten, were in the place. Some quickly cast their glances in other directions while others looked disgusted. I couldn't care less.

Tone walked out of the cantina behind his father, and I soon followed. Meanwhile, Bella started yelling and squealing at the top of her lungs. You would have thought somebody had poured scalding hot water on her naked body. Benita and her sidekick snatched Bella by her hair and dragged her, kicking and screaming, to the van. What they would do with her I had no idea.

I also had no idea where we would be staying for the night, as I knew Caltrone wouldn't sleep in any hotel bed he hadn't had thoroughly inspected. So it wasn't a surprise when we pulled up to a Mediterranean-style mansion that sat at the very end of a dark and dusty road. Traveling through Mexico City at night was a very scary experience especially if you had heard the tales of the Cartel. That would be a different story for another day.

I couldn't see the color of the house under the night sky, but I was surprised to see Antonio's niece and nephews were already there, ready and waiting for their grandfather like the good toy soldiers they were. Tone hadn't said anything to me on the ride over. I sat on the front seat behind the driver and passenger seats of the van, a stoic expression on my face. Tone sat behind me. I didn't know what was going on in his mind. Probably the same thing going on in mine as I stared at the picture of our daughter on the phone we had found.

I couldn't get over how wide the smile was on Jewel's face in the photo. She looked to be in love. That look was familiar to me. Many days

I'd had that same look when I was a teenager and her father had been around. I remembered the days when I used to be stone-cold pissed off, ready to fight any chick or boy who wanted to catch a beatdown. And all Tone had to do was look at me and shake his head or grab me up from behind to pull me away and all the anger I had in me would subside. Tone and I were good back then, before the baby and before the pressures of growing pains got us. But I shook those memories off, as Tone and I were over.

I thought about my fiancé, Isaac. He was a good man. Since the day I'd met him, he'd been good to me. Jewel liked him and he worked damn hard to get her to. Isaac had always been afraid of not being able to meet Jewel's expectations for a stepfather. So when he found something they were mutually interested in, he jumped on it. Jewel liked anything to do with science. I always chuckled at the fact that a doctor and a lawyer had produced a future scientist. Isaac was into all that chemical mixing shit. He and Jewel would talk for hours about whatever the newest shit Neil deGrasse Tyson was talking about.

I chuckled to myself. No matter how good an attorney I was, I was no match for that kind of talk. There was a time when I'd prided myself on being able to find a mate whom my daughter accepted and one whom Tone approved of; at least, that was the lie I told myself. I wasn't really sure what Tone thought of Isaac, as he'd never said a word, but I was sure since he hadn't forbade me to have the man around his child that he was somewhat okay with him.

"Kenya, you going to get out of the van or what?" Tone asked from the back seat.

I jumped at his intrusion into my thoughts. For some reason, his voice annoyed me in that moment. I didn't even realize I'd just been sitting there. Caltrone had exited the van already. Benita, her sidekick, and Bella were all gone as well. I glanced behind me at Tone then hopped out of the van. I pulled my cell from the black bag I carried. I had forgotten I'd placed it there. I had fifty missed calls. I eagerly scrolled through the log to see if any were from numbers I didn't recognize. My heart deflated when I saw they were all from Isaac.

The mansion sat regally like it went back to the Spanish roots of architecture in Mexico, and beyond that to the Mediterranean culture of the classical period. A peristyle, or inner courtyard, was the central element around which the house was organized. The various rooms of the house surrounded the interior space. That was where Bella had been strung up. She was stripped naked. Her stretch marks made trails like a road map over her bottom half. Tears rained down her rosy cheeks and she looked to be in more pain than she cared for. The way her arms were above her head made it appear as if they were about to be pulled from the socket.

There was no need for me to make any bones about what was going to happen to the woman. If she was alive after it was all over, she would never be the same. Mark was already eyeing her like she was his last supper. Frederick and Maria-Rosa were standing off to the side, guns strapped on them as if they were going to war. I didn't need to question how they'd gotten here or when. That wasn't of importance. My heart was broken because my daughter had run off with some lowlife piece of shit and that was my only concern.

"Don't get too comfortable," Caltrone said as soon as Tone and I walked in. "We have to move quickly, as word travels fast. Catch a quick nap; then we're on the jet to Texas before daybreak."

I nodded but didn't say a word. I looked at Tone, I mean really looked at him for the first time in years. I didn't give him enough credit for being a single father. His load was much heavier than mine. To be honest, after my run-in with Lu

Orlando I'd dropped the ball as a parent. Wasn't mentally fit to be a parent after all the mess I'd gotten myself into. I found that I wanted to apologize to him. Maybe that would make me feel better. Maybe that would take away the guilt I felt behind letting my personal demons interfere with being a mother.

But I didn't get a chance to. My cell rang and before Tone could ask me what the fuck I was looking at, I pulled it from my hip and found my way to an empty room. It was Isaac calling. I'd meant to call him sooner to let him know I'd made it to Cuba and that I was okay, but I hadn't had the chance to. The room I was in was dark and the only light came through the floor-to-ceiling window because of the moon. I could see that different furniture pieces had been covered with white sheets. Statues made ghostly shadows along the wall and I was willing to bet any amount of money that there were cameras all around the place.

"Hello," I answered.

"Hey," he answered quickly. "Kenya, baby, what's going on?" Any other time, hearing his country baritone would make me feel at ease. It did nothing for me now.

"Hey, Isaac," I responded, my tone about as dry as I felt.

"You find anything? Did you get the help you went there for? You okay? Did that man touch you in any way?" he rattled off at me.

Isaac knew I was coming to see Caltrone Orlando. I'd told him as much. He didn't really know the man, but he knew the name Orlando and that had given him pause. The only way a person didn't know the Orlando name in the South was if they lived under a rock.

"I'm okay, Isaac."

"I've been calling you."

"I know and I'm sorry. I left my phone in my bag on the flight—"

"Flight? What flight?" he asked as the tone in his voice changed a bit.

"Caltrone traced Jewel to Mexico. Me and Tone—"

"Mexico? What? How the hell did she get to Mexico? And Tone? You didn't tell me Antonio would there," he said, his voice taking on that jealous note it always did when I mentioned I'd be somewhere alone with my child's father.

Shit. Isaac didn't know about Tone being here because I hadn't known Tone would be in Cuba once I got there. Quiet as kept, Isaac liked Tone about as much as a person with arachnophobia liked pictures of spiders. He always tried to play it off though. I never really knew his beef with

Antonio, as Tone had never said a disrespectful word to the man.

"I didn't know he would be in Cuba, Isaac. He showed up a few hours after I did," I explained.

Isaac was quiet on the other end of the phone. I could hear Bill Nye talking about something in the background. That was Isaac's thing. He always had to be in the know, always had to know what his white counterparts did so he could stay one step ahead.

"So you mean to tell me that you both randomly showed up in the same place to ask the same man for help?" he asked.

I knew that sounded like too much of a coincidence even to my ears, but it was the truth. "It's the truth, Isaac. I had no idea he would be there," I defended myself, feeling myself become annoyed.

Isaac grunted. "And now you're both in Mexico," he said with a tone that told me he didn't believe shit I was saying.

"*Dios,* Isaac, I don't have time for your male pride and jealousy bullshit right now. My child is missing," I snapped into the phone before I could catch myself.

"Don't yell at me, Kenya. Don't ever yell at me like that again. I told you before," Isaac said. This time there was no tone in his voice. It was a low and even monotone. The same one he always took when he felt my voice was at a level too high for him. Isaac never liked for me to yell. He felt because he never yelled or cursed, even when we argued, that I should grant him the same respect.

I sighed and shook my head. I wasn't able to deal with his bullshit and handle all that was going on at the same time.

"You didn't tell me he would be there because you knew I'd have a problem with it. You knew I wouldn't have let you go had I known he would be there," he said. Anytime Isaac said the word "he," it was with so much venom it poisoned my ears.

"'Let me go?'" I barked back into the phone; then I pulled it from my ear to look at it as if it had offended me. "Like you could have stopped me either way."

I heard Isaac sigh. "It's always something with you and this motherfucker," he mumbled under his breath and, to be honest, I had no idea what the hell he was talking about.

"What? What are you talking about?"

"And, let me guess, you two are staying in the same hotel? Same room as well?"

"Oh, my God," I spat. "Isaac," I called then took a deep breath. "We aren't even at a hotel right now and if we were, no, we wouldn't be in the same room. I can't believe you're doing this to me right now. Where is the man who was supportive of me doing whatever it took to find my daughter?"

"He's still here, but that was because I didn't think Antonio was doing enough. That was why I gave you the okay to go globetrotting over to Cuba to speak to the man who you said could help you."

"Whoa," I said. "You better stop while you're ahead. Antonio was and is doing everything in his power to get our child back. What has gotten into you?"

"Does that include you?"

"What?"

"Nothing. Nothing at all, Kenya. I have to go," was all he said before the phone went silent on the other end.

I was left standing in the dark trying to figure out what the hell had just happened.

Later, I didn't get much sleep. Bella's screams through the mansion kept me awake most of the night. Thoughts of Jewel kept me awake as well. I missed my baby so much. My heart was broken into thousands of little pieces. I'd give anything to hear her voice, to hear her speak to me in Spanish when she was upset or to see her eyes turn to slits like her father's when I said something she didn't like. I'd give anything to see her pout or whine about something that wasn't going right in her world. I closed my eyes as tears fell down my cheeks. I'd trade everything I owned to have her hug me and sit on my lap like she would do from time to time. Yes, she was seventeen and would still sit on my lap.

I was in a room in the west wing of the mansion, with Tone in the room next to me. It seemed as if Caltrone always made it a point to put us in a room next to one another. I had no idea why he kept doing that, but I didn't care to press the issue.

There was a knock on the door to my room. I didn't have to open the door to know who it was. There had never been a time when Tone and I were around one another that he couldn't pick up on when something was wrong with me. Even when he wasn't in the same room, it was like something, some kind of connection we had to one another at the soul level, would allow him to pick up on my moods. This time was no different.

I got out of the bed and trekked across the cold marble flooring. "What, Tone?" I asked without opening the door.

"You okay?" he asked.

"I'm fine," I lied.

"You're lying. I know you, Kenya."

I sighed and laid my head against the door. For a moment, I thought about not opening it as Isaac's words replayed in my head. But after a few seconds, I turned the locks and opened the door. I turned to walk away without looking at Tone as he strolled in. It was after two in the morning. Neither of us would be worth anything once we landed in Texas if we got no sleep.

Tone locked the door behind him as I crawled back in bed. I finally looked over at him when I got settled in, and I wished I hadn't.

I groaned low in my throat. "Antonio, where's your shirt?" I asked.

I didn't need him in my room, in the dark with only the moonlight shining through, in low-hanging jeans. I didn't need to see the tattoos or the toned chest and six-pack abs. I most definitely didn't need the wild, thick coils of hair sitting unruly but sexy on his head. And God knew I didn't need to see the low droop of his eyelids and the sexy way his eyes seemed to glow against the moonlight in the dark.

"I guess the same place your pants and bra are," he quipped back at me.

I shook my head, remembering I only had on Calvin Klein boy shorts and a thin T-shirt

with no bra. So I didn't have a rebuttal for his
comeback. I slapped the tears away from my face
as Antonio sat on the bed next to me. We both
sat there in silence, looking out over the land
from the open bay window.

"We're going to find her," he said to me after a
while. "And soon. You have my word."

As badly as I wanted to nod or say something,
I couldn't. All I had left at this point were my
tears. In that moment, I was grateful for him
being there as I broke down crying. I couldn't
hold it in any longer. I was hurting. My child was
gone. Tone wrapped his arm around me then
pulled me onto his lap. Just like Jewel could still
sit on my lap, I still fit in Tone's lap like I always
did. There was nothing sexual about the way he
held me in that moment. He was simply a man, a
father comforting the mother of his child. And I
needed that. I needed him in that moment.

The bond between two people who had history
the way Tone and I did could never be broken.
Even when the love and the sex were gone, even
when the lust had gone from a blazing inferno to
a simmering coal, the bond Tone and I shared as
best friends never wavered. So when he held me
and allowed me to cry until sleep overtook me, I
welcomed it.

Chapter 7

Antonio

Sleep didn't come easy that night for me, if at all. The shared pain between Kenya and me, along with the thoughts of Jewel, kept me on edge. There was no way that I could mentally keep my chill on her kidnapping, but I was trying. Momentary flares of aggression that I had against those who would try to keep my daughter's whereabouts hidden kept me on edge. I let all that out in the privacy of my bathroom, gripping the porcelain bowl as my body shook in response to my sealed emotions; and the sounds of Kenya's cries added to the agony in my spirit.

I was a lot of things, but accepting that I could be a natural born killer was still conflicting with my psyche. The part of me that led me into medicine with a desire to heal those in need was fighting with what was in my blood. Even now, as I held Kenya, the doctor in me was at the surface. Once her cries softened and her hold against me became lax, I gently laid her on the bed, got up, left, and came back with a black duffle bag that held my med kit. In it was everything I needed in case any of us were hurt, and extras to use as what I knew best: medicine against my foes.

Settling back on the bed, I had gauzes, antiseptic, natural aloe gel, liquid stitch gel just in case, and square cotton pads. Kenya had gone ham on that Bella woman, so much so that she had effectively bruised and cut up her knuckles. From how she held me, I knew they hurt, which was why I carefully took her hands and began to quietly work on them.

"You're still trouble, baby," I muttered in Spanish while I cleaned her cuts.

The light, sweet scent of soap, mixed with her natural honey smell, traveled over my nose. It made me study the way her body had inched toward me and how her thighs peeked from under the bedsheets I had laid over her. In another place and time in our past, how she was right now, how she always was when I was near her in bed, inching toward me, would have me folding myself around her to give her the intimacy and comfort she needed. Or, it would have me waking her up with heady kisses, my fingers playing against her covered slit until moisture dampened the fabric and until her moans created a sweet crescendo in our room.

Rolling my shoulders, with a grunt, I tried to shut off from running across my mind that quick memory and internal truth that no woman could ever match her moans, but I wasn't fast enough. Carefully, I pulled the sheet back over her to cover her fully; then I went back to work on her. As I did so, the sound of something vibrating knocked me from my thoughts. Shifting in my seat on the bed, I looked around for that muffled sound until I reached under her pillow to pull out her cell.

The image of Kenya with her fiancé Isaac standing in front of the bakery they had opened together drew my attention. Considering how late it was, it annoyed me that he was calling, but it wasn't my business. I just knew that Kenya needed whatever rest she could get, so I tapped her cell and moved the call to voicemail. Nigga might have been upset about it, but it was what it was. He'd get over it.

Honestly, I didn't care if he didn't. This thing going on was about one thing, our child, and I'd be happy enough to explain it to him man to man. No lie. I had no issue with the dude even though I felt at times when Isaac looked at me that he felt some type of way about my presence. It took a long time for me to fully accept him in my daughter's life. Naturally, I let him know that when Kenya first introduced him to me. I mean, what man wouldn't question or do a low-key background check on a nigga he knew nothing about but who would be around his child, let alone his daughter? Blame it on how I was raised, but it took me a long time to trust.

Back then, I still was determined to keep a respectful decorum with the homie because I wanted him to know that if he stepped the wrong way I would not be a very responsible brotha. I also didn't want him thinking that I was still hung up on Kenya.

But you are.

Shaking my head, I glanced down at Kenya then let her hand go. That pesky secret place within me was acting up and I wasn't about to deal with its BS or its memories. I pushed up off the bed.

We had a good friendship at one time. I had embraced being a father and husband in the beginning until real life and college, then later her distancing behavior, got us both fucked up. But, in the end, we still were friends at times. We could be cordial.

Now that the anger was settling down, it kind of felt like we were getting back to being adults. Walking to the bathroom, I washed my hands then studied my face. I was getting a five o'clock shadow. I had a bruise near my jaw from where I was hit in my scuffle with Jesus. Near my ribcage was a similar bruise. Nothing on me was severe but everything was sore.

It had me rolling my neck until the muscles and tendons stretched and relaxed. I reached in my pocket and pulled out my untraceable cell. Dialing, I waited and moved to sit on the edge of the steel clawfoot tub that sat in the middle of the large basilica-style bathroom. My gaze took in the archway designs on the wall, with its golden touches and Spanish tilework.

"*Mijo,* are you okay?" I immediately heard in my ear.

Sliding my palm down my face, I sighed. "I'm tired, Mama."

"*Sí,* it's late, but I know what you really mean, my son. What have you learned?" my mother asked in the way that always was an additional healing balm.

Just the simple sweetness helped put strength back in me and get my head in check. As the son of Satan himself—not the legend that is Lucifer, but the title that is Satan—being weak was not allowed. Not how I was right now. Not with the way my voice cracked and my eyes itched with unshed tears. So it was spilling some of my frustrations out with my mother that kept me together.

"Found pictures of her. She was happy and it pisses me off. It pisses me off that my baby girl could put herself in the type of situation where she'd go with a complete stranger. It's fucked up, Mama. I mean, I thought I did everything right. Thought I taught her how to pick the right type of person to stand by her side."

"Listen to me, *mijo*. Remember what I told you. A parent can only instill a strong foundation. It's up to the child to lay the right bricks. You and Kenya took that and elevated it by offering her the first bricks then letting her gain her own footing. *Mijo,* sometimes those bricks are wrong but you have to trust that she'll replace them with the right ones," my mother lovingly explained.

"*Sí,* I know. However, I must bring her back alive and unharmed in order for her to continue building," I replied, gripping my cellphone.

My mother's light, sleepy chuckle tickled my ear and made me sigh as she said, "Yes, and you will. Stay strong, *mijo*. You are my child, but you are your father's seed. Continue using that to your advantage and be better than he ever could be."

Quiet for a moment, I let her words settle in, then I stood. "Yes, ma'am. I love you. Forgive me for waking you up."

"No, thank you for calling your mama, and I love you more, *mijo*. Please come home safely with my grandbaby," she said.

"I will. I promise you on that." I hung up and moved to the sink.

Turning off the running water, I stepped back into the room. My soul was weary. I watched Kenya sleep while I stood in the middle of the room lost in my thoughts. I felt as if I should leave and I was about to, but her whimpering began. How she was muttering in her sleep reminded me of a time several years back when she woke up in a sweat, screaming. She had come to Miami to visit me and Jewel. I had just tucked our daughter in after reading to her when I heard Kenya's scream.

It was one of the times in our then union that I instinctively was ready to pull out my gun and go after an invisible threat. When I made it to the room, she wouldn't look me in the eyes. She wouldn't tell me what her nightmare was about. All she said was it was stress; then she lay in bed. Taking her at her word like I always did, I climbed in ready to hold her the way she usually liked; but, instead, Kenya turned her back on me and kept her distance. Back then, that was the start of our emotional and physical separation.

This time though, without missing a beat, her thrashing had me quickly sitting on the bed. I slid off my black slippers, threw my legs up to lie against the headboard, and pulled Kenya to me. When her arms wrapped around me tightly and she whispered our daughter's name, I sighed and sent a prayer to the universe until I eventually fell asleep. We both missed our baby girl and needed to get her home safely.

Early morning was our friend when we left after a large breakfast. The sun was blazing as we strolled past the roasting, battered body of Bella. Eyes glazed over looking at the skies, her body had literally ballooned from the heat and internal gasses of her body. Blood caked her skin and, from what I could see, insect bites marred the flesh. A memory of my childhood immediately let me guess what torture Bella had been put through before her death. My father was a very astute type of man, meaning he was a watcher of people's behaviors. When I was young, he learned that I had a fear of enclosed spaces and dogs due to running from a dog on the beach and getting caught in a cave. One day, my father decided to teach me a lesson. For several days, I was locked up in an old dirt cellar used for his wine.

From where I sat, all I saw were twinkling stars in the night sky. By the time I was pulled out of the cellar by my furious and teary-eyed mother, I was a changed child. When she managed to get to me, I sat knees pressed to chest in nothing but my underwear with dead dogs and insects around me.

I'll never forget it. My usually rambunctious self sat rigid with my body pressed against the smooth dirt walls. I wasn't really cognizant of the fact that my mother was there. I sat with a blank expression on my sweat-drenched, sooty face. All around me were broken wine bottles, blood, a pool of wine from an empty barrel, dead dogs, and roaches. In my hands were two large pieces of bloody broken glass. My father gave me two guidelines in order to get out of the cellar toward a rope waiting for me: I had to either walk through a makeshift pit of roaches and attacking dogs, or kill them.

Fear can make a human accomplish the most amazing feats. Thinking back, I still didn't know how I made it out, but I did. My first attempt had me trying my best to go through them, but the dogs bit me, as did the roaches, which crawled over me. I was so scared, I pissed myself. For several days with no food, just water, I tried to conquer my fear and wade through them again, but fear got the best of me.

When my father visited me and saw how I soiled myself and pleaded through tears for him to let me out, he stared at me in disgust. The man who was Caltrone, my father, ignored all of that and had me dragged into the pit of roaches and tied down. The dogs were chained back, barking at me as they watched. Eventually, several days later, I was released to the other corner of the cellar but the rope was taken away.

After that, my young mind decided that enough was enough. I chose to play with fire and used what I had at my disposal to gain my freedom. When my mother got me out of the pit, I had marks all over me. It was my mother's loving help that healed me, and the way she went in on my father that inspired me to stop being scared. I was eight years old and it was my birthday. That was the day I knew that I wanted to be a doctor, to help kids like myself. It was also when the love I had for my father disappeared.

Fisting my hands at the memory, I glanced at the bloated body, figuring that she had gone through something similar. The woman had erred by incurring the wrath of this family by lying and keeping the truth not only from us, but from my father. A humanistic part of me was disgusted, but the vengeful father I was felt nothing for the woman. She had crossed the wrong family and she needed to pay for it, and that was the Orlando running through my veins. Though the memory of my childhood and the emotions attached to that scratched at my mind, I hated my father; but, above all else, I feared the man at the same time.

Arriving in Texas didn't take as long as I thought it would. We landed on a private airstrip attached to a forty-acre, plus several mules, cattle ranch outside of Houston. After climbing into a blacked-out Bentley, we passed through iron gates that featured the crest of a lion with the name KING MEADOWS RANCH over it. I remembered this place, having come to it only once.

It belonged to Caltrone as a spoil of war and was run by family allies. I never understood as a child why he hated coming here but wanted to own it. The staff he selected were nobodies and family never came here; only unsubstantial business people came here to rent it out. As we rode over cream-colored bricks, in the distance a grand chateau-style mansion greeted us. Waiting in the blaring heat were several cousins and attendants who wiped their brows on the sly.

I stared up at a symbol that, as an adult, I knew goaded my father; then we walked inside. From the bad vibes kicking off my father, I knew that the Satan in him was riled up, which meant he was going to be a foul fucker. I slowed my stride to walk in tandem with Kenya.

"Keep out of his way or keep your language to a minimum, I'm warning you," I muttered low for her to hear. I watched Kenya open her mouth to question me and I quickly shook my head. "Above everything, trust me in this. This place doesn't make him as commendable as he was before coming here, okay?"

Crossing her arms over her chest she nodded. "As long as we get our daughter, I'll do whatever."

"Be careful in how you express that, especially now." With that I walked forward then was stopped abruptly by my father.

With his back to me, he stared ahead as if lost in a daze but spoke with a chilling tone in his rough voice. "I want you to head to the back. There's some things that I feel you need to be schooled on again as a refresher. You are too in your emotions and I will not tolerate that, Antonio."

Turning his head to where he stared at us from the side of his face, he grabbed a tablet from Mark, muttered something to him, then returned to speaking to us.

"Ms. Gates, for as much as I find your raw candor in handling that woman in Mexico intriguing, it is just that: intriguing. You need to learn structure in how you go after someone. Tone will teach you. Get out of my face," he said with quiet finality.

I could tell that Kenya wanted to ask about going after Hector, but I shook my head. When my father had handed Mark the tablet, I had noticed a file with the name Hector Sanchez on it. He was already steps ahead, so all we could do was follow his orders. Placing a hand on Kenya's arm, I pointed and guided her to the back where we stopped in a sunroom.

"We don't have time for this. We need to go after Hector," Kenya urged, her eyes wide with anger.

She paced back and forth, her feet thumping on the Moroccan tile flooring as I took in the surroundings. Exotic vines swung low like ivy against the brick wall of the sunroom. Several plants blossomed around us giving us shade, and Moroccan lounge chairs and couches begged to be reclined on. Behind Kenya on a large table were clothes: black pants, white tanks, and black kicks. Next to them were several types of guns.

I stepped up to the table then began undressing. "I know and I agree. But, like I said, we need to do what we gotta do. I told you this wasn't going to be easy."

"How can you say that with ease? This is our daughter," she said whipping around at me with a turned-up face, her words trailing when she saw me. "What are you doing?"

"I know. But he's calling the shots on this part of the game, Kenya," I said while looking up at her as I unzipped my pants. "I know nothing about Hector, so my own intel is dry at this point and I'm getting dressed. Looks like I'm teaching you gunplay."

"Gunplay?" Kenya continued watching me before shaking her head and reaching for clothes. "I have to change too?"

"Yeah, you do. Let's hope these lessons aren't like what I had to deal with as a child," I grumbled while working on my shoes.

After we both finished dressing, we walked across the lush green grass of an immaculately cared-for garden. Ahead of us sat Mark in a golf cart. He watched us with a mischievous expression on his face. He sat with one boot-covered foot swinging from the side, and he leaned on the wheel of the cart as a huge black bag seemed to twitch next to him.

Shaking my head, I ran a hand over my hair. "Nigga is about to be on some next-level shit. Be warned."

Kenya glanced up at me then looked back toward Mark. "I'll kick his ass if he tries something."

I chuckled then put my game face on. "Is that our target?" Jutting my chin toward the body, I heard another cart and I turned to see Caltrone stepping out of it. He had also changed. Like me, he wore a beater and dark jeans with boots. In his hand was a golf club and his face was marred by anger.

"Very astute, *mijo*," he said. How he called me that sent a chill down my spine every time. "I see that you aren't too out of the game," he said, taking several aggressive strides toward the golf cart. "Set our target free, Marco." Waiting, Caltrone stared our way with shades over his eyes. His jaw was tense and I just kept my distance.

"Show us how fast you can run, homie." I heard Mark cackle as he drove the cart forward then pushed his bag out.

"Today's lesson is this: are you a killer, *mijo*? Can you take down a man in cold blood? A woman? A child? Can your woman do the same?" he asked harshly.

I kept my eyes on my father and nodded watching the body of a young kid pick himself up and look our way with anger in his eyes. The boy looked to be maybe three years older than my daughter. He stood fisting his hands in front of him with his chin pointed up as if he was ready to buck up.

A sarcastic laugh left me as I sized the boy up then stopped in recognition. The kid matched the face that was on the tablet. Sharp, heated anger took over my thoughts and I strode forward.

"Hector?" I said not taking my eyes off him while moving forward.

"*Sí*, so tell me why you're hesitating," Caltrone said.

Rolling my shoulders, I walked forward, snatched away the golf club that was in my father's hands, then headed toward Hector. "I'm not."

As I approached, Hector stepped back. The closer I got, the farther he got until his eyes widened in fear and he turned to run. Hunkering low as if I were playing football I broke into a sprint with the golf club in the air. Swinging, I caught that little nigga on his leg, causing him to fall on his face. As he fell, so did my golf club as I shouted curses at him. Red was all I saw as I screamed at him and asked him what his part was in my daughter's kidnapping.

"Don't kill me, please. I was paid. I was paid," Hector shouted between my punches.

When I heard the sound of a gun going off and then the sharp scream of Hector as he cradled his hand I knew Kenya was behind me. When she started shouting too, I knew she was just as angry as I was. I guessed we were passing our first test because my father watched on in pride.

Chapter 8

Kenya

"Oh, fuck," Hector screamed out. "You shot me. This bitch shot me," he yelled.

"Next time, I'm aiming to kill," I spat. "I'm no longer in the mood to play around. Tell us something or you're dead and I put that on everything."

I was losing my patience with the whole thing. If we didn't find Jewel soon I was liable to lose all grip on reality. I kept having images in my head of her being tortured and sexually assaulted. It was all threatening to drive me mad.

"*Vete a la mierda! Perra estúpida,*" Hector hurled at me. "Why you so worried about her now? Why are either of you so worried? Especially you, *bendejo,*" he then barked at Tone. "You're the reason she ran off anyway. Ain't nobody kidnapped her. She left willingly and all I was paid to do was pick her up in Miami and drive her to Mexico. Shit was easy. Bitch had all the papers she needed, passport and her ID. So nah, nigga, ain't nobody kidnapped that young bitch."

Hector was sweating now, clutching his bleeding hand to his chest. I looked over at Tone and I could tell by the way his lips had thinned out and the way his jaw was set that he was about to walk over that thin gray line of sanity to lunacy.

"That young bitch, huh?" Tone repeated while shaking his head. He walked over to pick up the golf club he had dropped, looking at it like he was seeing it for the first time. I knew shit was about to go left.

"Who paid you?" I asked Hector.

He frowned at me, inched away from Tone like a slithering snake then, surprisingly, looked at Caltrone. "Hey, man. I don't want to talk to this crazy bitch. I'll tell y'all what you wanna know, but I ain't talking to no cunt with a gun and shit," he said then flinched when he thought Tone was walking toward him. "And I don't want to talk to this nigga either. Way I heard it, he was a fucking asshole who always kept his daughter locked up and shit. I don't wanna talk to you, nigga," he spat at Tone. "Fuck you."

I turned to look at Caltrone, who looked on with a curious gaze adorning his features. I took a deep breath and tried to calm my nerves. Something fragile in me was coming undone. But, before it could take root, I heard something crack. Then the yells and screams of Hector seemed to make my ears bleed. I turned swiftly then jumped back. With a deadpan look etched on his face, Tone beat Hector with that golf club. High above his head then a hard slam down on the sternum of Hector, Tone beat him. Hector's chest went from blood red to bruised purple and black.

Each time Tone hit him, his body jerked like a fish flopping out of water. Hector tried to roll out of the way, but Tone just kept following him, swinging that golf club until it broke skin. Blood started to pool from the boy's mouth as lesions, breaks, and tears in his skin decorated his upper body.

"Tone," I called out to him.

He didn't pay me any attention. That rage I'd seen in him the night he had attacked Johnny for hitting me was the same rage that encompassed his every move now.

"Pl . . . please, h . . . help me," Hector barely got out as his wild eyes gazed at me.

I saw fear. I saw panic. I thought I saw the boy's life flash before his eyes. He knew he was knocking on death's door.

"Antonio," I yelled again, this time louder, but to no avail.

He was gone and there was nothing I could do or say to stop him. I looked at Caltrone and Mark, knowing I would find no help there. Caltrone stood with his hands clasped in front of him and a posture that told me he wouldn't be moved. Legs spread shoulder-width apart and shoulders squared, he looked on with pride. Mark stood there with a sick smirk on his face, one that told me he was surprised to see Tone snap but was elated to see it nonetheless.

"Now," Tone said through deep breaths as he took one last swing. Hector was facedown by now, barely breathing but still trying to crawl away. "Two things: one, don't ever call the mother of my child or my daughter a bitch again or I'll flay your ass, nigga; and two, who paid you? Talk now and I'll let you live . . . for a little while anyway." Tone kicked Hector in his ribs then reached down to flip the boy over. I doubted Hector even knew where he was anymore.

"Shorty knew . . . This shorty knew my homie, Fallon. She asked Fal to do a pickup for her. Her name is Donna. Fal pulled out last minute and gave me the dough to do it." Hector was wheezing now. He coughed, spit blood, then took a deep breath like it pained him to talk. His eyes rolled around until they rolled to the back of his head.

"And where can we find Fallon and Donna?" Caltrone asked coolly.

"North Houston, Greenspoint Area. Moonlake Mills Apartments," Hector wheezed out.

"Thank you, Hector. I do believe your services are no longer needed," Caltrone responded. "Kenya," Caltrone called out to me.

I snapped my head up to look at him. "Yes."

"No witnesses," was all he said.

I swallowed, as I knew what he wanted me to do. I turned my attention to Tone, who had an unreadable look on his face as he watched.

"Please," Hector cried. "I . . . I got babies," he pleaded. "I didn't take her," he cried. "She came on her own. I ain't take her, I swear."

"This nigga lying, sexy," Mark's voice cut in. "Let me show you something. Some shit I found on this nigga's cell."

Mark pulled from his golf cart the tablet Caltrone had given him earlier; then he strolled over to me. He took his time scrolling through the thing before landing on a video. "I sent the shit to my e-mail and downloaded it to the tablet just in case," he said. He grinned like the Cheshire cat then pressed play. There was a sparkle in his eyes as he pointed to the video.

"No, don't do that," I heard Jewel's voice cry. "No, stop, stop," she wailed as a man kept trying to snatch the sheets she had covering her body.

My eyes widened. There she was, naked on a bed. There was apprehension in her eyes.

"Don't be yelling, bitch. You knew what it was." Hector's voice could be heard in the background.

I didn't know where they were, but the walls were shit green and the bed was unkempt. The red sheets were a bit dingy and Jewel looked about ready to jump out of her skin.

"Keith, what are you . . . What's going on?" she asked, panic all in her voice.

"Shut up, Jewel. You said you was down for a nigga so be down for me. Let the crew hit. You owe me anyway."

"No," she yelled then tried to run from the room.

Hector chased her, slapped her, and then threw her back on the bed. She jumped back up and punched him in his face before he swung and his fist landed in her eye. The sight tightened my insides and made my muscles coil in my stomach.

The camera panned across the room and I saw two more guys walk in.

"Yo, Fal," Hector called out, "told you this bitch was pretty. Keith been letting me watch him fuck shorty. Prettiest pussy you ever did see."

I saw the two men speak to Keith, who was behind the camera so I couldn't see his face. I swallowed hard, already knowing what was about to happen. When Jewel started screaming and Hector hopped his naked body between her thighs, I let out some kind of sound, something akin to a wounded animal. But when I saw Hector finish and the one called Fal flip my daughter over and sodomize my child, I lost all grips with humanity. So much so that I didn't even see that Mark was getting a kick out of watching his cousin get raped. I was angry at myself because, for a moment, I felt some kind of remorse for Hector. My humanity made me feel for the children whose father would never come back home.

It all happened in a flash. Caltrone yelled for Tone not to watch the video, telling Mark to put the tablet away before Antonio could snatch it away. In the back of my mind, I slightly remembered Caltrone body-blocking Tone from Mark so he wouldn't beat the boy down to get the tablet from him. Nobody was paying attention to me. I walked over to Hector and emptied the gun into him.

Each shot that rang out echoed in my mind. As my finger pulled the trigger, I felt a little more of my sanity melt away. I couldn't get Jewel's yells and screams out of my head. Couldn't take away the images of my child's body being violated over and over. I felt numb. Felt as if my humanity had left me. Once done, I dropped the gun on Hector's chest and walked off. I didn't know where I was going. Just knew the old Kenya was slowly dissipating.

Getting to the apartments Hector had given us took no time at all. I hadn't uttered a word since I'd put bullets in Hector. The images of my daughter being raped haunted me. She may have left willingly but, clearly, the game had changed. Tone and his father had gotten into a heated argument. Something about not allowing him to see the video.

"Antonio, *mijo,* watch your tone with me. You don't need to see that video," Caltrone had yelled at his son.

"Fuck you. I heard her screaming," Tone hollered, a wild look in his eyes. "I fucking heard her. I want to see—"

"Yo, Grandpops said no, nigga, so chill," Mark had foolishly chided him.

Tone's anger turned quickly. He went from being ready to square up with his old man to pummeling Mark's face.

Somewhere in my mind, I remembered Mark's brother, Frederick, trying to pull his uncle off his brother, which was his mistake. Tone had lost all of the mind he had left at that point and the only person who could bring him back was his father. I watched on, kind of like having an out-of-body experience, as Caltrone bear-hugged Tone and forced him backward. I didn't even think Tone knew or cared that Frederick wasn't trying to fight him. He was in a fit of rage and whoever was in his path could get got.

"Kenya," he screamed out at me wildly as Caltrone forced him back. "What was on the video? Did they hurt her? What? Why? Is she okay, baby? Just tell me, is she okay?" he rattled off at me.

Pain was in his eyes. He was like a rabid dog foaming at the mouth. I couldn't tell him what he wanted to know. Couldn't tell him that our baby had been violated in the worst way. Wouldn't tell him about the absolute fear in her eyes, the terror it was clear that she felt. No way would he ever know the wild, catlike way she was clawing and fighting until two men had to hold her down while another forced himself on her. So,

I turned away from him. I turned away from his
bloodshot eyes while his father was holding him
back, and I walked away.

Now, Tone was angry at me. I could understand why. But I wished he could understand
why I chose to remain silent.

"Shut the roads down," Caltrone ordered into
the phone.

Northborough Drive was where the apartment complex was. It was after ten o'clock at
night and children still littered the street. The
place smelled. Dumpsters were overflowing with
trash. Broken-down cars sat about. She-men and
he-bitches blurred the lines of male and female.
Curtains hung haphazardly on windows. Blinds
hung on by thin threads. This place looked as if
God had forgotten about it. Caltrone was muttering under his breath in Spanish. He wasn't
pleased that he had to come to the slums. Even
though he was in a face mask and latex gloves,
being here didn't agree with his OCD.

Building K was where we were to look. People
watched on as two black vans rolled through.
Most of the dope boys took off running for fear
of us being the cops. Tone was out of the van
before Mark could park it. Building K, door
three was where he ran. There was no knocking.
He stood back and then planted his booted foot
right through the door, knocking it off its hinges.

A woman screamed, kids scrambled about, and a tall, brown-skinned male tried to jump from the front window. Tone quickly rushed in and snatched him by the collar of his shirt to yank him back in. Tone pulled the boy so hard he went flying back into a glass end table.

"Hey, I ain't steal that shit, man. That was all Hector. I ain't take the drugs," the boy yelled.

The fool thought we were there about fucking drugs. That angered me. The fact that he didn't readily assume someone would come to avenge Jewel made my blood run hot. Caltrone casually strolled in and looked around the place like it stank, because it did. It smelled of mold and old chicken grease. The furniture was tattered. From the front room, I could see the dirty kitchen, which looked like it hadn't been cleaned in weeks. The floor was sticky, as the bottom of my combat boots made a tearing sound against the floor anytime I moved. Two children ran around with snotty noses and saggy diapers. They both looked too damn old to have pacifiers or to still be in diapers. A white girl who was built like the Michelin Man ran and snatched them up, trying to protect them as best she could.

Just looking at the filth of Fal's home and the beaten down way his woman looked angered me. She looked diseased; and the fact that he had been fucking her then stuck his dick in my child made me grit my teeth.

"This isn't about drugs, young man," Caltrone said.

"Then what the fuck you niggas kicking down my door for?" Fal snapped, a wild look in his eyes.

"This is life or death and you have only one time to answer incorrectly or I tell this man what you did to his daughter," he said. "I'm going to say a name and you're going to tell me if it rings a bell. Jewel Ortiz."

Fal's eyes widened at the mention of her name. He looked from me to Tone back to Caltrone before making a foolish attempt to get up and run for the window again.

Caltrone tsked then let his eyes roam around the dirty front room we were in. When several roaches made their way up the wall, he flinched like something hot had been thrown on him.

"Let's make this quick," he said. "Bring in the Judas Cradle," he then told Frederick.

I didn't move for fear I would kill the man before we got the information we needed. I didn't know what a Judas Cradle was but I was sure if Caltrone wanted to use it, it was brutal.

"Tell me where Donna is," Caltrone then said.

"Who?"

"Donna. The woman who asked you to pick up my granddaughter."

"I don't know where that bitch is. She dipped out about two days ago. Hey look, man, look. She was here all right, your granddaughter. But I told that nigga he had to get her up outta here."

"Where did he take her?" Tone asked.

Fal bunched his face up like he was confused and then annoyed. "Fuck if I know. I just told that nigga he had to go. Too much fucking heat, especially when they kept fighting."

Caltrone asked, "Who is he?"

"Man, I can't tell you that. Them niggas will kill me. You don't fuck with them. You don't fuck with that family."

I frowned then looked at Tone. *That family?* So, we were dealing with a whole family now? I didn't understand.

"Father, I need to know what happened to Jewel," Tone said, lips balled tightly. "Somebody tell me," he yelled when Caltrone didn't answer quick enough.

"This man raped your daughter, *mijo*. He was one of three," Caltrone finally revealed. "Kenya already killed one."

I saw all color drain from Tone's brown face. His eyes turned to Fal and I knew the boy's demise was eminent.

Frederick and Mark came back in with something I didn't know the name of, but I guessed it was the Judas Cradle Caltrone had asked for. It was about five feet high, the top built like a pyramid-shaped cradle. They both had brown braided ropes in their hands.

"Today, Fal, the sins of the father will be visited upon his children. You're going to die in the most painful of ways and your children will bear witness to your demise," Caltrone said. "Once you're dead, I'm going to hand your girlfriend over to my grandson, Mark. I can assure you, she's going to wish for death once he's done with her. He's going to do to her everything you did to my granddaughter. Also, your children . . . Well, your legacy ends here."

I looked over to the pasty white woman. She held her crying, dirty children to her chest as tears rolled down her face.

"*Mijo,* do you remember how this works?" Caltrone asked.

Tone didn't respond. He snatched the rope from Mark, which made him bristle, but I didn't think he was stupid enough to run up on Tone again. It took all of ten minutes for Tone to nail the ropes to the wall at different angles. He then stripped the man down to nothing as Frederick and Mark held Fal down. Just for the hell of it, I walked over and kicked Fal in his dick over and over.

"For my daughter," I said to him before spitting in his face.

"*Dios,* Kenya. That is disgusting shit, *mija,*" Caltrone said.

I said nothing as I watched Tone tie the man's hands behind his back. He then did the same to his ankles, only this time there was a spreader bar between them. Fallon's feet were tied to each other in a way that moving one leg would force the other to move as well.

"There shouldn't be a need for me to tell you why I'm using this method for torture and death, Antonio. I believe in tit for tat. This is his tat," Caltrone said, telling Tone without telling him what Fal had done to Jewel.

I didn't know what I expected, but it wasn't for Fallon to be sat atop the triangular-shaped end of the Judas cradle or for it to be inserted into his anus. The shit was brutal. Mark and Frederick added weights to his legs and, each time Tone yanked the ropes, Fallon was hoisted up. Tone would let the ropes slack a bit and Fallon's asshole would be ripped farther open as the tip of the Judas cradle would be inserted again. The mucus mixed with blood and defecation dripping from his backside sickened me. The smell burned my nose hairs but, for the life of me, I couldn't feel any remorse for the man.

Chapter 9

Kenya

"Let's move out."

No one had to tell me twice. I didn't know how much longer I could stand around and watch the dismemberment of an entire family, including children. If I had any doubt in my mind that Caltrone and his brood were evil personified, I didn't anymore. Fallon had made the mistake of having a hand in taking our daughter. For his sins against an Orlando, Caltrone had made him pay dearly. He along with his kids' mother and their children had all been killed.

"Come on," Tone said to me.

He knew I was on the verge of a nervous breakdown. To take a blade and slice a child's throat had taken me past my limit. I'd taken two lives in one day all in the name of my child. Did I have no morals or compassion left? How much further would I go to meet my own agenda? Sooner or later I would have no soul left and I was desperately trying to keep even an inch of it.

Once we got in the van, Tone looked at me, trying to assess where I was mentally. "You good?" he asked me as he slid in the back seat next to me.

Outside, Caltrone was giving Benita and her sidekick instructions on what he wanted done before some woman named Lilith returned. Benita visibly bristled and Caltrone scolded her for it.

"Keep your feelings to yourself," he said to Benita. "Do as I asked and nothing more."

It was clear that Benita didn't care for whoever Lilith was. From the first seat, the woman whose name I didn't know, Benita's sidekick, laid a hand on her left shoulder where Caltrone couldn't see it. I had no idea what that was about.

I turned to Tone. "No, I'm not, but I get what I paid for, right?" I said to him.

He studied me for a long moment. Sweat beaded his brows and blood stained his shirt. His curly, coiled hair was pulled back into a ponytail. The way his hair was lined gave definition to his facial features. In the dark, he was every bit as beautiful as he was in the light. He snatched his shirt over his head then caressed both my cheeks in his hands as he looked me over, using his shirt to wipe excess blood from my face. He gently turned my head from side to side examining me. He even lifted my shirt to look at my abdomen. I wasn't sure how well he could see in the dark, but it was Tone, and he was always above average in certain areas. Fallon's baby mother had put up a fight to protect her babies. Crazy bitch had come for me with a knife.

"Thank you," he said to me after he was satisfied I wasn't hurt in any way.

"For what?"

"For not telling me what was on the video. For doing what you have to do for Jewel. For taking this insane fucking journey. For losing your soul the same as I lost mine."

All I did was nod. I didn't want to think of what was on the video any more than he did. I wanted to scrub my brain of the images burned there. I didn't know if I would ever be able to "unsee" them. Tone may not have seen what happened to Jewel, but I knew just hearing her screams were enough to take him over the edge, as was evident in the way he had dismembered Fallon. However, I used my daughter's screams of pain to deafen the sounds of my conscience when I killed Fallon's oldest child.

Tone laid a hand on my thigh and gave a tight squeeze. I swallowed back bile and tears. I was shaking badly. So much so it looked as if I were vibrating. I looked at my ringing cell then sent Isaac to voicemail. I didn't have it in me to speak to him right now. I watched silently as Benita, her sidekick, and Caltrone exited the van.

"I feel like we've been playing cat and mouse. We find one person, only for them to lead us to another and another," I said. "From place to place. And now we have to find this Donna woman."

"The old man says he's certain she will lead us to Jewel," Antonio said, his words spat out in exhaustion.

I cast a glance at the back of Caltrone's head then back over at Tone. I wondered if he had thought about what I had. Since Hector had looked at Caltrone and spoken directly to him about not wanting to talk to me or Tone, I'd had a niggling feeling in the pit of my stomach about something.

"How do we know he isn't behind this, Tone?" I finally asked. "How do we know he's not just using us to further some sick agenda of his? Why did Hector look at Caltrone and speak directly to him as if he had known him?"

"Baby Kenya, listen to me, okay?" he said. "Don't, all right? Don't do this to yourself. Don't do this to me. Don't put that in my head. Please. I'm already knocking on hell's door."

I studied his eyes. "Something's not right, Tone. I feel it. Something ain't right. Fallon thought this visit was about drugs. Why would he—"

"Kenya!" Tone yelled. "Stop."

I was crying now. I kept seeing that child's blood pour over my hands out of his neck. I'd killed a child. My eyes were wild as I studied Tone. My mouth was agape and I felt I couldn't breathe. The reason I was questioning Caltrone's motives was because I couldn't deal with what I'd done.

"I killed . . . I . . . Tone, I killed a child all in the name of finding mine," I blabbered out. "I can't . . . What . . . Why did we come to this man?"

I couldn't breathe. My heart was in my throat; it had blocked my ability to inhale and exhale properly. I'd become the criminals I'd put away. Lu Orlando flashed in my mind. Would thoughts of that man ever leave me alone? I'd taken him down with a vengeance. I was happy to hear that someone in prison had taken his life. Meanwhile, it seemed as if his spirit had infected me as I'd just sliced a child's throat. I'd watched as Tone

did the same, killing a child mercifully so they
wouldn't suffer. Then I'd watched as Mark did
with Fallon's baby mother as he saw fit. Once
all was done, the dismemberment commenced.
Watching Tone surgically remove body parts
and organs sickened me.

Caltrone had too much power. During the
time we had done all our evil deeds, not one
person called the cops about the noise I was
sure they heard. The neighborhood had stilled.
As we walked out to the van, I saw not one
man, woman, or child. No one Caltrone hadn't
ordered to be around could be seen for miles. I
wanted to yell. I wanted to scream. I wanted to
wash myself in holy water and scream a million
Hail Marys.

Antonio roughly held both sides of my face
now. His cool eyes stared into my panicked
ones. "You need to breathe and calm down.
Understand? We signed up for this. I told you
that this would happen. I gave you the option
to turn around and walk away, but you refused.
So, no, you don't get to have a mental breakdown on me right now. You don't. You suck
that shit up. Leave your conscience back in
that damn apartment because I can assure you
this isn't the worst of it. I. Told. Your. Ass. This
would happen."

I heard him and, yes, his words that I should have left were coming back to haunt me worse than I thought they would. This was the one time I agreed that I should have listened to him. The shaking in my body was worse now. I couldn't stop, couldn't be still. The blood of an innocent child was on my hands.

"I can't . . . I can't do this. I want . . . I wanna go home," I cried. "I quit, Antonio. I quit. I wanna go home." I was hysterical at this point. I was no longer myself. I was having an out-of-body experience.

"No, nah. You don't. You stay. Because if you don't, he will find a way to kill you and that would kill me. Do you understand, Kenya? Snap the fuck out of it," he barked at me.

I shook my head. Over and over I shook my head, screaming no. I screamed that I was done and that I wanted to go home. The more I screamed and yelled, the more Antonio said no. It went on that way until a hard smack across my face silenced me.

I gasped, eyes wide with shock and dismay. Antonio had slapped me. The hit was so hard, lethal, and swift that, for a moment, I had no idea where I was.

"I'm sorry," he said quickly. "But I had to bring down your hysteria. Snap out of it, Kenya."

Any other time, he and I would have been fighting, as I hated for any man to raise his hand at me to strike me; but something in me recognized Tone's need to bring me back to rational again. He needed me to be coherent so I could comprehend what he had been saying to me. My face burned, as did my eyes. I looked around before my eyes settled on Caltrone, who had been watching Tone and me from outside the van.

Tone still had my face in his hands as I brought my eyes back to his. "We're in this together no matter what, you hear me? Even if I meet death on this path, I'll still be with you. We have to find Jewel and that's all we can think about right now. We can pray or whatever else you need to do later. But remember we came to him for help to find Jewel. We left our souls back in Cuba. Nod once if you understand me."

I gave a slow nod. Tone was used to this from me. He had seen me panic and freak out many times before when we were teenage parents. I was sure from the outside looking in Caltrone was probably proud that his son had smacked me and put me in my place. From the outside looking in, I was sure it didn't look like I was having a panic attack and that it looked more like Tone had gotten tired of my mouth and had finally smacked me to shut me up.

"I've thought about everything you just said. I've even thought about whether he could be behind this, but I don't have proof. I don't know that he is behind this or that he would even do something like this. That ain't his style, not when it comes to family. But, trust me, if that old man had anything to do with this, I'll kill him myself," he said with finality, the coldness in his voice chilling me to the bone.

Chapter 10

Antonio

Kenya's breakdown had me on edge, as did her comments about my father. What she said was no doubt based on fear. Could my old man be manipulative to the point that he'd hire people to go after his own blood to teach a lesson? Yes. Would he take it to the point of where it was with my daughter being assaulted? No. Could a situation happen where his minions might have gotten out of control even for Caltrone? Thinking about everything I'd been learning so far being back under his watchful eye, no. The no was simple. No man or woman was allowed to touch the blood of Caltrone.

From the high to the low, everyone who worked for Caltrone knew that and would never test it in the way that it was going now. Caltrone would gut, burn, dismember, and dissolve in acid anyone who touched the flesh of an Orlando.

He didn't fuck with rape. He just helped in trafficking, sick as that was. Besides, finding what I found in Fallon's apartment dictated otherwise. When I was in the apartment, I made sure to study my surroundings as my father taught me. There was nothing out of the ordinary in the dingy apartment, home to a well-known dealer.

Mark worked on removing the medieval torture device, while I staged the place by taking some money, and the shoes off of Fallon's body. Eventually I moved to the back rooms checking that no witnesses were around. Landing in Fallon's room, I trashed it and rummaged through the place. Banging on the wall and searching through his closet and dressers for any hidden spots, I found his stash of weed and some pills. I grabbed his Js, a notepad, and a variety of random-ass drugs: molly, heroin, meth, weed, and more.

As I was about to exit the room, I noticed, strewn on the floor with the sheets, a black iPhone. Dropping on the bed to sit, elbows on my knees, I rolled my shoulders and listened to them make that popping sound.

Ready for whatever I might find, I began looking through the cell. "The fuck do you have on here, Fallon?" I muttered to myself while I looked on.

A series of numbers shifted past my eyes. I checked his trashed files, then went to his pictures where I saw Fallon with several women. When I noticed one with my daughter outside of some building, I frowned deeply. She stood smiling next to two other young women. One was a toffee-toned girl with colorful hair, tiny shorts with black-and-white striped leggings, black high tops, and a cropped off-the-shoulder shirt. On her right shoulder was a chess piece and it piqued my interest. She stood with her tongue out, head tilted to the side, causing teal-blue hair to fall like a curtain with both her hands up curled in a sign that I knew represented Houston's Fifth Ward, while her other hand was around Jewel's shoulder.

Syncing his cell with mine, I transferred everything that was on his cell. I then switched gears and went through his videos, also transferring those. There was one marked Tight. I clicked on it and my eye twitched when I saw my baby girl being assaulted. Anger had my jaw clenched tight again. My gloved fingers dug into the palm of my left hand as I almost broke the cell from gripping it too hard. The room started to spin, and red washed over my vision. Kenya had been smart in keeping me from seeing this. Had I seen it before getting my hands on Fallon, all the

torture we put him through would not have gone
down and I might have fucked it up on a level
where it would have jeopardized everything.

A sour laugh came from me as my mind went
to the worst of places. *Nigga was going to try to
profit off my child? Share this sick, twisted shit
with people in the street? Use it as leverage for
money or something?* It was a damn good thing
that Fallon was dead. I wanted to storm back
into the living room and bring him back from the
dead just to rip him apart again. I had nothing
to put this anger in right now, but I knew that I
would soon.

"Tone?" I heard rattle my thoughts from my
memory.

I shook away from my thoughts and focused
back on Kenya. The sadness and fear in her voice
bothered me. The desire to go off on her was back
and left a sour taste in my mouth. Everything
she did was exactly why I had been pissed off
about her meeting with my father. But of course
I expressed that to her and let it be what it was.
There was no turning back, but if she pulled a
stunt like she just did with my father, then the
issues she had now would not even compare to
what she'd experience with that man.

Jaw clenched tight like a steel tension wire, I
stared ahead at the back of the seats in front of

us. "Sorry. Listen, keep your emotions in check, Kenya, and don't let even a tear fall in front of my father, understand?"

"Yes," I heard Kenya say softly. "I just need our daughter back."

"I understand, but any weakness he or my nephew see or sense, they will pounce on it and twist it into some mental mind games, okay?" I explained.

Reclining in my seat to watch her from my peripheral, I scratched the side of my shaggy face. The desire to wash myself suddenly hit me. I was covered in blood. I had stood in a tiny apartment and watched children be slaughtered by my hand and Kenya's hand. All in the name of vengeance. A weakness within me tried to seep through my mental walls, but I effectively locked it back. The death of those children would haunt me and I knew that I'd try to find ways to make amends for it but, at the same time, I knew that this was a necessary evil.

Any child who survived could grow up with an agenda. That child could make it their sole goal to come after me and mine, which I wouldn't blame them for, and the cycle of killing would go on. So, innocent in nature, they weren't innocent by default and they had to go. Each life that died, I mentally prayed for their passing, something I'd never let my father pick up on.

"Stay in here and get your mind right. We need to stay calm and make sure that's the only emotion we show them. Will you be okay?" I asked, turning to check if Kenya was here in the present and not about to fall by the wayside.

"I'm here," she said clutching her fist.

"You sure?" I said with a frown and a slight rough tone.

"I'm sure," she said back with a little heat to her tone. "I just want my baby."

"We'll get her back; trust me on that." Climbing out of the van I saw that old demon, my father, taking his sweet time speaking with Benita.

I went to where my father stood with Benita. When I had exited the apartment, I gave everything over to Benita. She now stood handing a notepad to him as he looked through the cell phone, hands still covered in latex gloves. Once in front of them, I crossed my arms over my chest and watched him thumb through the notepad before he tossed it and the phone to Benita.

"There's names of people he does business with and product sales in the notepad. The phone looks promising as well. Follow the trail and we might find the female. That picture alone gives me faith that she'll lead us to my granddaughter. What do you think, *mijo?*" he asked me.

My gaze stayed on the van, mirroring how my father addressed me without looking at me. "Yes. I feel that the phone will help. The contacts on the notepad might not lead us anywhere. You know how closed-mouth street goons try to be, but it doesn't hurt to see and take them out while we at it. We need to hit up spots that Fallon would occupy and then trace his steps to Donna."

"That slows us down," Benita said looking my way.

"No, that slows down you and the people we assign to go through the streets and hunt every person associated with Fallon. Just because you burn a flea-infested bed doesn't mean there aren't more fleas, *mami*."

A low chuckle came from my father when I said that. It made me look his way. Made me notice how he stood with authority, the sun shining on his sunglasses. My father knew I was right, which was why he said nothing in return. I was proving that I remembered his old lessons and I figured that it was helping in the long run.

"Yes, sir," she said in a tight, constrained tone. "I and my team will surveil his most recent deals and report what we learn."

"Good," my father said. He turned to clap a hand on my shoulder and walk us to the van.

"Houston is not a place I desire to take over. However, cleaning out some of it can only help the *familia* rather than hinder it, so we will use this situation to our advantage."

I said nothing as he spoke to me about the family corporation. We all headed out to the van and returned to the ranch. During that time, I learned that the family base was not only centered in Cuba, but we were also expanding and working on a second home base in California. Los Angeles was my pops's other goal, along with expanding his transporting business already running in Vegas. Since I was a doctor, my father felt that he could use my services in opening clinics in these hubs.

"Father, right now all I'm focusing on is getting my child back," I said once we made it to the ranch. Kenya and I were left alone in the foyer with my father.

"*Sí*, as am I, but I am also thinking of the future of our family." He held his hand out, and a glass of chilled amber liquid was placed against his palm by one of the females he had walking about.

He took a sip then focused back on me. "I'm reacquainting myself with you, *mijo*. Though I hated how your mother took you from me, I see that two good things came from that. You will be the head of our health foundation. I learned that you did a tour of duty to help the Marines?"

When he laid out that info, I wasn't shocked one bit. I took a quick glance at Kenya, who stood by my side looking exhausted and worn. But when my father mentioned the tour of duty I went on, all her energy seemed to plunge back within her. It was as if she was suddenly anxious and I wasn't sure why.

"Yes, sir. I did, for about a year and a half," I responded with a nod.

Caltrone gave a slight smile as he took a slow drink of his liquor then looked Kenya's way. "And this was when you were in Atlanta, yes?"

"Yes. Yes, it was," Kenya quickly said with an odd tone to her voice.

"Hmm," my father said then chuckled. "That was the period you both trained in your own ways and grew your strengths in your prospective careers. This family needs that and I demand it. When we get my grandchild back, you will be working to opening the clinic, *mijo*. You will also work over our health foundation and build your base in Miami for our Cuban *familia* and extended relatives. Now, Kenya, my dear, I have plans with my legal branch for you as well, but we will speak on that later. The little bakery of yours will need to be managed from a distance."

Kenya's mouth opened and her body language changed to one of sadness. "I invested my time in the bakery. It is my world. Named it after Jewel. I have no desire to return to law."

"You may not have a desire to return; however, law desires you. We'll work out the logistics later. If you both will excuse me." With that my father walked away and left Kenya and me alone.

"Tone, I don't—" she started and I shook my head.

"No point in arguing about it. I suggest you call your fiancé and talk about that with him and give him a fair amount of warning. When we stood in front of my father, we both signed over our lives. He controls them now. We might be able to counter, but he always maintains the control."

"Jewel works there. I don't want to leave it," she said following me as we walked up the grand staircase of the foyer.

"I know, baby, and you might be able to keep it. This is all a contract with my father. You need to make sure you tailor it just right for your own needs because this is all his world, not ours. I'm sorry," I explained, stopping at my door.

"I just wanted Jewel back," she spat out, anger in her eyes.

"As did and do I. My practice is being taken from me. We lose what we love in dealing with the devil, baby." Carefully, I reached around her, opened the door to her room, and then stepped back. "Prepare yourself; that's all you can do."

Kenya stared up at me with pain in her eyes. I reached out to give her a reassuring hug, then headed to my room.

Once inside, I took to the bathroom, turned on the shower, and undressed. Carefully pulling my shirt off, I grunted then sat on the edge of the toilet. Taking off my boots, I reached into my right one, pulled out the blade I had there, and set it next to my cell phone on the sink.

My stomach was in knots. I was a failure of a father and now a cordial ex. I remembered when Kenya opened the bakery. It was her pride and joy. When we were in college, as a way to break away from her stress, she'd always find a way to bake the best cupcakes and sheet cakes in the world. Her cookies were slamming too. Even now, thinking of their taste, a warmth spread to my heart. Back then, I used to tell her that and she'd tell me that, one day, she planned to open up a spot to reflect that and name it after Jewel, because our baby girl was the fire in our hearts.

Now, Kenya was going to lose what she worked hard in building up. I felt responsible but, at the same time, it was her own doing. Standing up, I walked to the sink and hunched over trying to keep my emotions in check. I was changing. Caring about others' welfare was becoming harder by the day. Killing was starting to come easy to me and the dark thoughts in my mind were more frequent. I was becoming something different and I shook my head at my reflection before stepping into the shower. Hot, stinging water sloshed over the planes of my sore and tired body. I cupped my hands to gather water and splashed it over my face, scrubbing at my beard as I tried to keep from roaring in my mind the flashes of my daughter fighting, and her screams. All I wanted was my daughter back, along with her safety. Why did this shit have to happen?

Slamming my fist into the shower, I slapped my hand against the wet wall then pressed my forehead against it as the emotion poured out of me and down the drain. It took me twenty minutes to get myself right before I stepped out of the shower with my towel around my waist. It took another ten before I headed out of my room dressed and looking for something to eat.

Briskly walking down the hall, I adjusted my watch on my wrist and went in my head about where I had my hunting knife, my Glock, and whatever else I needed on my outing. Taking the steps down, I stepped in the foyer and noticed my nephew.

"Where you going, *pinja?*" Mark asked in his usual snarky way.

Homie was standing in front of me drinking a beer with his arms crossed. On his hip was his Glock, and he wore a gun holster over his white beater. From where I stood, I could see that he had a fresh line up and of course he was clean from the previous massacre we both partook in.

Locking my gaze on him, I continued forward and walked past him to grab from a bowl of keys. Then I stopped outside the door. "Out. I'm hungry and I got some things on my mind."

"Ah, yeah? Well, a nigga like you can hit up the kitchen and get all you need; besides, you don't have that pretty wifey of yours by your side. Don't you want to check in on her?" he said behind me.

"There something in there that can get me over this craving for some Texas barbecue?" Raising my eyebrow, I frowned. "If so, I don't give a fuck. I'm going out, mongo. And Kenya got here on her own; she'll be all good on her own."

I said that to keep Mark off my back. He annoyed the fuck out of me with how he watched me, and Kenya for that matter. Ever since we were kids, he was trying to be Caltrone and I saw that it hadn't stopped. I hit the remote to unlock the car. I waited for the chirp then headed to the driver's side door.

"Nigga, only dumbass here is you," Mark said laughing sharply. "Since ya riding out, I'm ya shadow. You know the game."

Annoyed, I opened the door of a blacked-out Range Rover. "Where's the old demon? Shouldn't you be sniffing his balls and shit?"

As I felt the heat of the Texas sun heating up my flesh, Mark and I stared each other down. His jaw twitched. My jaw twitched. The distrust for each other was strong to the point where we could almost taste it. It was then that Kenya came out and headed my way when she saw me.

Crinkled hair braided back so that it was a loose afro in the back, Kenya moved like she had no care in the world. Rocking tight jeans, black boots that matched mine, a checkered shirt that was tied around her waist, and a black tank, she slid on a pair of glasses and moved past me to go to the passenger side.

"It's full, Mark. Tone is about to take me to the store for some women's stuff. Now, if you want to chill in the feminine aisle as I shop for tampons and pads, then ride out, nigga."

Playing with the ends of her hair, she smiled then climbed in the car.

"I didn't invite you either." Hopping in, I slammed the door, rolled the window down, and glared at Mark. "You coming?"

Mark stared at Kenya then shook his head. "Naw, I'm good. Fuck that. Bring back some food."

That was when I pulled off without a thought. Speeding away, I turned up the music and reached in my pocket. Pulling out a black box, I turned it on and waved it around then passed it to her.

"I didn't invite you, *mami*," I said motioning for her to lift the box and wave it around.

She did as I said, unbuckled her seat belt, and leaned to the back to scan. "I saw Mark being a dick, so I decided to save the drama. You know how you men can be."

"Fuck that, how we can be. Mark and I have legit beef," I said, knowing she knew that already.

"I don't care," she said as she sat back down. She mouthed, "Clear."

We sat in silence as I drove and glanced in my rearview mirror. "He's trailing us, too, so we'll be going to Walmart or Target."

"Do Target," Kenya said calmly. "What are you doing anyway, Tone?"

"First, what's up with you? I thought you were going to rest," I said eyeing her from the corner of my eye.

Kenya sat quietly, her fingertips tapping against her plump burgundy bottom lip. "I called Isaac. He's pissed. Like, we got into it heavy and I just can't deal with that; and I'm still shaken from . . . from . . ."

I quickly looked her way. The way her voice cracked put a pit in my stomach. When a fat tear slid from under her shades, I gripped the steering wheel harder.

"Look, none of this is going to get easier but, at the same time, I don't want you to cry. I'll try to help however I can in keeping Isaac chill, okay?" I asked while reggaetón thumped in our ears.

"No, no, it's okay. I'll be able to work it out. I just need this quiet right now and I didn't want to be in the house," she said. Kenya sat back, tears falling down her face, with her finger against her temple. She was reclining, legs wide, tapping her nails against her inner thigh as she always did when in thought.

Honestly, I didn't want to be an asshole, but I couldn't stop myself. I just wanted her to stop crying. It hurt and added to the tension between us and how I felt about her being here.

"You should have stayed away," I grumbled in my throat. "I knew this would be too much for you."

"I don't care, Tone," Kenya spat back. She turned in her seat and glared at me. "I made my choice but, at the end of the day, I was the one who helped kill those babies. I did that. For our daughter. You might be able to live with that but I can't."

Frowning, I made a turn, and decided hit up Target later. "I'm not sitting here asking you to live with it, and you don't know me well if you think that I am able to, Kenya," I barked back. We whipped along the interstate going off on each other, letting our pain ride us until I parked outside of a Jamaican restaurant. "'At the end of the day.' All I'm saying is—"

"All you're saying is what, Antonio?" Kenya spat at me, undoing her seat belt. "Be a fucking emo? Have no feelings? Kill with no regard?"

"Yeah. Yeah, you have to in this type of world. You asked to be a part of it, so deal with it. Swallow your tears and hide them until you're in private. That's all you can do. Otherwise, it'll get you killed in the street or by my father's hands. Understand that, please! I'm trying to keep you safe."

"I didn't ask you to," Kenya shouted at me, wiping under her shades.

"Well, I am. We might not have been able to keep our vows, but I'm a decent man, *mami*. I'm going to try to keep the blood off your hands as much as I can. Now get out." Climbing out of the car, I slammed the door and walked ahead.

Heading inside, I passed by a tall, Amazonian sista with a large afro, sharp hazel-green eyes, and beautiful cocoa skin. She stood out in a nice way that had me turning to watch how her ass quaked. While I was checking her and holding the door waiting for Kenya to follow me, I saw that she carried a blade around her thick thigh. Food was in her hand, and she let out a light laugh as a tall brotha, who leaned against the side of a large black truck, watched her with a smirk on his face. He opened the door for her, speaking in Portuguese. She glanced my way, smiled, and closed her door.

Shaking my head, I focused back on Kenya, who gave me a stank look. "I'm sorry. We're tired and need to just chill. Mark is watching us, so let's just eat and work on being on the same page, okay?"

Saying nothing, she walked in and I followed, watching how her ass shook also. It was an old habit of mine. When she was mad, she always switched a little harder. I sighed at the memory, ordered us food, got us a seat outside, then thanked the staff when they brought us our food five minutes later.

Using my fingers to dip my bread in the rich brown sauce as I quietly thought, I then reached in my pocket, turned the phone on, and pulled up a picture. Sliding it to her, I gave a nod. "A'ight, this is what I know so far. The kid Keith, who took our daughter, had a chess piece tattoo. When we found Fallon, he had one too; and when I went through his phone, I found pictures of a young girl with the same tattoo."

"Do you think they are a part of some group?" Kenya quietly asked sipping from her bubbling drink and looking at the picture. "Did our daughter know this girl?"

I watched her quickly wipe under her shades again, and I knew it was from seeing our daughter.

"There's no doubt about it and I don't know yet. But we'll see what we find out when I question the old man."

"All right. We need answers, Tone. This relying just on him isn't working for me right now," she said.

"It's what we signed up for. We'll find our daughter and everything else will be what it is.

I'm tired to my soul like you. But we have this
picture and all we have to do now is dig up a
trail." Quietly chewing, I looked to the right of
me to see Mark walking our way.

"Agreed. Hey! The wall behind him is this
place," Kenya said sitting up.

Glancing at the distance between Mark and our
table, I quickly nodded. "That's why I brought us
here, because they came here. So I'm watching
and listening. I think that I can find something
on her. What do you think?"

"I think we can too. I'll do whatever I can," she
said with a sad smile.

"Good. We'll come back later after I speak to
the old man and you can pull out the lawyer in
you. Question but don't scare them. I think we
might be able to use their security footage," I
said as Mark plopped down next us then took
our plates of food.

Kenya gave me a light smile then quietly picked
at her food.

Plans were in motion. All we had to do was
wait to see what chips would fall from our digging and if Donna was anywhere around.

Chapter 11

Kenya

I studied traffic both ways before rushing back across the street to the Caribbean eatery. I didn't have much at my disposal, but there was a Kinko's across the street. I e-mailed to myself the picture with the girl and Jewel then I rushed across the street to print it out. Once done, I briskly made my way back inside. It had been awhile since I had to put my lawyering to use, but I had no choice now, especially since Caltrone had all but ordered me back into it once this ordeal was done.

I couldn't think about that at the moment, however. I stormed back in the place with new-found energy. My mental breakdown before be damned. Jewel had been in this place. For a minute, I stood still trying to imagine her here, laughing, eating, thinking she was among friends and safe. I opened my eyes and glanced around. I had no idea where Tone had gone, but I knew

he was around because Mark was and there was
no way Tone would leave me anywhere alone
with Mark. The man always watched me like
he intended to do bad things to and with me. I
detested him and he knew it. Still, he seemed to
get some kind of sick kick out of that, too.

I paid him no mind as I walked to the counter.
Behind it was a beautiful, dark-skinned girl who
appeared to be no more than a few years older
than Jewel. Her hair was pulled back into a
bushy ponytail and her white apron was stained
with grease from food.

"Excuse me," I said.

She turned to look at me. Although she was
smiling, I could tell it was forced. It was all a part
of her job. "Yes," she answered. There was no life
in the girl's voice.

"Have you seen this girl in here before?" I
asked her, pointing at the girl in the picture with
Jewel.

She took the picture and studied it a bit; then
a slow, genuine smile stretched across her face.
"Yeah. That's Caitlyn and the girl beside her is
Jewel. They're besties."

I quirked a brow. *Besties?* How the fuck were
they besties? I'd never seen, met, or heard tell of
Caitlyn before. "When's the last time you seen
her?"

"Why you wanna know? You the cops?"

"No, I'm not the cops. I'm her mother and I need to find her."

She handed the picture back to me and thought before answering. "Was a few weeks ago," she answered.

"Here?" I asked referring to the restaurant.

"No. I mean, yeah, they were here but, no, last I seen them was at the house party Donna was throwing. Jewel was sick though so Keith made her leave the party. Caitlyn and Keith got into a fight about it. Caitlyn was mad because she said Keith put too much stuff in Jewel's drink."

"What stuff? And who is Keith?"

"Caitlyn's cousin. Donna is his sister, I think. I don't know," the girl said then looked around like she was uncomfortable. "Keith is . . . different, you know. Somet'ing wrong wit' he, yuh?"

I was surprised when her accent jumped out. I felt my stomach muscles coiling at the thought of Jewel being drugged. "Different how?" I asked.

The girl behind the counter looked around to make sure nobody could hear her before she leaned forward. In an aggressive whisper, she said, "I bruk it down fuh yuh. Keith not right in the head. He watched his sister and cousin like he watch any other piece of ass walking around, yuh? He come from a family of nutters. Dem not right. Donna no better, but that boy special. Him fine like wine, but"—she stopped to shake her head—"him not fi tight in di mind, yuh. He like little girls fi much. He old, yuh know, and Jewel is young, seventeen. Him talk fi her since she was just sixteen."

I'd been around enough Jamaicans to know "fi" meant "to" or "too." I swallowed hard. "How did they meet?"

"Twitter. He direct messaged her after she put up something about doing stuff her father wouldn't like. She put up a picture of her in a bikini and cutoff shorts. Said her dad would probably freak on her but, oh well."

I frowned. "How do you know this stuff?"

"She my friend."

"How? You're in Texas."

"I went to school for a while in Miami. We used to hang. We met Caitlyn on Facebook in a private group. We all kinda like just stayed friends and stuff, yuh? Jewel always thought Keith was cute and all so when he started talking to her, she got all excited. Couldn't believe he had picked her to talk to. An older guy liking her? She couldn't believe it."

"Just how old is he?"

The girl glanced away like she was embarrassed. "Think like twenty-six," she said then shrugged. "I don't know really. Could be younger. Could be older."

"Did you know she ran away?"

The girl nodded. "Yuh. Keith said her pops was crazy. Said he was getting her away from him. He told us we'd be doing his family a favor if we helped him. His family a big deal 'round the way. He had this plan where they would go to Mexico first then here. Everything was all good at first then Keith started acting weird. He hit her and stuff. They started fighting because Jewel won't stand for nobody hitting on her. Shit just changed and got crazy. His family, the Kn—"

Whatever she was about to say got cut off when the door to the kitchen opened.

"Would that be all for you, ma'am?" she asked me, completely changing her posture, attitude, and the tone of her voice.

I caught on as the mean-looking man cast a glower at both of us. I hoped he hadn't heard what we had been talking about. Hoped I didn't get the girl in trouble and I prayed with everything in me that my daughter wasn't dead by now.

"Yes, that will be all. And will you add some coconut water with it, please?" I added on just to make it seem more genuine.

"That'll be $17.50," she said.

I quickly handed her a twenty. I looked behind me to see that Mark had disappeared. I took the food I hadn't ordered when the girl behind the counter gave it to me. When she slid the change in my hand, I noticed on the back of the receipt were the words, "the Knights." I wanted to ask the girl more, but I knew I couldn't.

The man—dark-skinned, tall, and lanky—was forcefully wiping down the white countertop like it had offended him. "Don't you get my gyal in no trouble," he fussed without even looking up at me. He just kept wiping down the counter.

"Excuse me?" I said.

"You heard me. Don't get my daughter in no trouble. She go to school. She gon' make somet'ing of she self. You ain't heard nothing from she. Yuh understand?" he barked out at me.

I nodded. "Yes, sir. I understand," was all I said in return. It didn't take a genius to figure out that he was telling me not to mention where I had heard all the information I had.

"Sorry, Daddy," the girl said, her head dipped into her shoulders like she was ashamed.

The man stopped wiping down the counter. "Ain't not'ing to be sorry fa. Get back yonder outside and see what's keeping your brother Mallock."

"Yes, sir."

I was just about to leave when the girl came running back up front to her father. "He ain't back there, Daddy. He gone."

The man shook his head and started fussing about his no-good-ass son being lazy. I didn't know why but, in that moment, I thought about Tone. I walked outside just as my cell started to ring. Tone was calling me.

"Where are you?" I asked as soon as I answered.

"You find out anything?" he asked.

"Yeah."

"Get in the car; drive out of the parking lot. Meet me down the street. There is an abandoned shopping center. Drive behind it and pick me up. Keys are in the car."

Before I could ask what was going on, the line went dead. I shook my head and got in the car. I did what he asked me down to the letter. I drove behind that shopping center. With half of his body hidden behind a big green trash can, I saw Tone covered in blood. My heart sank. I whipped the car to a stop then jumped out. I didn't know if he had been injured. There was another car there. The driver and passenger side doors opened.

"What—"

"Don't ask me nothing, Kenya," he said before I could get the words out.

I couldn't see him fully until I walked around the trash can. My eyes widened and I almost screamed. In his hand was a severed head. The locs on the head reminded me of serpents. The mouth was open like the male had been in mid-scream when Tone decapitated him.

Mark rushed around the corner with Frederick and Maria-Rosa in tow.

"What the fuck, Antonio?" Maria-Rosa yelled.

"Holy hell," Frederick commented.

"This nigga really is in touch with his dark side," Mark spat. "Get the body from over by the car," he told Frederick.

It was only then that I looked to see a headless body sitting upright by the open driver side door. Blood dripped from the bottom of the door.

"What did you do, Antonio?" Maria-Rosa asked him. She looked at her uncle with a deep frown, almost like she was disappointed in him. All the while Tone never took his eyes off me. He was gone. The Antonio I knew was no longer there.

"Leave that nigga alone," Mark told her. "Something off about that motherfucker."

My eyes were wide while looking at Antonio. If Mark, of all people, was saying something was off about Tone then something was wrong.

"Apparently," Frederick said. "Ain't no knife around this place. How he get this nigga's head off?"

"He used the door of the car," Mark answered. "Kept slamming it on his neck until it came off."

Maria-Rosa backed up a few paces from Tone, as did Frederick. These were the Orlandos. One would think they were used to seeing this kind of thing. But I think it was the fact that Tone was supposed to be the "good one" that gave them all pause.

"We gotta get this shit cleaned up and get the heat off Tone. If we let this nigga get caught holding any bodies, Grandpops gon' flip his shit," Mark said. "Call the cleaners. Kenya, y'all gotta jet. Get this nigga outta here."

Tone's nose and upper lip twitched as he walked to the car with the head in his hand. Once he got to me, he held the head up and asked, "Look familiar?"

"No," I answered, not really even looking.

"Say hello to Mallock, the other nigga in the video raping our daughter," was all he said before walking to the car. He popped the trunk, then tossed the head inside. I was cold on the inside, numb even, as I walked around to get back in the car. I was confused. How in hell would he know who was on the video?

We drove back to the ranch in silence. A team of people dressed in all-white jumpsuits and face masks met us outside. One asked me for the keys to the car. I readily handed them over. Another tried to take the head from Tone and got shoved to the ground for the affront. He carried the severed head into the house, dripping blood along the way.

Caltrone was coming downstairs, but came to a complete stop at the sight of Antonio and the blood on the floor. Caltrone didn't even have to say a word. Women started moving like the world was ending as they rushed to clean the mess Tone was making. He walked up the stairs and stood in front of his father.

He held the boy's head up and said, "Found another one," before dropping the head of the boy at his father's feet and walking away.

The old man swallowed hard, his fist balled at his side. "You let him do this?" Caltrone asked me.

"I didn't let him do anything. He's simply his father's son," I answered.

I knew what was bothering Caltrone: he wasn't in control of this moment. Tone had taken control from him by going out on his own and coming back with a trophy to show for it. It was okay for Tone to kill for Caltrone's enjoyment, but the minute Tone took control of the situation, it seemed Caltrone had a problem with it. It took control from his hands. In this moment, he was no longer Tone's puppet master.

Benita yelled to cleaners, "Get the gotdamned head off the stairs and away from Caltrone," as I walked past him. I knew Caltrone's OCD was in overdrive, not to mention I was sure his mood had soured. I headed to my room, but then made an abrupt turn to head into Tone's when I heard him yelling for someone to get the fuck away from him. There was a woman in the room with him, small in stature, demure even. She looked at me with pleading eyes.

"Please, make him give me the clothes. I have to get rid of them or Caltrone will get rid of me. I can't leave this room without those clothes," her squeaky voice said.

She literally looked like she was about to cry. What kind of fear had Caltrone instilled in these women around him? She would rather suffer Tone cussing her to hell before enduring punishment from Caltrone. I walked over to Tone to stand in front of him. He looked down at me. There was something in his eyes. Who he used to be was trapped behind them; who he was now scared me. He looked more like his father now than he ever had before. The Ortiz had been imprisoned and the Orlando had taken rule.

"Antonio," I whispered softly.

He didn't respond. He was looking at me, could hear me, but he wasn't there. "They raped my baby girl," he said.

For a second, I thought he had seen the video, but that was impossible, right? I hadn't shown it to him. Caltrone forbade Mark from showing it to him so how did he know who Mallock was? I didn't know who the boy was just by seeing his severed head. How in hell had Tone even known the boy would be at the shop?

As if he had read my mind, he said, "He was in the picture I showed you. You didn't see him?" he asked me. "He was in the video."

I'd been so busy looking at Jewel, I hadn't really paid attention to anyone else in the photo other than Caitlyn, the girl she was standing next to. "No, I didn't see him, Tone. And who showed you the video?"

"Fallon's phone . . . When I was setting the scene at the apartment, I found his phone. Saw the video."

I swore Tone was talking to me, but he wasn't. He seemed to be somewhere else in his head. I didn't say anything else. I kneeled down to take his shoes and socks off, then his pants and underwear. His shirt was last. I handed it all to the timid woman who rushed from the room like hell was on her ass. I took Tone by his hand and led him to the shower.

I didn't know what to think. Didn't know what else to do. I stripped off my clothes and stepped inside with him. I took the time to wash him down. I washed his hair too and was happy he let me do it. There was no fight from him as I cleaned him up. After I was done, we both stood there, me gazing up at him and him staring down at me.

"I'm sorry," he said.

I nodded then licked my lips. I knew what he was saying to me without him having to say it to me. He was past the point of no return. There was no coming back. I thought about Mama Carmen as tears clouded my eyes. She had raised one hell of a son. People often said a woman couldn't raise a boy into a man. I begged to differ. Carmen had raised a gentleman. He wasn't perfect, but he for damn sure was nowhere near the worst. It would hurt her to know that the man she had raised had died by default.

"You did what you had to do," I said. "Any parent would." In a sense, I was sad but, then again, I'd do and had done anything just so I could get Jewel back. I pushed the doors open to the stall and stepped one foot out before Tone grabbed my arm to stop me.

I closed my eyes. His hands on me, the look I'd seen in his eyes before trying to walk away told me what was on his mind. I prayed Antonio wouldn't make me take this path.

I shook my head. "No, Antonio," I whispered low. He didn't let my arm go. I looked back over my shoulder at him. "Don't do this to me." He pulled me back into the shower with him, closer than I had been before, and he slid the door closed behind me. "Please, don't do this to me."

He knew what I was talking about. I'd never been able to say no to him. Never. Not when it came to us joining together as one, his body inside of my body.

My body shook as my nails dug into the palms of my hands. The closer he pulled me to him, the more I thought about Isaac. It had been years upon years and the only man I'd been with other than Antonio was Isaac and one other dude whose name I didn't remember. I liked to lie to myself, tell myself I didn't miss Tone or miss how it felt when we used to tear into one another when it came to sex.

By now I was so close to Tone I could feel his heartbeat.

"I have a fiancé," I said. I didn't know why I said it like it would make a difference.

Tone shrugged. "Yeah, I don't care," was all he said before his mouth met mine.

In that moment, all my resolve faded. That fire that no man could light inside me came roaring to life. I moaned; or was it a whimper? Water rained down on us from the shower. The steam fogged up the bathroom, telling of the heat we created. My hair stuck to my face and neck. His hair did the same.

Tone's hands slid down my back then cupped my ass in the way I liked, in only the way he could. His mouth moved from mine to the side of my face then down my neck and shoulders. Hands came up from my ass to massage my breasts. Only he knew the pleasure I derived from pain because he had introduced me to a part of myself I didn't know existed.

So when his mouth found my nipples and his teeth bit down on them, blinding pleasure ripped through me. When his nails dug into my sides and back, my pussy blossomed and leaked like it hadn't in years. When he roughly spun me around and pressed my face into the wall with a handful of my hair locked in his fist, Isaac faded from my subconscious. Tone growled in my ear before biting down on the left side of the space between my neck and shoulders. It wasn't a light bite, no. This bite was sure to leave a mark. It was deep and I could feel the pain penetrate my psyche.

My head fell back and I orgasmed on the spot. But it was only when he slipped inside of me from behind and whispered, "Mine," that I remembered what I'd been missing.

"Mine," he said in my ear again once he was in to the hilt.

I couldn't deny him in the moment. My mouth was agape and water threatened to strangle me as my body fought to adjust to his girth and length. He didn't move for a while. All I could feel was his dick thumping inside of me. His nails made scratches down my back. The water stung, even burned in some places, but I liked it. It was only when he started to move that my moans rent the air. I was his for the taking.

It was an hour or so later that Tone finally told me what had happened. After I'd told him what the girl at the restaurant had told me and I showed him the receipt with "the Knights" written on it, he pulled out the photo and then Fallon's phone with the video. He pointed at the boy with the locs in the video then pointed to the picture with Jewel and Caitlyn. In the back was Mallock, grinning with another male whose back was turned to the camera, but there was another girl there as well. Tone said he could see Mallock through the glass in the kitchen door. He saw when Mallock walked outside so he went out back to see if he was still back there.

Tone pretended he was interested in some weed. Mallock was more than happy to take him to get some. Didn't even know the man, but for the promise of sharing a blunt, he would take him to get the best weed in Texas. They never made it to the weed man and Mallock would never make it back to his sister and father.

I woke up the next morning to Lu Orlando standing over me. The scream that erupted from my lips could have awakened the dead. I wrestled with the covers, bucked and kicked my legs. I had to get away from him. *Not again,* my mind screamed. *Not again!* I swung out, fighting with everything I had within me.

I was in my office again, in Atlanta. Lu had just walked free. I was the laughing stock of the DA's office. Everyone but me had gone home for the day, and I found myself face-to-face with a maniac.

He hadn't given me time to say a word. I had always thought men like him sent others to do their dirty work, but not Lu. Lu came to see me himself. The first hit sent me flying over my desk. I got back up. If I was going to die, it would be on my feet. All I could think about were Tone and Jewel. They would be alone, free to move on without me. That was what I'd always been afraid of, Tone and Jewel moving on without me. I'd never thought I was good enough for him or her.

Even though I was at the top of my game, I still felt they deserved more. Jewel deserved to come from a better stock of mothers. That was why I didn't put up that much of a fight when Tone said he could do better at raising her. Deep down inside, I felt that he was right.

So, when Lu Orlando punched me again, I took it. Even as I fought back, I knew it was a fight I wasn't going to win. He was too big, too strong, and came packed with way too much aggression and evil. He had a hold of my collar while he punched and slapped me to his content. I tried to claw his eyes out. Blood dripping down my face, teeth bared like that of a scalded cat. I tried to rip his eyes from the socket as my nails dug into his face. I would have succeeded had he not tossed me across the room. I almost went flying out of the window had my thigh not gotten impaled by a piece of broken wood. Too scared to feel pain, I pulled my leg off the wood and tried to run.

"Nothing better than pussy that fights back," Lu had said. "Always loved me a strong woman, ADA Kenya Gates," he snarled as he stood over me.

"Somebody help me," I screamed.

"Nobody's coming and even if they could hear you, they wouldn't hear you, know what I mean?" he taunted as he stalked me.

Eyes dark and narrowed, I could see the evil that lurked just behind the surface. His lips were in a cruel snarl that sent chills through me. He shrugged and brought his fist down into my face again. I thought he had killed me this time. My brain rattled around in my head. Punch after punch to the face, chest, stomach, and kicks to the ribs, back, and neck.

"That is enough," I heard a voice rumble out. *"You have lost all the mind you have left, boy!"*

"Kenya." I heard my name yelled again.

This time I recognized it. Knew it meant me no harm. By the time I came back to reality, Tone had my naked body locked against his, my back against his chest as he held me. Caltrone was in the room. Had come to wake us up so we could move out when I woke up screaming, swinging, and kicking.

"Kenya, calm down. What's wrong with you?" Tone asked.

I gawked at Caltrone, whose eyes looked to have darkened. "I think it's time you told Antonio the truth about what his brother did to you. What you just displayed is a weakness I won't allow. If I find this is a hindrance to you, I will exploit it and I will force you to confront it until it no longer bothers you. Your hands touched my face, Kenya."

He said that last part as if I had committed a great atrocity against him. He hated to be touched unless he invited you to and, even then, you had to be careful. When I opened my eyes, I was half asleep and half awake. Seeing Caltrone standing over me must have made me think he was Lu. My fight-or-flight instincts kicked in and I chose to fight.

"I expect you two to be dressed and down-stairs in twenty minutes," Caltrone said before turning to leave the room.

Tone dropped his hold on me then asked coolly, "What did he do to you?"

I sighed then shook my head.

"What did he do you, Kenya?" Tone roared.

"He beat me. Lu beat me pretty badly. You were overseas doing that stint with the military and I was in my office. He came in and he beat me. Caltrone stopped him, got me to a hospital for treatment. Everything was done on the low. I didn't want anyone to know what happened. I had nowhere to turn. Everybody from the police to the mayor were in the Orlandos' pocket. Felt like that man beat me within an inch of my life, but Caltrone, he came in and he helped me. Afterward, after I had healed and was back to work, that was when Caltrone approached me about putting Lu away."

Chapter 12

Antonio

A harsh splash of a chilly sensation washed over me as if I had ice water thrown on me. I was taken aback. I was stunned. I was hurt and I wanted to kill. As I stood looking at a woman who lied to me by omission, all the old angst between us flooded back. I watched her without feeling, an empty void growing bigger every minute. In my mind, I heard my father's voice, quoting his favorite military strategist, Machiavelli: *"'For among other evils caused by being disarmed, it renders you contemptible; which is one of those disgraceful things which a prince must guard against.'"*

That quote played over and over as I stared into Kenya's eyes. I heard her explaining that it happened while I was overseas working for the military with Doctors Without Borders. Heard her say that she was still frightened to tell me anything when I came home, and all I could think was that she had lied to me and her actions could have put our daughter at risk back then. Jewel visited her mother often and Lu could have easily targeted baby girl to get back at Kenya. The nigga had been touched in the head like that. I was genuinely pissed.

My life was not my own. No matter how hard I had fought to keep clear of my father, his shadow always reached me once it stopped reaching for my mother. Lu, my older brother, had come for the mother of my child. He had almost killed her for his own twisted bullshit and she kept that shit from me. Kenya was a liar. She was a manipulator. She was a risk.

A slap against my chest barely drew my attention. Had Kenya not appeared in my face screaming at me, I thought that I would have stayed where I was, in a catatonic rage, for hours.

"Tone," she screamed, tears running down her face. "Tone, breathe. You're scaring me. Baby, your nails are cutting into your palms and they are bleeding. Antonio."

In a daze, I glanced down at my fisted hands then back up toward Kenya. To my ears, my voice was a cold monotone, devoid of everything as I mentally went over what she told me and started putting the pieces together during that time when we were trying to work it out, again for the hundredth time.

"When I came back from doing a Doctors tour, you told me that you wanted nothing to do with me anymore. Said it was foolish to try to work this out. Told me the fire at the DA's office was the writing on the wall that we just couldn't work it out," I muttered.

"I was scared. I needed to get away from Atlanta and if that meant dropping you, I had to do that for my mental state. And I had to be able to heal without you asking questions," Kenya explained. "I didn't know you were an Orlando and I was scared of what could happen to you and Jewel."

She stood with the bedsheets wrapped around her and it reminded me that we had just dropped to our rawest moment and used that to fuck. To release emotions and tensions that this whole ordeal had put us through. She was mine in that moment, fuck the world and her fiancé, and now we were back to the way it always was between us: her over there and me over here, a large wall rising between us.

"You ran. You told me nothing and a year later you hooked up with Isaac," I quietly said, ticking it all off in my mind.

Reaching out to take my hand, she carefully pried my fingers open and used the sheet to dab at the cuts there. "Please understand, I didn't want to put you in danger. I lied to protect my family and to protect our daughter." Kissing my palm, she looked up at me with tears in her eyes.

"You put me through bullshit. Anger, fights, hate . . . You should have told me." See, to me, that part came out soft and understanding of the trauma she had gone through. I turned away from her. But, in reality, hazing out of the red zone, something I hadn't experienced since childhood, I stood by a broken lamp breathing heavy, shouting, "If our daughter hadn't been with Mama in Miami, she could have been at risk because of you! You should have fucking told me!"

Behind me Kenya stood away from me in fear clutching the sheets to her petite form. For a second I thought she might run, but when those tears fell and her eyes narrowed, I saw a different side to Kenya that I recalled from our younger years.

Foul words spewed from her lips as she walked up on me shouting, "You lied to me too, you know. You put me in the center of a goddamned spiderweb, all controlled by your evil-ass father! But you have the goddamned nerve to talk to me about I lied? Yes, I lied. Yes, I put you through hell. I was wrong, but it was all I had to protect myself. And even after all of that, all I had was Isaac."

"You could have had me! I would have fixed it. I wish you would have told me—" I started, knowing what I said was irrational.

"And then this shit with your father would have started even earlier. Antonio, I was terrified, traumatized! You weren't there when it happened and I started to resent you for that. I'm sorry for that part of it. The rest I couldn't stop." Kenya's words came out in a strong vibrancy with the tremor of weakness.

My father was wrong that she was weak from it. Scared? Yes. But I saw something deeper: a woman trying to survive a traumatic experience put on her because of my family. My fucking terrorist family. Because of that, I came out of my dark rage over her and channeled it toward a brother I hated with my very soul.

"If there was ever a time that I needed you to understand, it's right now. I need that small sliver of clarity because all the nightmares are coming back and I don't know what to do. I feel like I'm falling into a void." Standing in front of me, Kenya was pleading with me.

Being with an Orlando was dangerous. I knew that the day I fell for Kenya. Essentially, had I kept my distance, she might have had a normal life with a normal man like Isaac. Instead, she fell for me and her life had been nothing but the worse for it. It was my fault.

"I'm sorry. I'm sorry I wasn't there. I'm sorry you couldn't tell me. I'm sorry." Dropping my forehead against hers, I closed my eyes then kissed her temple as I whispered those words. "I'm in that void right now. If Lu were here, I'd kill him."

Feeling the soft sweep of Kenya's small hands against the surface of my abs, I shuddered feeling the old me within aching for her. I couldn't crumble to this weakness. I was taught to turn that into power, and so I would.

"I'd let you." Softly she kissed my chest. Gently she let the tip of her tongue trace over where her name used to sit against my ribcage.

Then, like the confident, sexual powerhouse I knew and taught her to be, Kenya scraped her teeth over that spot and whispered, "Mine."

I lifted her around my waist, fisted my hand around her hair and then her neck, squeezing; then I dropped to a knee to place her on the bed as I found my way back inside her. Screwing had always been our thing—mentally, spiritually, and physically—and right now it was mad good. Thrust for thrust, we made the bed quake. With it we both growled out like animals as our flesh slapped against each other. This was no love shit. This was old-school animalist shit. I punished her cookie for her lies and the agony she'd put me through. She returned the favor by throwing it back and leaving my skin covered in her passion marks.

We were locked into old patterns and we didn't give a fuck. I knew after this if she wanted to go back to Isaac I'd have to let her, because I knew this life wasn't for her. But, for now, she was mine and I planned on making her kitty remember each stroke I initiated against her when we first made love back in our youth.

Our quickie put us back in order and had me clamping down my emotions. After, we found ourselves downstairs in my father's war room. Computers and screens where everywhere. The pictures from Fallon's cell were on a few of the monitors while programs played with algorithms meant to search out a person through face recognition.

Kenya went to Benita to debrief with her about what she learned. I moved with purpose around that busy room, hands in my jeans, to position myself near my father, who stood akimbo with his arms crossed.

"You rectify the weakness?" he said staring at the group picture with my daughter.

John Coltrane played low over the house system. Collective click-clacking of keys melded with the low mutters of my father's tech team handling business. My niece, Maria-Rosa, oversaw that part while typing on her own computer.

I stared at the faces in the picture. Two of them we had crossed out. Three were left. The bastard who was turned away from the camera, I felt in my gut, was Keith. Then there was the young girl sticking her tongue out, and Donna. She leaned against Fallon, smiling; however, her eyes were on the brotha who had his back turned.

Her hair was mermaid blue. Her blue jean shorts were cut so high that she might as well have been wearing panties. She wore a tank that had KILLER MOB scrawled on it. Little Miss Donna seemed like her goal in life was to be a trap queen and a leader in her own right. Focusing on the varied chess pieces of the group, I reached up to rub my jaw and answer my father.

"Yes, sir, it's handled and it won't be an issue for you again," I coolly stated.

I felt the tight squeeze of my father's hand on the back of my neck. We kept staring at the screen as I listened to him.

"You'll never be me, but you know that and don't want that. But you will make a strong right hand once you cleanse yourself of the emotions you allow to lead you, Antonio, my son. There is a place here for you, this is your *familia* and my lessons shine bright in you. You will help teach the next generation how to keep this family strong."

I turned my head to stare in his intense eyes. My father cracked a menacing smile and continued, "We kill out of need; we don't kill in excess. Each kill is our mark, our art, and we paint the streets in blood to show the world who we are. Never let another enemy dictate your steps. You make their movements lead to you."

"*Sí,* Father. And like a roach running from sunlight, Mallock was that; and through his stupidity I learned a lot," I calmly said, staring at my own reflection, albeit different, in my father's face.

"Tell me," he ordered in an even tone.

"Donna's spot is two blocks over from where Fallon's complex is. We should case it and scrape up whatever information we can find, because she's not in Houston. She ran off to L.A., I assume to be near the home base of the Knights."

A sharp hiss escaped my father's lips. For a second, I thought that he might flip; but when a cold calmness washed over him, I knew that he wasn't going to reveal a thing.

"What do you know about these Knights?" Caltrone asked me, removing his hand.

Feeling as if I had the control, I smirked, "I know they are all over the U.S. in pocket factions, just like us. I know they gun hard in Miami and seem to be trying to grow there; but, above all that, I remember a meeting with you and their duel kings: Emmanuel and Yasmine Knight. I think it would be wise to get to Donna before she makes it to the Knights, Father. Right?"

Just like that, my father's jaw began to twitch and I knew that he was holding something back from me. He turned away from me, glanced at a wall that held the insignia of a lion with a crown, then walked out.

"Pack your bags. We're going to L.A.," he said as he walked passed me. "Benita! Scour Donna's apartment. Find whatever you can and meet us on the jet. If you are late, we will leave you. I expect a phone call," he shouted behind him then slammed the duel mahogany doors of the room behind him.

I didn't know what secrets that old man was holding but I knew one thing: the Knights and the Orlandos were on tight leashes with one another. From the whispers I heard as a child, those leashes were held by old-world gangster respect and territory lines, nothing more. I knew on day one when I caught a glimpse of that inked chess piece and it triggered an old memory that nothing good was going to come from our hunt. When Kenya relayed the information she learned, I knew a war was going to come if we weren't careful.

Too bad that was after I took off that kid's head.

Following my father's orders, we all packed up our gear. Once Benita effectively trashed Donna's apartment, we took to the air and ended up in sunny L.A. Loose ends needed to be tied up and I was anxious to learn what Benita found.

Dropping a bag between our feet as we rode down the interstate, Benita glanced at Kenya and me, then frowned. "I found a bag of your daughter's clothes, and shoes. Found her cell phone, found her laptop. Looks like Donna was going to sell it for parts because it was in pieces," Benita said.

I felt Kenya tense by my side. She slowly slid forward and reached down to rummage through the bag before she asked, "What else?"

Exhaling, Benita was about to speak up but stopped when Mark took over. "Dumb bitch was scattered. Her place was fucked, which I took to mean she was running. Guess she got word about Fallon because the *punta* just left according to neighbors."

Focusing on my hands, I flexed them in thought. I used to be a healer and now I was the angel of death. "So, nothing worth shit to go off of?" I asked quirking an eyebrow.

"Naw, I didn't say all of that," Mark said chuckling. "Found out the bitch is a honeypot. Maria-Rosa found some scattered notes with girls' names, ages, and Twitter and Facebook tags with dollar signs by them."

Both Kenya and I glanced at Maria-Rosa, who sat wide-legged watching the cars and clicking on her cell.

"I'm still doing some searching but it doesn't take a rocket scientist to see the setup. Looks like Donna friends the girls, and gains their trust and eventually gets their information. Then, I'm assuming, Fallon and his niggas swoop in," Maria-Rosa said.

Kenya, who had been clutching the clothes, now threw them down and sat back. On the slick, her hand dropped between us and I felt her pinch my thigh hard. I knew that was her way to keep her emotions, and mine, in check. "So that's how they got my baby girl?" she asked in restraint.

"Partially. We believe Donna had been stalking our family, mainly you two and Jewel, for months now," Benita answered.

That puzzled me. *What the hell for?* "Why do you say that?" I started until Kenya abruptly leaned forward.

I watched her rip through the bag and pull out a tablet and pictures. On display were images of young girls and Donna over them, laughing, frozen in several sexual positions. Anger flared in me for the young girls. But that wasn't what had us pissed; it was the picture of a guy in a college jacket that drew our attention. Donna stood against him kissing his cheek, their hands locked, while she wore Jewel's clothes, shoes, and a necklace her mother had given Jewel. Under that picture were notes on Jewel, our personal information, addresses, and where we both worked.

"There's always a sloppy bitch," Mark said, breaking the silence.

"Found her," Maria-Rosa said with a smile. She then turned and said, "You get that, Benita?"

"Yeah. Heading there now," she said, driving.

The whole time, my father sat in the front of the truck in silence. His jaw still twitched, which gave me a clue that he was in his thoughts. When I looked at Kenya she sat in the same way. Donna had to die. There was no way around it, and we just needed to make sure that we got to her before anyone else did.

Heading off the turnpike, we ended up in Inglewood, from what Maria-Rosa told us.

My father then spoke up, "We have representation here. Take us to our house in Baldwin Hills. We'll wait for Donna to come to us."

I could tell by the way we all looked at one another, everyone in the 4x4 wondered how Donna would come to us. But from the stoic expression on Maria-Rosa's face, I gathered she had worked some magic that I didn't know about.

An hour later, I stood pacing back and forth in an old Tudor-style home. Plastic covered the dark wooden floors. We all wore rubber boots with plastic bags tied around our feet. Rubber gloves were on our hands, our bodies in sanitation suits, and our hair tied back. Kenya sat in the same attire watching me as I paced.

"Are you sure she'll come to us?" I heard her ask.

Tension kept me on edge. "I trust in my father in this part."

"She helped take our daughter. She stalked us and she helped, and she watched, and—"

"I know, baby," I quietly interrupted.

It was then that a loud scream and scraping could be heard. The door swung open and both Mark and Maria-Rosa strolled in, pulling the thrashing body of a female. Two unknown men were behind them and I figured they worked for my father. I watched them shut the door then glance up behind me.

I turned to see my father standing on the top step looking down at us all. A disgusted look was on his face and he seemed to burn holes into the screaming female.

"Let me go! I . . . I didn't have shit to do with whatever you got me here fah. Let me go!" the girl screamed.

Hair was everywhere, and as they stood her up and made her look our way, I realized it was Donna. I felt a flash of cool air brush my jaw. With it came a loud, animalistic scream. Kenya had rushed forward. In her hand was an iron poker, one she had grabbed earlier from the fireplace. Wielding it, she slammed it against the girl's face. Blood went everywhere, along with teeth.

"You took my daughter," Kenya spat out.

Donna stumbled and fell to the floor. Tears fell and she cupped her face, blood pouring. "I don't even know you," she managed to get out.

"No shit, bitch. But you know Jewel. You know all those girls you lured into your sick, twisted world to hurt. You know that, huh?" she said stepping forward.

I stood, quiet, watching Kenya lose herself piece by piece as she stalked Donna.

"The girl is smart. She knows not to talk," my father said from where he stood.

"Oh, she's going to talk," Kenya spat out. She slammed the poker into Donna's thigh.

The girl screamed and tried to get away. "Stop, please. I don't know no Jewel," she said; yet the lie just didn't sound like truth in the least bit.

"We found her on the Knights' block," one of my father's men stated. "She had Jewel's ID and purse."

"Motherfucker, you lie," Donna said heatedly. She slapped her hand against the door, leaving a bloody streak, and she tried to stand.

Kenya swung again, connecting with Donna's skull. Rage turned Kenya into a monster. She smashed then stomped Donna and, before she could kill her, I stepped forward and carefully pulled her back.

"My turn," was all I said.

Squatting down, I grabbed Donna by her leg then dragged her out of the foyer. "Now, Donna. You say you don't know shit, didn't see shit, ain't hear shit, as they say? But all the evidence and your actions say otherwise. You dig?"

Of course, I got no answer. She just lay there breathing heavily as I dragged her to the kitchen. On my way through the hallway, I stopped only once to see if she was able to comprehend what was going on. Donna's head lolled around, her arm strewn over her face.

When her head bumped a door, she groaned as her eyes fluttered. "You killed my man's grandparents. You . . . you raped my best friend."

A deep sigh came from the hallway. "No, girl. My *familia* and I didn't. What you think is the case, isn't."

"You did," she spat out trying to fight but failing.

It was then that my father walked forward and looked down at her face. "That's what you all say, *pero* my method of killing and my intellect are far superior than to lower myself to such a thing. Your family was attacked by a false faction: people who wanted to be Orlandos but weren't. Los Lobo Royals. We've since wiped them out for using my family's name in vain. However, this anger does not excuse your foul treason and actions against us, now does it?"

We watched Donna weakly swing at us. My father moved in disgust, which allowed Kenya to walk up to her and stomp the girl in her face. I was pretty sure Kenya would have spit on Donna; however, she knew the law of DNA: don't share it.

Positioning the girl in the middle of an opulent white French-style kitchen, I motioned for Kenya to stretch out Donna's arm.

"Now that that is settled, Donna," I asked in a sing-song voice, "where is Keith?"

When the girl said nothing, I chuckled. Then the sound of metal, namely a cleaver cutting and chopping through flesh, tendon, and bone, mixed with a sharp scream that rent the air. When that didn't elicit a response, I tied off where I cut through, then moved on.

By the end of the night, Donna and I became close. With every piece of her, truths spilled from her bloody lips like rain. By the end of it, we learned that Ms. Donna was Fallon's sister and that it was Keith who was the mastermind of the grand scheme, and that he had taken Jewel away to some place in Georgia.

With Donna's last breath, I watched Kenya slice Donna's throat open with a box cutter as the girl choked on a final word: "Caitlyn."

Chapter 13

Kenya

"We need to see someone here before we head to Georgia. It's imperative we cover our tracks here as cleanly as possible. For as much as I want to find Jewel, we do not need another blood feud on our hands. The Orlandos have had enough of that to span generations," Caltrone said.

Something other than what we had going on was bothering the old man. There was a mutilated body that a cleaning team was getting rid of in the kitchen. Tone had asked them to leave the head and one arm. He was collecting souvenirs. For what, I didn't know, but there was always a method to Tone's madness.

"Are the Knights that big of a family or do they have enough power to tackle you?" I asked, curious as to why Caltrone seemed to be put off by the notion of having to go to war with them.

The old man looked at me, pointedly. "It's not about the size of the family or the amount of power they have. It's about lines that have been drawn in the sand that all parties agreed not to cross. Emmanuel and Yasmine Knight are not ones to trifle with. They were formidable foes once and I'm sure they won't hesitate to become so again. They're like rabid wolves: once poked with a hot iron, nothing will stop them until their thirst for blood has been quenched. To go to war with them will not just affect the Orlandos. It will reach past us, to those who we've made enemies of before. It is a war we can't afford to fight nor lose."

"Yeah, but if they had something to do with Jewel being taken—"

Caltrone held up a hand to stop me. "She wasn't taken. She left on her own. I seriously doubt the Knights would have had anything to do with that part. However, just like me, if someone kills blood for reasons I feel are trivial, I will seek revenge at all costs."

"My daughter isn't trivial," Tone cut in.

"No, *mijo,* she isn't, not to us, but to them she means nothing, especially if she willingly left home. If Donna in there is indeed the daughter or any close kin of the Knights, we will have a serious problem on our hands."

I looked at Tone, not sure what to make of everything Caltrone had just said. On top of worrying about whether we would get our child back in one piece, we also had to worry about stepping on the toes of another family I'd never heard of before. Tone glanced at me, but quickly turned his eyes back to his father. I could tell he wanted to ask him more questions but decided against it for the moment.

A flight and one hour later, Caltrone, Tone, and I ended up in Fresno, California. We walked into a cathedral so big it was intimidating.

"We came to a church?" I asked just to be sure Caltrone was at the right place.

The church had a Roman Catholic feel. It was constructed of red brick. The facade had a triple entry framed by two square towers with spires. Above the entry sat a small rose window. Inside was impressive as well, but I didn't have time to get a good look at it. My attention was diverted to the two men who were meeting Caltrone down the long aisle.

The man in priest robes could have passed for Caltrone's twin had he had gray hair. They both had a full head of hair, but the priest's hair was coarser than Caltrone's. I looked at Tone to see if he knew the man. Judging by the stoic look on his face, I'd have said he did.

"There is an Orlando priest?" I asked him.

He grunted. "Don't let the robes fool you. He's a good dude, but he is still an Orlando," Tone told me.

"Speak your piece, Carlos, then leave these grounds. They are for the holy or those looking for redemption and you are anything but," the priest said as soon as he came face-to-face with Caltrone.

His voice surprised me as it carried a timbre that would make any woman drop her drawers on command. I blinked a few times, trying to figure out what relation the priest was to Caltrone. "Who the hell is Carlos?" I asked.

Tone grabbed my hand and pulled me back a bit. "Kenya," he called out to me. "Your mouth, keep it closed," he said.

"I need your help," Caltrone said.

"Why?"

"Because you're the only one who can help me."

"No, why should I care you need my help?"

"You're a priest, Rueben. To not help me would go against your religion, *sí?*"

Rueben's jaw twitched and his eyes darkened a bit. Priest or not, he was clearly an Orlando and he most definitely did not want Caltrone to be in his presence. "It's Father Rueben to you, and don't use my religious beliefs against me," the priest said.

I was so caught up in the exchange between Father Rueben and Caltrone that when I caught another man staring at me, I yelped and jumped behind Tone.

"Can I touch her?" the man asked Tone.

Tone visibly bristled. "No, Uncle Savoy, you cannot touch her."

"She's pretty," Savoy said while tilting his head. "Like a porcelain doll."

My mouth hung open like my jaws were unhinged. One side of the man's face was burned beyond recognition. The other side was perfectly fine. His good eye was as black as the night was long. The other socket had a milky-colored glass eye that seemed to roll around on its own. However, on one side his head was a full set of auburn ropey locs. He literally had two faces. All three men were tall and statuesque, with Father Rueben being the tallest by two inches or so. Any time Father Rueben looked at Caltrone, his honey brown eyes blazed like a fire was burning behind them.

While Father Rueben was dressed in priest robes, Savoy looked like he belonged to a biker gang. He wore a leather jacket that had the same Orlando symbol as the ring Caltrone wore.

Black biker boots adorned his feet, and tethered jeans sat loose around his hips but tight enough against his thighs that I could see the muscles strain any time he moved. The gym was his friend, as his chest and arms were sculpted with muscle. A diamond earring sat in his left lobe and drew attention to the burned side of his face. Clearly the man had been handsome before the burn to his face. Even as he was smiling now, the burn did little to hide the attractiveness he once possessed.

"Stop staring, Kenya," Tone said to me. "Don't stare at him. He'll think you want him or are making fun of him. Either way, don't stare."

I quickly cast my glance down at the floor.

"Is there someplace we can talk that isn't out here in the open like this?" Caltrone asked.

"No," Father Rueben plainly stated. "You wanted me and Savoy here, we're here. Talk," he said to Caltrone but then looked at Tone. "Antonio, I'm sorry for my bluntness but, as you know, where your father goes, trouble follows. How have you been?"

"My daughter is missing, Uncle Rueben. I'm not doing well at all," Tone answered.

Father Rueben nodded once. "Understandable. And is this your wife?"

Tone nodded a lie. "She is."

Father Rueben stepped forward and extended his hand. "Pleasure to meet you. I'm sorry it had to be under these circumstances."

"Pleased to meet you as well," I responded.

Savoy stepped forward but Father Rueben, Caltrone, and Tone stepped in front of me. "Savoy," Father Rueben said.

Savoy put his hands in the air as if he were being robbed. "What? I can't introduce myself to the lady?"

"No," they all said at once.

"Carlos, tell me what you need and please be on your way. I can keep Savoy in here for only so long," Father Rueben said.

He was calling Caltrone Carlos and it baffled me. I made the mistake of looking at Savoy again. He was watching me like an eagle did prey. There was a smirk on his face and he rolled his shoulders as he did so. I frowned and looked over at Tone. I had so many questions about the trio and why Father Rueben seemed to be able to talk to Caltrone like he wasn't the head of the biggest criminal enterprise on North American soil. However, today wouldn't be the day I got to ask them.

"The Knights; we need you to keep any mention of me being in California off their radar until we leave and for as long as you can after we're gone," Caltrone said.

Father Rueben frowned. "The Knights, Carlos? You've crossed that line?"

"I've done no such thing, at least not intentionally so."

I stood by quietly as Tone and Caltrone explained all that had happened over the last few months all the way up until we had killed Donna an hour or so ago. While Savoy had taken great interest in me moments earlier, as Father Rueben and Caltrone spoke, he paid close attention to what they were saying. Once Tone and Caltrone were done, Father Rueben took a deep breath, closed his eyes, and then shook his head.

"I'm not sure what I can do with such short notice, Carlos, but I'll do what I can. I want you to know I'm only doing this for Antonio . . . and for Carmen."

When Father Rueben said Carmen's name, Caltrone's face contorted and he looked at the priest as if he had just cursed him. There was history there.

Savoy laughed and tsked. He said, "Carmen, Carmen, Carmen." Savoy sang her name like it was a soulful melody. "Surprised you didn't learn your lesson the first time around where women were involved, big bro. First Moses and then Rueben." Savoy tsked again and shook his head. "At least Rueben is still alive, *sí?*"

Caltrone made a move so quick toward Savoy that it was like lightning. Rueben stepped between the two men and Tone grabbed his father's forearm. That wasn't the kicker, though. From behind doors and confessionals, men in robes came out as if they were guards. Shit reminded me of some Knights Templar shit with how they all homed in on Caltrone. There were serious gazes on the faces of the ones I could see and they looked as if they meant business. Father Rueben lifted a hand and then waved it. The other priests disappeared as quickly as they had come.

Caltrone spat out Spanish venomously at Savoy while Rueben shoved Savoy back and asked Caltrone to leave.

"*Di una palabra más a mí y yo te corto la lengua*," Caltrone said. "Say another word to me and I'll cut your tongue out," Caltrone had told Savoy.

Savoy fixed his lips and pretended to spit Caltrone's way. "Not unless you have gloves on and wash your hands at least thirty times you won't, *estúpido*."

"This is a place of worship and you two will respect my house!" Father Rueben shouted.

Savoy backed down quickly. Caltrone looked as if he was still ready to fight. And, judging by the looks on both Tone's face and mine, we were baffled by the events unfolding before us.

Chapter 14

Kenya

Caltrone stormed from the church like the hounds of hell were on his ass.

I had so many questions, but I knew the answers would not come easy. I'd seen Caltrone in a different light in the past few hours. While most of us assumed Caltrone was larger than life, he had shown a more human side, one I thought he was incapable of possessing.

"Are you going to explain to me what just happened in there?" I asked Tone once we were back on the plane and heading to Atlanta. I had thought Caltrone would take a day or two to rest and regroup, but I was damn glad he didn't. I was anxious to get my child. I had no idea what else her kidnapper would do to her and the thought of it made me uneasy.

There was a stoic look on Tone's face when he answered. Caltrone was in a private cabin on the

plane. Tone and I were sharing the main cabin.
Tone had changed out of the clothes he had on
earlier. He'd replaced his old attire with sweats
and an all-white T-shirt. He had pulled his hair
from the ponytail it had been in and there was a
constant frown on his face.

It had been eerily silent on the way back to the
airport. Caltrone's face was emotionless but he
sat rigid. Something about what Savoy had said
rattled the normally cool, calm, and collected old
demon.

"Which part?" Tone asked.

"Who's Moses? And your father's real name is
Carlos?" I asked.

"No one calls him by that name."

"Father Rueben just did."

"Father Rueben is the oldest son. He can do as
he pleases. No one else would be foolish enough
to call the old man by his name as such. Moses
was once Pops's best friend."

"Was?"

"He's dead now."

"Oh. And Caltrone had something to do with
that?"

"More or less."

"And what is it about Uncle Savoy that makes
my flesh crawl?"

Tone sighed. "For starters, he's a sociopath with a narcissistic personality disorder. And he has a weird fetish for collecting women."

"How is that any different from what your father does? Doesn't Caltrone have a harem of women at his beck and call?"

"Uncle Savoy collects women. The emphasis is on collect. He doesn't procreate or have sex with them. He just collects them. He calls them his porcelain dolls. So, think of it this way: he has a house full of dolls."

I guessed by the way Tone shook his head as he watched me that my face showed my disgust or disdain, whichever was etched on my features at the moment. "How?" I asked, still aghast afterward.

Tone shrugged. "I don't know the particulars, but it's always best if a woman doesn't stare at him too hard or too long. Once he gets it in his head that you want him or that you're making fun of him, you're pretty much fucked."

"So he's a serial killer?"

Tone took a deep breath and sighed. "No. None of those women he collects are dead. They probably wish they were though."

For a moment, I sat there, puzzled as hell about what I'd just heard. I couldn't form another question to ask even if I wanted to. So

I didn't. I didn't think Tone was in the mood to talk anyway. He sat down in one of the plush seats on the private plane. The scowl on his face would stop the devil in his tracks. We still had a huge problem. Our daughter was missing.

"So we're headed back to Atlanta?" I asked after we had been in the air for a while.

"I'm not sure what move Pops is about to make next. I know I'm anxious and I won't be able to take this shit for much longer," Tone said.

I could feel his tension, the angst. Shit, I knew what he was feeling because I felt it too. Every time I took a breath, I thought about Jewel. I thought about what her body had endured. Wondered what this shit would do to her mind. As her mother, just knowing the things that had happened and what could be happening to her was enough to drive me mad.

We landed in Atlanta a few hours later. I would have said it felt good to be back home but in no way did it feel good. My daughter wasn't here with me. We had been all over the world it seemed only for it to bring us back to Atlanta. I wasn't even sure she was here anymore.

The private airport was alive with life. Men and women dressed in all black flanked the plane. Most had guns on their person. Others rushed to flank Caltrone as soon as he stepped off the plane.

Caltrone barked out orders as he took powerful strides toward a black SUV. "I need every available body we have in Atlanta at the safe house no later than nine in the morning," he ordered, his strong baritone laced with a tone that said he meant business. "Nobody and I mean nobody should be late. Are we clear?"

The woman he had been speaking to nodded. "Would that include your grandson Damien, señor?"

Caltrone stopped then scowled down at the woman. "What part of 'every available body' did you misunderstand, Danielle?" he asked her.

She nodded, lowered her eyes, and rushed off. Tone helped me into the truck after Caltrone got in. I was so out of it that the name "Damien" didn't quite register with my senses yet. We were all silent for a moment. Caltrone looked to be so deep in thought, I didn't even think he was with us in mind. What his brother Savoy had said to him really shook him to the core. Or could it have been that the threat of whoever these Knights were rattled Caltrone's cage as well?

Either way, none of it mattered more than getting Jewel back.

"I have some information," Caltrone said once we were all in the truck.

"Let us hear it," Tone said.

"Damien has seen your daughter," Caltrone said.

"Damien? Damien Orlando?" I yelled. My heart sped up. Damien was a pimp and if he had gotten a hold of my daughter . . . I let my thoughts trail off. I couldn't fathom even thinking about that possibility.

"How do you know?" Tone asked. He had leaned forward, concern etched on his features.

Caltrone said, "I had her picture passed around when you first came to me. He told me someone brought her to him to sell her before he knew it was her."

"So why didn't he reach out to someone?"

Tone's question confused me. "He didn't know it was her," I said.

"Bullshit," Tone snapped at me. "An Orlando always knows another Orlando," he said to me then turned back to his father. "So why didn't this nigga reach out to someone and ask some fucking questions?"

"Antonio, calm yourself," Caltrone said.

"I am fucking calm. When did he see her?"

Caltrone took a deep inhale. "It was as recent as last week."

Tone's whole body shook violently before he yelled, "And this is after you had already put out a BOLO? And that nigga didn't think to—"

"Antonio," Caltrone yelled his name, his accent thick.

"Fuck you, old man. That nigga Dame has seen Jewel, has been in her fucking presence. She is an Orlando. One Orlando always knows another. It has been that way since we became a faction. One Orlando is never in another's presence without us knowing who they are even if we have never seen them before. It is the way of the Orlandos. I'm going to kill this nigga," Tone roared then started rocking back and forth.

"You will do no such thing. Damien can point us in the right direction," Caltrone said sternly. "We need him alive."

I knew Tone was livid. He had gone from Harvard to hood in his vernacular within seconds. My soul was tired and scared. I was shaking so badly that my teeth ground. Jewel had been close. So fucking close. *How dare Damien play with her life?*

"I have already spoken to Damien about this. Once he learned that Kenya was the mother of your child, I suppose his anger at his father being put away and subsequently murdered clouded his better judgment. We need him alive, *mijo*. Atlanta is his domain. He can tell us who and where," Caltrone continued.

Tone cut his eyes at his father. "Then you had best keep him away from me."

The next morning, I sat next to Tone in a mansion near Alpharetta. Being in a room full of Orlandos and their relatives made my flesh crawl. There were so damn many. All the men were similar in looks. No matter if they had olive complexions, brown skin, black skin, or caramel skin, they all had that Orlando look to them. Even the ugly ones were appealing. However, the ruthlessness that emanated from them couldn't be denied. They all spoke to Tone. Smiles were on their faces. Most of the women treated him like royalty. Everyone was shocked to see him for the most part, but the general consensus was they were happy he was home, so to speak.

Tone took it all in stride. He never smiled but he acknowledged everyone. He gave a nod here, gave a wave of the hand there. But he never said more than two words to anyone but me. He seemed to be cool, calm, and collected, until Damien Orlando walked into the room.

That could have been because I stiffened. My whole spine went rigid. That man had tried to help his father kill me. I'd never forget the boy in the hoodie warning me to leave my office. Damien was every bit of Lu, his father. He walked with an arrogance that could be matched only by Caltrone. In his hand was a cane that I was sure hid a sword on the inside. Damien was dressed in a tailored Armani suit that fit his athletic frame perfectly. It was easy to see how he was so successful at being a pimp. Women flocked to him like stank on shit.

The man carried an all-knowing smirk on his face as he walked to the long dining table and took a seat across from me and Tone. His smirk deepened when he laid eyes on me. Tone bristled. Damien noticed and turned his gaze to his uncle.

"What's up, Uncle Tone?" he spoke. Damien's voice carried a sexy but deadly undertone. "How did you manage to get this bitch in your stable?"

Tone sat forward, his eyes cold and unmoving. "If you value your life, it would do you good not to say another fucking word to me."

The room got silent. All eyes were on us. There was a chill in the air when Damien's smile turned from a smirk to a full-on grin. He showed all thirty-two of his perfectly white teeth. His light eyes sparkled with evil intent. "Or what?" Damien challenged.

"Or what your father got in prison will be considered child's play once I'm done playing with your entrails."

Damien's grin left his face. A scowl took up residence. "You threaten me when I'm the one who passed up on whoring your daughter?"

Before the words finished leaving Damien's mouth, Tone had jumped across the table. Dishes went flying; broken glass and falling utensils could be heard hitting the floor. Tone had tackled Damien. I wasn't sure who threw the first punch, but the men in the family rushed in to pull them apart before any real damage could be done.

Tone had a knife in his hand and Damien was bleeding from his neck. I didn't know the men holding Tone back, but they were family. The Orlando eyes didn't lie.

Damien's eyes widened when one of the women screamed and started cussing in Spanish. She was calling Antonio crazy. She kept yelling that she couldn't believe he had tried to kill family.

"You shut the fuck up or I'll come for you next," Tone yelled as he pointed the bloody knife at her.

The woman gasped and jumped back. She clamped her mouth shut but stared at Antonio like he was the devil incarnate. Damien rubbed his neck where he had a fresh cut and then looked from his hand to Tone.

Tone turned the knife back to Damien. "You're lucky they pulled me off in time or I would have ended you. Don't fuck with me, Dame. Not today. Not tomorrow. Not fucking ever," Tone spat.

"I didn't know she was your daughter until Grandpops showed me a picture, you irate motherfucker," Dame shot back. "Even so, I had enough sense to pass on her when she was brought to me. You should be thanking me, nigga. I could have made her just another Orlando whore"— Dame turned to look at me— "just like her mother."

I kept thinking about how close Jewel had been to being rescued, how easy it would have been for Dame to take action and bring my baby home. Yet, he'd done nothing. All because he felt like he had to get some kind of revenge against me. All because of me, my baby was still out there somewhere. Now it was my turn to lose what little grip I had on reality. I couldn't jump across the table like Tone had done, but Dame was close enough for me to spit on. So that was what I did. I spat right in his face. *Fuck him. Fuck him and his demon-possessed father.* I hoped Lu Orlando was rotting in hell.

A few people in the room gasped. Dame's whole face turned red, and I knew when he checked out of reality. I didn't know much about the man, but judging by the way disgust overtook his features, I knew I'd angered him. He reached out to grab me. Tone broke loose from the men holding him. I tried to wrestle free of Damien. He was so busy trying to choke me that when the butt of the knife Tone was holding caught his face, he didn't know what had hit him.

Chapter 15

Antonio

"Motherfucker, have you lost your goddamn mind?" I roared as the back of my blade made contact. "I will erase you."

"Ha ha! Damn, I forgot how mad Uncle could be," Dame taunted between my punches.

Fury had me going in on my nephew. At this point, I gave not a damn that I was going against the grain and taking out my vengeance in front of family, against a family member. This shit was fair exchange because if my daughter died due to something he could have stopped, then his right to life would be forfeited.

"Listen as I tell you this one more time, nephew . . ." How do you put a monster in his place and make him feel it in his black soul? A small part of me didn't know at one time. Now, everything was different. A bastard with the same blood as me, the blood of the head of our family of monsters, the devil himself, lay under my foot. The pressure of it had Damien choking. His fingers clawed at my shoe as I pressed down on his throat.

We all were aware of how much Damien liked to play sadistic mind games. How much he got off on his masochistic ways. Everyone here turned a blind eye to it, until me. The one thing that he was not going to do was put family in harm's way and get away with it. Not with me. Not my daughter and not the mother of my child. Damien was not and never would be his grandfather, my father, and I aimed to teach him that.

"What you're not going to do is touch what is mine, feel me?" Slipping from my lips was pure ice, seething hatred for this waste of cum pumped from my brother's dick. "Not again. You disrespected this family by allowing an enemy to this family to have my daughter. Strike one. Then you come for my wife, again? Strike two."

Damien gagged but he wickedly smiled as he did so. As if he were enjoying this crap. The shit pissed me off so much that I pressed harder, close to getting a snap. I was at the edge and if killing him threw everything out of order, at this point, I truly didn't give a fuck. The devil in me was coming out more every day, and I had that legacy straight from the pure tap, unlike my nephew. Watered-down-ass nigga he was. Close in age we may have been, but that did nothing for me in retaining loyalty to his putrid blood. He allowed my daughter to be taken. Played with the idea of selling her off, all for his own machinations.

Today wasn't the day that I was just going to let him off without showing him how much like my father I could be. Without a thought to the matter, I pressed down again, swiped his favorite cane, and slammed the end of it against his face. The satisfying sound of pain he made had me unlock it, and pull out its blade.

I knew his secrets. I had been there for a short while when his father was the first to learn them. Wasn't shit original in Damien's style except that it was a pale imitation of the better model. From what I was hearing anyway, his brother Dante was the one carrying on the legacy of a devil better than this asshole right here. But, that was just me being the motherfucker I could be by minimalizing the insane genius that ran through all of us.

"Dame." Something like sick, dark laughter came from my soul. It had me toying with my nephew, giving him back what he gave out in energy to us all. Pure, unadulterated insanity. There was something in me that would get joy from dismantling his body, limb from limb, and peeling his flesh from him, layer by layer.

The demon in me flashed across my face in a quick, twisted grin, and showed itself to let Damien know that I could be my father in every way imaginable. If pushed, I could be a sicker bastard then Damien could ever be. The humanity in me was the only thing that was keeping me on a calm level higher than that of my father.

"Strike three will mean your death. I might not be able to kill you right now because we need you but, one day, if it's not me, one of your many whores is going to show you just how much of a dickless motherfucker you really are and cut your shit off then feed it to you."

The fire in me had me momentarily glancing around the room at the rest of my family with a "try me if you want to" stare. This was my moment. If anyone outside of my father tried to challenge me, then they were going to get the same treatment.

As I focused back on the piece of shit under my feet, my lip curled up in a sinister snarl. "You don't rouse your elder's strife, nephew, and think nothing will happen to you when you do. This act of yours will never be forgotten or forgiven." That blade of his glinted in my hand as if in sync with my rage. "I'll personally skin you alive, do you understand me? *Entiendes?*"

Dame tapped my foot and I eased up. Of course, he swiped at me, leaving a thin line of blood on my jaw. Where he came up with that blade, I really didn't know. I was about to feed him my fist when I heard my father's cough. Both of us stopped our scuffle with me pinning him again, face against the floor, hand against the side of his face.

My ribs were sore from where he punched me hard and kicked me. He could hold his own. He probably could have killed me but he didn't. When Dame locked eyes with me again, I knew what he was going to do before he did it, which was why I gave a sharp laugh and playfully, yet forcefully, slapped the side of his head. My fingers dug in to shake his skull as I stepped back, challenging him with a hard stare to try it again.

Caltrone's slow stroll between us had me stepping back farther. He glanced between the two of us, his hands tucked behind the small of his jacket-covered back. Like the man he was, he spoke to us with superiority, shutting down our brawl without flexing one finger.

"Let this go. Enough time has been wasted on elementary emotions; and punishment will be handed out for the blatant disrespect toward our family code. But, until then, step back. *Entiendes?*"

Of course, when my old man laid down the law, we all listened. I moved toward Kenya and positioned myself in a manner that blocked her from any attack from Dame. A deep, rattling cough came from Dame. He casually took his time in brushing off his Armani tailored suit, as if what went down was just another ordinary day. However, being that the fuck boy had OCD, I knew his nerves were on edge from the imaginary dirt he felt was on him, along with his blood and Kenya's now-drying spit.

An arrogant but lethal grin spread across his face while he looked my way. "Another time, Uncle. Bet you won't get another chance like that with me again or your bi-atch, though she tasted good." Nigga slowly licked his lips then winked. He then pointed at me as if he held a gun. His thumb dropped like he was letting off several rounds.

His grandiose gesture didn't do a damn thing for me. There was no fear in me because that was what was innate in my blood. When Kenya bristled by my side, I calmly looked at her from the corner of my eye. My face went stoic. With it my posture became tense like a steel wire while I controlled my breathing to a calming pace. She knew what that meant. No words were needed. *It's chill and I got you.* Nothing more. Nothing less.

Once everyone in the room calmed down and the chaos cleared up, we all sat back in our places. Between those of us in our chairs was a massive carved marble table. The family crest with its signet carved in its center as a reminder about who we were. Framing us from behind was all white mixed with ultra-light colors. Modern mixed flawlessly with classic style. Slick ceiling-high curtains draped an opulent wall of glass that highlighted the vast emerald green Spanish-style gardens outside.

If one went around the room, they'd see period-piece art from various ages and a few gallery-quality paintings created by family members. Swarovski crystal sculptures and vases sat on either pedestals or wall tables, glinting from the sunlight and cascading on the warm wooden floor. Behind where I sat was a massive foyer where one would see a black iron double staircase. This place, though a safe house, was opulent and screamed Caltrone.

Near my side was Kenya, who sat fisting her hands on her lap. On the other side of me, surprisingly, was my father at the head in his own chair. Opposite of him was Damien, who sat rubbing his neck still smiling and staring between Kenya and myself. The art of getting under one's skin was Damien's talent and I actually respected and hated him for it. It was an asset I rarely used.

"Now that we are at ease, tell us what you know of this boy who took my granddaughter,

Damien. Your reckless actions have allowed him to become a bigger threat to our *familia*. What say you?"

Damien behaved how Damien does: like a lowlife, entitled asshole. I sat back as staff—who were family members because the old man didn't trust outsiders unless they grew up by his side, and even then he didn't trust but his own self—set preparations of warm and comfy-smelling foods out in front of us. Each dish reflected our Cuban heritage, along with a couple dishes reflecting our Black American sides. Basically, it was a soul food pairing that flowed with the main Cuban dishes. Wine, ice water, and other libations were poured and mixed in front of all our faces.

Without blatantly looking around, I took in all the various faces of family, some as old as my father and many younger. No one reached for their food, except for Damien. His disregard for our dysfunctional traditions had him reaching for his wine. He took a deep drink, and smiled at us all.

It was then that I looked at the old man. His older, handsome features, which matched my own, became a blank slate. The very few and light creases upon his face deepened and his mouth became a hard edge. An uncomfortable tenseness filled the room. Family shifted in their seats. The few small infants who were allowed at the table with us started to fuss until their mothers plopped a titty in their mouths. Everyone at the table knew the rules: only the king of the clan took the first drink, sip, bite, or taste of food.

"Mmm, that's quality, Grandpops," Damien said with his lips to the edge of his glass again. There was a slight jarring edge to his voice and he continued. "I'm curious about this boy you mention, Grandpops, because there was no boy who was presented to me. There was a hippie-looking mayo nigga with stringy brown hair. Kinda looked like Robin Thicke. He was with his lanky, nerdy-looking black friend with glasses, but that is all."

Calmly, as if what Damien had done hadn't irritated him, Caltrone gathered his glass, and resigned himself to taste his red wine. He swirled his wine around, inhaled its scent, then took in its rich, dark coloring. In my mind, I saw the old man snatching Damien by his throat but, yeah, that shit didn't go down. "And you, again, allowed them to go? Interesting."

He began taking meticulous bites of his non-touching food. That then signaled us all to eat and relax. Though, both Kenya and I watched in tense quietness.

"The only interest I had was in the packages of snow they transferred to me as a deposit for bringing me fresh pussy." Damien glanced our way with a wink then continued speaking while spearing his food with his fork. "Once they left, after I decided not to go with their female, I had my boys trail them. Shit still felt suspicious to me, which is also why I didn't just kill them and keep her for myself as a prize."

I almost leaped across that table. My composure was about to snap as this nigga explained it all away as the nature of business. I was trained not to care about the regard of anyone, including family, but loyalty to family was something that never should have been disregarded. This nigga sat here practicing the first half, while fucking his loyalty to family. I wanted to slice his throat to the bone and stuff my hand in his voice box.

"Had you touched her or allowed her to be abused in any way, you do understand that you and I would have a bigger problem than we already do, due to your insolence? *Sí?*" The old man's stoic voice was even and cold as he issued that reserved threat.

Damien sat in silence and we all knew that he definitely understood.

Taking a sip of his wine, Caltrone continued. "Now what did you learn?"

"That Pinky and the Brain were really being led by a third nigga. I guestimate that he must be the boy you're speaking about. Keith, correct?"

When Caltrone gave a nod, Damien seemed to relax his resolve. "My men watched them leave, and heard mention of Savannah as the destination. That's all I have." Dame gave a dramatic pause.

It was clear that he was toying with us. Part of me, frankly, didn't believe that Keith had another set of connects he'd trust to present Jewel to Dame. But, considering how the trail went cold once we got here, I wouldn't put it past the crafty bastard.

There was a sharp pain against my palm. When I glanced down, I realized that I had pressed my fork against the surface so hard that it had broken skin. The games being played had my anger boiling over. I was about to pop off at the mouth but Dame's wicked smile cut me off at the pass.

"Oh, that and where they dropped off Pinky and the Brain."

Plump, fresh steak with garlic herb butter sat on my plate, cooling. I stared at the juices and the *arroz blanco* with various vegetables on its side becoming chilled due to me not touching it. "Give us the location," was all I gruffly stated. More like demanded.

The light touch of Kenya's hand against my thigh was her way of letting me know that she was by my side. It gave me a moment of peace that was broken by the reality that our baby girl was lost to us still. Bodies had dropped in our search for her, and it could have ended if only this had been a different life.

"*Sí,* that and the real names I know you have, grandson. You're a thorough man, so I know you did more than just trail."

Damien noisily cut into his steak. His utensils clanked against the plate. Head bowed then tilted to the side, he gave a calculating smirk and popped a sliced portion of the tender meat in his mouth. That conniving expression was back on his face, and he calmly reached for a napkin to wipe at the corners of his mouth. He was fucking with me.

"I can do more than just give you names, Grandpops. I can personally take you to where I'm holding them and their family." Dame glanced our way again.

Through all his masochistic bullshit, Dame was still an Orlando. Once my hands got on the two motherfuckers who dared to sell my daughter and I politely introduced myself to them, then I might, just might, not attempt to end my nephew's life. I had a specific nigga named Keith to fry.

Chapter 16

Kenya

I found it odd that Caltrone allowed Damien to be so blatantly disrespectful to family rules and traditions. While other members of the family didn't even look at the food before Caltrone did, Damien had seemed to forget his manners. I figured there had to be a method to the madness. Although my nerves were still going haywire, the fact that Tone had gone hard for me, like he had done so many times before we had broken up, reminded me that we still had some unfinished business between us.

I'd cheated on Isaac. I gave in to something that had been simmering inside of me for a long time. And it felt so damn good. I felt shame in admitting that. Yeah, Isaac's sex hadn't been bad. Yet, no man could do to me what Tone had always been able to do. Nobody could make me moan the way Tone did. No one could tap into another part of my soul and make me lose my mind the way Tone did. I'd actually missed him in the most intimate of ways; and, even though we had been just kids when we started having sex, Tone knew things that I didn't and he gladly taught me everything he knew.

I looked over at Tone to see he was still in fight mode. His jaw twitched and his eyes were narrowed. It felt as if at any minute he would make good on his threat and try to kill Dame, for real this time. I held his hand a little tighter, trying to see if he was still with me or if he had snapped, so to speak. When he squeezed back, I relaxed a little.

"Let us finish fellowshipping," Caltrone said. His voice was controlled, like he was trying to remain calm even though he wasn't. "Once done here, Damien will take us to where he is holding the heathens who dared to take an Orlando. Finding my grandchild is of the utmost importance to me. However, this thing with Jewel has opened another can of worms for this family. Maria-Rosa, Frederick, and Marco are all back in California. We have a Knight issue."

Forks stopped midair to mouths. Someone choked on their wine. A few of the women gasped. "A Knight issue?" an older gentleman repeated like he hadn't heard correctly the first time.

A beautiful Amazonian, dark-skinned woman leaned forward. She had hazel eyes and her natural hair was braided into four elegant goddess braids. "Why do we have a Knight problem, *papi?*" she asked.

Caltrone looked around the rectangular table, and made eye contact with every person there, including me. He then took a deep breath and said, "We may have killed a girl who was directly related to them."

The shock around the table was palpable. "Was such a thing needed?" the dark-skinned woman asked.

"Believe it or not, *sí.* Yes, it was. She knew information about Jewel and wouldn't talk. We had to do what we had to do."

"And there were no other options?" the older man asked.

Caltrone turned and pierced the man with a scathing look. "Have I ever gone in half-cocked, Xavier?"

"My apologies," Xavier said then picked up his wineglass to drink.

"Uncle Rueben knows about this?" the dark-skinned woman asked.

Caltrone nodded. "*Sí.*"

"I'll fly out tonight to give Uncle the backup he needs."

"Savoy is there."

The dark-skinned woman nodded once. "I'll keep him leveled."

Caltrone nodded then looked back at Tone. "Son, we must get moving. Time is of the essence. But, before we leave . . ." Caltrone started. He stopped talking then took a long swig from his wineglass. He set it down and, with a quick sleight of hand, he punched Dame so hard, blood went spilling from his nose like a faucet.

Dame almost fell out of the chair, but he caught himself. He jumped up, expletives leaving his mouth in rapid Spanish. He was angry. Like a caged wild animal who had been poked and prodded too many times.

"If you want to behave like you have no manners, like you do not know the rules in my domain, in my presence, then you shall always be dealt with as a peasant," Caltrone stated calmly.

Even I knew there would be punishment for the disrespect Damien had shown his grandfather. The room was deathly quiet. No one said a word. Tone chuckled. Dame scowled at his grandfather, who sat unbothered; then he shot daggers at Tone before turning back to Caltrone.

Caltrone sat like he hadn't just assaulted a man, although he kept eye contact with Dame.

They stared one another down like they were two opponents as opposed to family. Dame's chest heaved up and down, his lips pulled in, and he had fire in his eyes. He yanked the chair he had been sitting in backward. He yanked it so hard that the chair went flying back into a wall, knocking a few paintings down.

"My dearest grandson, if ever you feel the need to test your manhood, let it not be with a man who takes pride in breaking men down to their bare minimums. Your father learned it from me and he was nothing compared to what I am capable of. So, I must ask of you, do you feel . . . froggy?"

Dame took one step toward Caltrone and every woman in the room stood. Dame took notice as well and, wisely, stopped. He looked at each of the women and snarled. Every last one of those women had a look in their eyes that said they had no intention of letting Dame leave alive if he got an inch closer to Caltrone. I was wishing, hoping, and praying he was stupid enough to go up against Caltrone. In my mind, I saw the women come down on him like a swarm of killer bees.

I'd come to notice that in the presence of Caltrone Orlando, women could be fragile and yet fighters. The dark-skinned woman who had spoken so freely to Caltrone stood like she was ready to launch an attack. She had inched her chair back. Her feet were planted shoulder-width apart. A gold fork was held tightly in her palm. For Damien Orlando to be a pimp, he would have no control over the women in the room now. They were ready. Even the ones with infants had smoothly passed babies off to the men sitting beside them. They, too, stood ready to take down the grandson foolish enough to disrespect the man of the house.

If I hadn't known any better, I'd have thought it was odd that the woman who had just moments before tried to fuss at Tone for going after Damien was now standing, ready to take Damien out herself if need be. That was the way of the Orlandos. You didn't come for the head of the table.

Caltrone stood and washed the hand he had punched Dame with in a bowl of soapy water that one of the women from the kitchen had brought to him. He dried it with one of the white cloth napkins then closed the gap between him and Dame. He slapped a hand on the back of Dame's neck and whispered something in his ear. Whatever he said didn't sit well with Dame, who jerked away once Caltrone was finished talking to him.

"Go clean yourself up," Caltrone ordered. "Meet us in the garage in ten minutes. Not a minute later. Antonio and Kenya, follow me."

Ten minutes later, we were behind the black SUV Dame was in as we followed him to wherever he had stashed the men who had tried to sell my daughter to him. I looked at Tone, wondering where his mind was.

"We're close to finding her. I can feel it," I said, trying to get him to talk to me.

Only then would I have any inkling of what he was thinking. Tone grunted but kept quiet as we hopped on I-75 South headed toward Locust Grove. When I saw he wasn't going to talk, I sat back and sighed. My cell rang. Isaac was calling me again. I ignored it. We'd fought the last time we'd spoken and I wasn't in the mood for his ego trip. Not to mention so much had happened since our last conversation. I wasn't ready to be confronted with my infidelity.

I looked up and saw a billboard advertising the Tanger Outlet as well as other restaurants and rest stops. Traffic moved at a steady pace. Caltrone was in the SUV with Dame while Benita drove Tone and me. She and her sidekick, whose name I still didn't know, were in a heated discussion.

"Just let him be until this is over, Tiffany," Benita said.

Tiffany, who was all of five feet five, petite with perfectly rounded hips, and dark-skinned, snapped her head around to look at Benita. "Why? I kept my end of the deal. He should keep his," she said.

"Because he has a lot on his plate. He's trying to find his granddaughter. Leave him be before you piss him off."

Tiffany scoffed and shook her head. Her bone-straight jet-black hair swayed back and forth as she did so. "I'm going to say something to him," she said to Benita.

Benita made a sound that said she was annoyed. "Don't fucking come crying to me when he hurts your fucking feelings, either. Just don't."

Tiffany snapped, "Fine, I won't."

Benita got ready to say something else until she looked in the rearview mirror to see Tone and me paying attention to their conversation. Silence engulfed the truck again.

"Go to Frederick," Benita whispered; at least, she tried to. I could still hear her.

Tiffany shook her head. "No."

"Marco?"

"Hell no. Fucking deviant."

"Can't you just wait this out?"

"No," Tiffany all but screamed. "I have waited. I've waited damn near two weeks. No."

"He's going to hurt your feelings, dumb ass."

Tiffany was silent for a moment as she stared straight ahead. Then, in a soft voice, barely above a whisper, she said, "I'll risk it."

Benita shook her head and mumbled something under her breath. Clearly, she was annoyed with her sidekick. A few seconds later, she reached out to hold Tiffany's hand. I had no idea what all that had been about, and I didn't have time to care. My daughter was missing.

We got off at exit 212. Drove for another ten miles or so and ended up at our destination. Locust Grove was country as shit. So much so that it almost seemed as if we'd gone back in time. All the houses were ranch style or bungalow. There were gardens and small farms. I almost thought I was going to see the Amish riding on the road in the carriages.

We took a loose dirt road until we got to a small farm. There was an aging red barn in the back of the bungalow-style house that had four armed men guarding it. The land looked as if it hadn't been used in some time. Most of the grass was a brownish yellow. The faint smell of horse crap clung to the air. Two old cars had cinder blocks for tires. Pecan and peach trees sat about. They looked bare.

Benita slowed the truck down. Tone was so anxious to get to the men that he didn't wait for her to fully stop the truck. He jumped out, and didn't wait for me either. Each stride he took was more powerful than the last. Once Benita parked, I hopped out of the truck and rushed to catch up with Antonio. I was just as anxious as he was until I saw the faces of two of the young men guarding the barn.

I'd seen the big one and the other young man before. His locs were a little longer but I'd never forget that face. As usual, he had on a hoodie. His face held a dispassionate look, but there was an aura around him that said he wasn't to be taken lightly. He was a little on the skinny side, but definitely stockier than the last time I'd seen him. He watched me from underneath his hood. Hands in his pocket, he turned to look at his boss.

I could hear men screaming in the barn. It sounded as if their souls were being ripped from their bodies.

"Who's inside, Trigga?" Dame asked the boy in the hoodie.

"Enzo," Trigga said.

Dame smiled. It was so wicked that it chilled me. He looked at his grandfather, who I noticed had donned latex gloves and a surgeon's mask. "A boy after your own heart," he said to Caltrone.

I had no idea what he meant by that, but once the big, beefy guard slid the barn door open, I got my answer. One of the men was hanging in the air. There was something that looked like a double-ended pitchfork. One end was pushed under the man's chin and the other to the sternum. There was a strap used to secure the man's neck to the tool as he hung from the ceiling.

"When's the last time that man has slept?" Tone asked as he moved closer.

"Answer him, Enzo," Dame ordered.

The boy slipped the Nightwings cap back and looked over at us. I almost gasped. It was another gotdamned Orlando. How young did they start training these motherfuckers to be so damned evil? Yes, Enzo was an Orlando, but it was as if there was a calm nature about the boy. He reminded me of Tone, which probably meant his mother had kept him away for as long as she could before the Orlandos came claiming what was theirs.

Judging by the way Caltrone tilted his head and looked at the boy, I knew I was right. However, Enzo didn't even look at Caltrone. He focused on Tone.

"The purpose of the device is so he can't sleep. If he does, the prongs will pierce his throat and chest. Nigga didn't want to talk. Since he won't talk, he won't sleep, not unless he wants to die," Enzo answered.

Damien smiled like he was a teacher proud of his student.

"A heretics fork," Tone said.

Enzo nodded. Tone studied the kid.

I could tell Tone was thinking along the same lines I was. One Orlando knew another one. Any other time, Tone would have probably been lucid enough to question why Damien had two kids doing this kind of dirty work, but not today. Today we came to learn the whereabouts of our daughter. That was all that mattered.

"The other one was more pliable," Enzo said.

I walked over to the other table. There was a silver instrument on the table that looked like an expensive rattler. It looked as if molten lead and tar had been sprinkled on the man's face, eyes, and stomach. The man was breathing raggedly as he shivered and shook on the glass table. He was bound by his ankles and wrists. A gaping hole had been burned through the man's guts. I could have sworn I was able to see vital organs in the man's abdomen on display. And the smell was so putrid, bile rose to my throat.

"You used a lead sprinkler on this man?" Tone asked Enzo.

He answered without blinking, "I did." There was no pride in Enzo's voice. More like he was content in the role he had been given.

"What did he tell you?" Tone asked.

"Said once Dame didn't want to buy the girl, they dropped her back off to the head nigga. Last he heard, they were headed to Augusta."

"You believe him, kid?"

"I believe he told me all he knows. But the nigga hanging up there knows more."

Just as Enzo said that, there was a loud clap that rang through the air. The man's yelps and screams made me whip my head around. Dame had put some gloves and a surgical mask on. In his hand was a two-by-four that had nails protruding from it. He'd hit the man so hard that the plank was now stuck in the middle of his back. The man's body jerked violently as blood trickled down his ass crack.

Caltrone handed Dame another two-by-four. Dame walked around to the front of the man. "Care to talk?" he taunted him.

The man said nothing. I didn't think he could talk, he was in so much pain.

Dame took a stance like he was about to hit a homerun. This time, he hit the man right in the abdomen. Again, the two-by-four stuck into the man's flesh. Tone picked up the lead sprinkler and made a move toward the man, but Caltrone held out a hand to stop him.

"Allow Damien to do the dirty work for his insolence earlier," he said.

Tone laid the torture device back on the table and watched on. I was quiet. In my own head I was trying to figure out how much of the information we had been told so far was useful. Had he taken our daughter to Savannah or Augusta? Had she been violated again, by different men? There was no doubt in my mind that all her innocence was gone. Being raped changed a girl. I never thought we'd be here. I worked hard and Tone worked hard to ensure that Jewel would never have to go through what I did. And, yet, here we were.

Chapter 17

Father Rueben

Back in Fresno, California . . .

As I knelt at my altar, I felt my soul was bogged down. Being born into a family that was inherently evil wasn't something I was proud of. I abhorred it. Yet, when my brother, Carlos, came calling, I always answered. It was the way of the Orlandos. To not do so would be blasphemous in the family's eyes and, sadly, my own.

It was in our blood to answer when called upon by family. It was like some kind of innate sixth sense within the Orlandos. Sometimes I detested my younger brother. No, sometimes I hated him. I'd had many confessionals about him. However, I couldn't hate what he was because he was I and I was he. We were cut from the same cloth. Endured the same kind of abuse at the hands of our father.

My hate for him deepened when he befriended Moses Ekejindu. Carlos had been able to escape the madness that was our home. He found a family who wasn't repulsed by the sight of him. Found a friend who genuinely loved him for who he was. I was the elder son. My fate had already been sealed. No one looked at me without seeing our father. The people in our small town hated me, but they feared our father. They feared the light brown–skinned man who stood six feet six with a temper that would put the fear of God into God Himself.

I didn't understand how Carlos could find the love of family and friend and yet turn out like the man who was our father. I'd always thought that if we could all just find someone, some adult to love us, we'd be different. I was wrong. Caltrone had found that love and, in the end, he ended up just like the man.

A loud tapping against my door brought me out of my thoughts.

"Father Rueben, you have guests, sir," Father Delaney said.

"Who is it, Father?" I asked.

"It is Emmanuel Knight, sir."

I stood and straightened my priest robes. My spine stiffened and my face became unreadable. It was time to be about my father's business.

Chapter 18

Antonio

There was nothing but the sound of my boots meeting dirt blending in with the shrill sound of a sharp scream. The clandestine clink of chains rattling, along with Dame's occasional manic rumble of a chuckle, were in the background. Like a smooth soundtrack, both created a rhythm that provided a sinister song marking me as what I was: an Orlando. This was hell. But I'd never let on.

None of the men here would ever see the revulsion etched inside my blackening soul. Not in the reflection of the emotions in my eyes. Not in my body language. No. I remembered and reflected what I was taught: to be a blank slate of controlled emotions. It was strange enough with the young kids surrounding us, soaking up everything like a sponge, especially the one named

Enzo. I could feel a connection with them, that they were like me. We all were just surviving.

However, emotion was formulated in vengeance and rooted in evil.

I was ready to go after my daughter, but nothing was making sense. Dame had said the men heard them mention that Keith was heading to Savannah, yet this motherfucker who was strung up mentioned Augusta. The fact that we were even in the same state as my daughter and her kidnapper riled my soul. I wanted to blaze a burning trail through all of Georgia just to get my child back, but I understood that action would be a brazen, reckless one. I was better than that, smarter than that, and now with so much blood on my hands, more calculating than that.

No. It was time to make Keith show his own hand. The fact that he let these two live showed that he was borderline sloppy due to running out of connections. That was our genius in snipping away at his network. There'd be no goons in Mexico or Texas who could help him. The only thing that was keeping him as hidden as he was, I felt, was his link to the Knights, however deep that was. Which brought me around to my father.

He stood back, akimbo, but with his arms crossed over his chest. There was a deep pride in what was going on here. A small part of me was disgusted; however, growing up around his mythos dictated that this was who he was. Even watching him in his element, I knew it was just ingrained in my father's bones: pride over the eradication of weakness and underlings all in the name of Orlando. With that in mind, I rested a hand against my father's shoulder and spoke low against his ear.

I was ready to get this done and, strangely, the hippie Robin Thicke was holding up against Dame's torture antics. Must have been all the coke running through the idiot's system. When my father gave a nod at my request, he pulled out his cell phone and began making contact. Stepping away, I moved to Kenya, who stood as far away from the scene as possible. The shadows of the barn cloaked her in a veil of blackness. She reminded me of Morticia Addams because the light seemed to shine only around her eyes.

This whole world was changing her. I wasn't a fool in seeing that. We both had been ripped down to the primordial core of ourselves, letting whatever evil that lived there manifest itself. There was no pride in that at all, which had me reflect on the tone of the budding torturer, Enzo.

He had removed himself from the scene, standing close to the two young henchmen Dame had brought with him. All three flanked the door of the barn and watched on with stoic expressions.

The kid with the locs and hoodie had his head bowed in a manner where you'd think he wasn't watching, but staring at his feet. However, something in me knew that wasn't the case. His shadow, the big, quarterback-looking brother, stood as if he were a bouncer ready to take on whatever came his way. While Enzo . . .

Everything about him screamed Orlando. I mean, he had a different look to him where, if I didn't know what I was looking for, I wouldn't have guessed he was one. Kind of like myself. The tattoos on the side of his neck and hands kind of obscured the signature Orlando looks in him, along with the eyebrow piercing and the medium-large earlobe plugs he sported. He'd slightly fade to the back if no one was paying attention. However, his work on our two friends hanging in the barn stated otherwise.

A part of me wanted to tell each of those kids to run away, to find another hustle out of Atlanta and never again allow themselves to be found by my family but, of course, I didn't. We all made choices that linked up in this game. It wasn't my place to fuck with it, because there was no saving to be had here. I grew up with that mantra and when my father found my mother and me years later, that reality became etched in stone.

I prayed the kid wasn't what I thought he was, because my father's fascination was already showing. Quietly studying the three, when Enzo shifted his cap down over his eyes and crossed his arms to mirror the bigger guy's stance, I turned my attention away from them and back to Kenya.

"You should go back to the car. It's only going to become messier."

Kenya's gaze focused up at me. She had that dark look of madness in them with a touch of exhaustion. There was going to be no turning her away from journeying down this path with me. She already got blood on her hands. I guessed she now wanted to bathe in it.

"Please." She softly scoffed. "You have a collection of body parts traveling with us, Tone. I was there when you appraised them. This is nothing."

Clearly, she was lying and putting up a façade for my sake. I honestly commended her for that but, at the same time, I worried about her because of that. In a sick way, this whole situation had brought us closer together. I wasn't sure whether that was a good thing, or where it was going to lead us. I just understood that, all for the sake of our daughter, she had done something I once thought was unattainable. I just hoped that it didn't ruin her.

"Is there anything you need me to ask them on your behalf?"

Our voices were low in a manner where it almost didn't seem as if we were actually interacting. If you glanced our way, you'd think we were enthralled with how Dame had the hippie sniffling and begging. I waited for Kenya to speak up. Her unrelenting silence made me wonder just exactly what she was thinking. Was she mentally dismantling the two who attempted to sell our daughter to Dame on behalf of Keith? Or was she thinking of something else entirely?

Such as her fiancé. From how her cell phone kept vibrating on the ride over, I assumed that it was him. Her electing not to answer didn't surprise me in the least. We were at war and him checking on her just wasn't equating to the overall picture. I mean, I didn't blame the brotha for reaching out but, if he trusted her, he needed to keep as safely away as possible. Something in me had me smirking in thought.

If he trusts her? My shaft low-key hardened at the reality of that trust, the consequences of that trust, which had her here with me. I had her in the most biblical of ways because of his trust of her. But though the dog in me wanted to gloat about the fact that I still had that power over her and she over me, it was quickly tucked away at the sounds of screaming.

"I don't know anything. We . . ." Mr. Hippie's teeth were chattering. Part of his eyelid was sliced to the juicy, fleshy matter resulting in a swollen, bulging eye with drying rust-colored liquid dripping down his face. "We owed him. Had no choice to deliver . . . h . . . her."

No one was ever innocent in this shit. So, I didn't believe him. When he started to jerk and twitch like he was on drugs, I reached up to clasp my chin. That's when I heard Kenya's soft voice.

"Huh? Repeat yourself, baby," I said while glancing down at her.

"Did they touch her? Did they rape her? Ask them that."

Jaw clenching, I gave a nod. "I will."

More chains rattled. Dame laughed an evil laugh. One that made my flesh crawl. "Yeah, right, homeboy," he said in amusement. Running his gloved hands over a table of utensils, he clicked his tongue then picked up a thin metal barb.

With no thought to anything but my daughter, I took several strides forward and bent forward with my hands resting behind my back and I whispered to my nephew. His soulless eyes narrowed. A thumb swiped his nose, then he leaned back, head tilted as if he had been offended by what I shared, which were the full details behind what Keith had done to our daughter.

I knew that he didn't like what he'd heard by the way he abruptly stopped smiling. It was one thing for him to test the waters and cause us pain by entertaining the thought of selling our daughter, and making her his. It was a mark of showing his power by allowing Keith to take her again, but hearing about how Keith treated her was another thing.

I shook my head, then took some steps back for my nephew to handle business. Dame was a fucking nut and it worked to our favor because he was able to work out a second location where these two met up with Keith. Sloppy, sloppy. Or a setup.

"I hear your boy, your boss, has a reputation for touching what isn't his and allowing his 'boys'"—the last word was accentuated with a midair quotation—"to sample the same goods as him. You owed him, a'ight. I get that, but touch her? Touch my blood? No. That I don't understand."

Mr. Hippie began fighting again. His head lolled to the side in a deep drop. My hand reached up in a vise grip. The fires of hell bore into his droopy gaze.

That's when he tiredly drawled, "Oh, shit. Dude. Just kill me. Please."

I looked Kenya's way. We knew that was an answer to her question.

Dame chuckled. His fiddling fingers held up a thin steel barb spike. "Now, why would I do that when I enjoy our conversation? Besides, I think that you'll love this penetration."

A sharp, ear-splitting scream erupted through the barn. Dame took that barb and meticulously ran it through Mr. Hippie's urethral opening, pushing it all the way back then curving it down near his sacs. I watched as Dame twisted that barb and blood leaked everywhere. All this fool had to do was open his mouth and talk but, of course, he and his friend had to stay tight-lipped. Their fault. This shit wasn't going to end anytime soon, especially once I got my hands on Keith.

The sound of a door opening behind where Dame's crew stood caught my attention. I glanced to see the door being held open. Standing outside of it, from how he was positioned, no one would really notice the tall cop in all black. He

wore a helmet that obscured his face. I knew
near the covered side of his neck were the Cuban
and U.S. flags merging as one. If he took that
helmet off, locs would fall out. The one member
of this fucking family I embraced as my own
blood, Fuego, stood outside. He nodded my way,
and I returned the same.

"What's going on?" I heard Kenya ask by my
side.

Fuego's appearance meant that he had escorted
someone here. That someone casually walked
through the door with a large plastic case. Running
my eyes over the newcomer, my jaw clenched.
I had seen her briefly at the family safe house,
standing off at a distance by my father's request.
She had dark hair with strawberry blond highlights
and blunt bangs across her forehead. Her hair was
pulled back in a knot at her nape. Sharp kohl-lined
dead eyes stared at me. By how she carried herself,
with power in her midnight blue suit and heeled
boots that carried her with a lethal purpose, I knew
that I was staring at my father's favorite: Lilith.

Walking toward my father, behind her, were
two of Dame's watchers, some fools I heard him
call Pookie and Slammer. They rolled two tires
toward us. There were no rims, just the outer
rubber rings. My lips curled upward at the cor-

ners. I then turned toward my father. When he gave me a nod of approval, I mentally readied myself for what I had to do.

"Tone? Did you hear me? What's going on?"

A wonderful warmth spread in my stomach. It had my abs constricting and my spine becoming straighter. I glanced down at Kenya and I softly said, "My turn to get some answers."

Lilith pointed toward Pookie and Slammer to put the tires near Dame. She then ordered them to exit, which they slowly did. Both fools casually looked around. They slid their hands in their pockets as if they had no cares then glanced at the other three members of their crew. An odd exchange occurred between them but it was quickly squashed. Whatever that was about, I didn't care. When Pookie and Slammer made their exit past Fuego, he ordered them to go back to their posts.

At that moment, my gaze went to Fuego. He gave another salute then closed the door from outside.

"I have what you asked for," Lilith stated while presenting the big black case. Her black leather gloves opened the case and she held it out for all to see. "Our people also inspected their homes and the location where these two met our enemy. It panned out as they said. We might have to lie over near Augusta."

"More networks?"

"*Sí*. We believe he has a few more, but barely."

"Hmm." My father rubbed his chin in thought. Something seemed to spark in his eyes then he turned my way. "Son, is this what you need?" Caltrone asked.

I felt Lilith's eyes on me. Her gaze was harsh as if she were absorbing every bit of me to her memory when I walked up on them. A huge part of me didn't like that; however, I was used to it. It was how my father trained his women. She was, in her own way, challenging me and when my gaze locked squarely on her she backed down as my jaw clenched. I knew that what she saw in me was my father's ghost. I wasn't okay with that, but if I had to play the game and show that I was his, then I'd do that.

Once that was handled, I gave a curt nod then held my hands out for the case. "Yes, this will do."

"Good. Now end this. We don't have the luxury of time on our side. His trail will get muddled again if we dally any longer; and I received word that we have a Knight sighting in ATL. No big-wigs, but the fact that they sent in foot soldiers, pawns so to speak, tells me something is afoot."

Shit, flashed in my mind. But, I nodded in agreement. I walked away as he spoke to Dame.

"Grandson, press home with your games and let him spill his innards. But, before that, turn him so that he can watch his friend."

Dame turned in his chair, pulled on the guy's chains, and positioned him so that they both could watch him. Tapping the hippie's face, he smirked, "Now watch. I heard my uncle is crazy when pushed but this is a treat to watch him work. Haven't seen this ever."

"No," the hippie moaned, barely alive anymore. Sadly, it fell on deaf ears.

Taking my seat, I stared up at the geeky one. The brother was so bludgeoned that his dark flesh was blue against his black skin. Setting my items out, I rolled my shoulders, then added on an extra set of black latex gloves. A cart was brought to me by Lilith. On it was a charged car battery. In the black case was a set of jumper cables. When I reached down, my fingers took hold of two copper wires. I straightened then looked up. "What's your name, kid?"

Mr. Nerd ignored me. I knew by his breathing that he hadn't passed out.

"Please, don't have me repeat myself."

When his eyes rolled under his heavy lids, I knew that he was mentally battling with his own will to stay alive and trying to stay coherent. "No One," was all he said.

I chuckled low. I accepted the fact that he wasn't going to say a damn thing, so I reached for a plastic bottle, squeezed it, and smelled the sharp scent of lighter fluid as it saturated him. When No One hissed, I stood and walked up on him. "I'm a doctor. I'm just trying to help you."

We all knew that I wasn't there to help, but I said it just to add to the mind games. No one believed the latter part. So, when No One spit on me, I sent my fist into his gaunt rib cage.

"Fuck you," I said maniacally. My pearly whites flashed in glee. I stared into his face. "Remember this face even in your death, motherfucker. Yeah, we all say that, but it never happens, right?" I taunted then pressed my hands together in prayer, giving a Hail Mary.

When I dropped my head to look at him, my dark eyes bore into him. I snatched hard at his belt buckle, rattling his jeans. The moment I did that, the kid started hollering.

"Wait, wait. No, please," he stammered.

How cute. Now he was scared after the medieval shit we had done to him. *Really?* I chuckled then dropped my hand only to snatch his hand. I was falling into darkness and there was no turning back. With an unnerving swiftness, I pushed the copper barb under the bed of his fingernail. The more this went on, the easier I dropped into my zone.

Damn, don't let me get in my zone.

"All you have to do is talk," I cajoled.

"But we said that we don—"

Another copper barb. His screaming became my melody. We continued the back-and-forth until I had wires sticking out from all his fingernails. I thought about his feet, and decided to go there as well. Once done, nigga was Edward Scissorhands.

Turning, I sighed. It was time to kick things up a notch. I picked up the cables. "I just want my daughter back." With a clink, I let this fool see that they were charged. "I just want to put Keith's skin on a mantle. So, what am I going to do about that?"

Mr. Nerd's body began to quiver. He shook his head. I looked behind me toward Robin Thicke then smiled.

The hippie let out a shout that would break the average man's soul. But for me, Dame, and probably Father, all it did was make our dicks hard.

"Dennis. No."

Pop, sizzle, snapppppp. The sound of Mr. Nerd turning into an electric fence was all I was greeted with. Oh, yeah, and the fun seizing of his body. Lilith stood by the battery cart with a menacing grin.

"Brotha got the moves, huh?" My attention had returned to Mr. Hippie. When I strolled toward him he jerked and tried to get at me, I guessed. Stupid move. Because all it did was pull at his flesh more.

"One more hit," I said to Lilith and she obliged.

Pop, pop, snap, pop, sizzle.

Spit foamed at Mr. Nerd's mouth. The thick substance drifted down the corner of his mouth and fell to the dirt. Bloodshot eyes rolled so deep in his skull that I thought the pupils might be lost. I waited for his body to stop its rock-steady seize. My fingers snapped with a frown.

"Dennis, wake up. Your boy wants you to suffer more."

Mr. Hippie's wails started again. It had me motioning to Dame's goons. I knew if I hit Dennis again, he'd die on the spot, and I needed him a little more lucid. So, I slowed my roll a pace.

Dame's henchmen came my way with the tires. When I locked eyes on the one with locs, I could see how he studied my battery and the method I used to electrocute Mr. Nerd. I smirked and walked over to the tires. Resting a hand against them I sighed.

"Look, that was a low charge. Something just to let your boy—Dennis, is it?—know that I'm tired. Are you tired?"

Mr. Hippie gave a nod.

"I mean, then what are you going to do about that? I have an idea, but you can stop me, if only you talk." Mr. Nerd's coughs sounded. I looked his way. "Yeah? What do you have to say, Dennis?"

"He drove off in a Chevy. License plate . . ."

I glanced to where my pops nodded, letting me know that he had the information.

"He has a house . . ."

"Yeah. Yeah, used to brag about it to us." Mr. Hippie added. "Was his grandparents', I think?"

Rubbing my jaw, I shook my head in fake disbelief. "Well, shit. You two knew him deeper than I thought, huh?"

When both fellas became quiet, realizing that they just erred by getting too talkative, I chuckled then ran my gloved hands over my face. "Shit, I'm just so tired."

"I can give you his number," Dennis pleaded.

As I walked to him, he didn't see when I motioned behind me. The big one came to my side holding the tire. "Collar him," was all I said.

The boy shook and screamed, not sure what was going on.

"Him too." I pointed to the hippie. "See, we already have his number and since you two clowns dragged this shit out, and wasted our time, shit's gonna happen."

"Probably on his orders," Dame interrupted. "I know it's some shit I'd have my goons do."

He was right. "Exactly. So, because of that, we have all we needed. Pack up, family."

Staying where I was, I waited until everything was cleared up. Eventually, while they did so, I reached in the black case. I pulled out a tub which had a clear gel-like substance in it. Walking up to each nigga, I slathered the gel that was in the tub on the inside of the tires.

"Oh shit, are you anointing them, Uncle? What are you about to do?" Dame asked in glee.

There was nothing for me to acknowledge by what he said. I walked slowly by and splashed each one with more liquid. The weight of the tires on their shoulders was enough to make them slump pulling at the hooks in their flesh. Their pain was palpable. The fear was intense and through it all I lost my humanity to where I didn't give a damn.

It didn't take long at all for our presence to be cleared up. In the end, my family stood behind me once I was done. As I stared at the two who had helped in keeping me from my daughter I reached in the case pulling out two long matches.

Lighting them, I gave a nod. "We bid you adieu and thank you for the informative information."

Urgent pleas sounded. When I tossed the matches at both men, their screams became a song again as flames burst around their heads. Rings of fires made their heads look like lamps as their faces melted away from the intense heat. Eventually, the fire would ignite the rest of their bodies, then the can that was nestled in the black case. That can contained a flammable liquid that made fire burn so intensely that it'd leave no trace of DNA, bones, or anything else in its wake.

A solemn sigh came from me. I looked to my father then Kenya. "We have his phone. We have his car. We know that he has property. Let's go."

Kenya tugged at my arm. "Where did you learn that?"

I gave a shrug. "Overseas."

With the screams fading to nothing behind us and Augusta on our mind, we walked out leaving nothing behind but our vengeance.

Chapter 19

Father Rueben

I walked through the halls of the church, knowing that I had only one shot at getting the Knights off Carlos's scent. It was as if they had a built-in radar where he was concerned. Carlos had pissed off a lot of people on his rise to the top. There was once a time when the beast in my little brother rested peacefully. Carlos had been content being the "good" guy, but then life happened. That was the lie I liked to tell myself, knowing full well that the beast that lived inside every Orlando male was hard to put to rest.

Emmanuel Knight stood in the same aisle Carlos had just hours before. He was flanked by his two sons. They all stood well over six feet and were built as if they were once Mandingo Warriors. Dressed in tailored black suits and dress shoes with wing tips, his sons looked every bit like him, even down to the different colors of their eyes. One brown eye and one blue eye would always be how people knew Emmanuel Knight. His brown locs were pulled back and he stood regally, as if he ruled the world and all its inhabitants. There was a black cape around his shoulders that resembled a king's robe. His hands formed an upside-down pyramid in front of him. He, too, was dressed in all black. The Knight family emblem—a king chess piece for Emmanuel and two knight chess pieces for his sons—was etched on each of their lapels.

Emmanuel and I regarded one another with caution. Priest or not, I was still an Orlando and he was still a Knight. There was equal respect, but there was also equal distrust. From the east and west of the church, more priests filled in behind me. They flanked me as his sons did him. They stopped walking once I made it a certain distance from Emmanuel just as his sons took steps backward, out of respect, so we could speak frankly.

"Emmanuel, to what do I owe the honor?" I asked, speaking his name with the diction and enunciation he was known to do when people pronounced his name incorrectly.

"Father Rueben, how are you?" he asked, eyeing me.

"I am well, and you?"

"I'd like us not to beat around the bush."

"I'd like the same. This is a place of worship and I'm sure you're not here to do such. So again, I ask, how are you?"

"A bit disturbed."

I gave a wry smile. "And how does this involve me?"

"Caltrone was on my turf without the proper etiquette."

"I am unaware of what etiquette you speak, Emmanuel."

"Set rules dictate that he should make his presence known, as I do when I come to Cuba, *sí?*"

"If we were in Venezuela, your homeland, I'd understand your concern."

"Let us not play semantics, Father Rueben. This is my territory. When I go into Atlanta, I make my presence known. When we go into Miami, or anywhere else he has laid claim as ruler, we do the same. He sets foot in California and not a word? Am I to assume he is up to no good?"

"You can assume what you will, but I would suggest you not make an ass of yourself in the process. How would you know if Caltrone was here?"

"Word around is that his people snatched up a young lady around the area. I find it too coincidental that now one of my nieces can't be located," he said, eyes darkening as he said that last part.

"Your niece goes missing and it is my brother who is at fault? My brother, who isn't in California at the moment?"

"At the moment?" he questioned. "So he was here before?"

"Those words never left my mouth, Emmanuel."

As alpha males, leaders of our own factions, we both recognized that there was a battle of wits going down. He gazed at me, and I at him. Our eyes never left the other's. I kept my hands underneath my robe for a reason. Same as he kept his hands a certain way for a reason. Just as I knew his sons were armed, he knew my priests had more than the word of the Heavenly Father to fend them off.

"Have you taken your place in this rift, Father Rueben? I've always thought you to be the sensible one," he said.

Just as those words left his mouth, Savoy pushed open the doors of the church. Behind him stood several men and women from his biker gang. Savoy, the baby of us brothers, smiled his most wicked smile. He was always ready for a fight, ready to kill at a moment's notice. Their boots sounded like they were marching as they walked into the church. They all moved to the outside aisles, closing Emmanuel and his sons inside the circle of us. Savoy took his place just behind me, but a bit to the left. Emmanuel kept his eyes on me. He was unmoved. Same as I or Carlos would have been if the shoes had been on the other feet.

"Again, I do not know this rift you speak of. I have no knowledge of your missing niece. Neither can I speak on whether my brother was here. However, I can assure you, Caltrone has done nothing to your niece."

That was the truth. Carlos hadn't killed his niece. Antonio did. The tension in the church was thick, so much so that Emmanuel rolled his shoulders and cut his eyes around the room. He said nothing for a while, just stared me down. I returned the favor. He turned and headed toward the exit. Just before he walked out, he turned around and looked back at me.

With a sinister smile on his face, he said, "Tell me, Father, how is the beautiful Carmen Ortiz doing?" He showed all thirty-two of his perfectly white teeth. His natural canines were a bit longer than the average human's, making him appear to be a bit supernatural, if you will. "I hear Miami is quite beautiful this time of year."

He said that, then chuckled as he exited the building. I growled low in my throat, but kept my composure. It was an intimidation tactic on his part. He wanted me to know that he knew my secrets. That he knew where the one person I loved the most was.

I gave no response. Never allow the opposition to know your hand.

Chapter 20

Kenya

Augusta. Our next stop was Augusta. I felt something akin to elation wash over me. We were so close to Jewel. So damn close. I'd lost track of how many days or weeks it had been. It didn't really matter. Jewel was close. So close. All I knew was that we left home in July and it was a few days before August.

I found it odd as hell that when Tone told Dame that those two men in the barn had sexually assaulted our child, Dame seemed to flip his wig. That was odd because it was well-known that he did the same thing to other girls and women. I guessed turnabout was not fair play when it came to the Orlandos.

I half listened as Caltrone spoke to Dame and Tone outside the truck. I didn't care what they were saying. I just wanted them to hurry so we could move on to the next plan of action.

Once they were done talking, Tone climbed in the truck with me while Caltrone got back into the other truck with Dame.

"So what's next? We're on our way to Augusta, right?" I asked, anxious.

Tone dropped his head a bit before looking at me. "Yes, but we're going to wait a few hours before we go, maybe even a day. We'll arrive at night when we can catch him off guard just in case he's got backup."

My leg started to shake and I scratched the back of my head. "I don't understand why we can't just go now."

"Because he'll be expecting us, Kenya. And who knows what else he may do to her if he sees us coming. As badly as we want to go speeding down the freeway, it's imperative we remain smart about this, a'ight?"

I blew out steam and sat back. To be in the same state with her and not be able to get to her right away was killing me. Tears clouded my eyes as I stared out the window at nothing and everything.

"Kenya, will you trust me on this? We've come too far in this journey for you to start doubting me when we're so close," Tone said.

I glanced at him then quickly turned back to the window when a tear slipped from my eye.

Tone waited a few moments. Then he used his pointer finger to bring my face back around to his.

"We got this, okay?" he asked.

I nodded or, at least, I tried to. My head was too heavy to hold up, really.

"Good. We got this and I got you. Trust me."

I nodded as did he and we remained silent on the ride back to Alpharetta. After getting back to the mansion, I locked myself away in my room to wash up and to get my thoughts together. Isaac kept calling. I finally decided to answer my phone a few hours later after I realized he wasn't going to stop calling.

"Hi, Isaac," I answered.

"Where the hell have you been?" he barked into the phone. "I've been calling and calling."

"Looking for my daughter, Isaac. I've been looking for my child," I answered wearily.

"You couldn't answer the phone? You couldn't let me know you were okay? Where the hell are you?"

Somewhere in my head, I heard him. I wanted to be rational, but I couldn't help but realize he hadn't once asked me how I was doing. He hadn't asked me if I'd heard anything of Jewel. He only wanted to know why I hadn't answered the phone.

"I'm doing fine, Isaac. We found some information on Jewel's whereabouts," I said in a calm voice.

He grunted. "Clearly, you're doing fine."

I took a deep breath. I had to remember that I was the one who had cheated on him and he didn't even know it. I had to remember I was the liar. I was the one who enjoyed having Antonio touch me. I was the one wanting that old thing back. In the midst of it all, I couldn't help but think that if Tone and I had stayed together, Jewel wouldn't have suffered such a fate.

"I'm in Atlanta," I told Isaac.

"You're that close to home and didn't think to check in?"

"I haven't even taken a minute to rest yet." It was technically the truth.

"Where is he?"

"He, who?"

"Antonio. I bet he's there with you."

"Yes, he's in Atlanta too. We followed the trail to Jewel here."

"You two in the same hotel room?"

I sighed and tried to remain patient. He'd assumed the same thing when I was in Cuba. He was accusing me of being untrustworthy without coming right out and saying it. "No, Isaac."

"Well, when will you be home?"

"When I get Jewel. When we find Jewel. Has she tried to reach out to you?"

"If she had, you wouldn't have known since you didn't think to call me."

"Isaac," I snapped, yelling his name then catching myself. Tears rimmed my eyelids again. I felt like I was losing my mind. I had already lost control of my emotions. I said through clenched teeth, "Can you stop? Will you stop making this about me and you when the most important thing is finding Jewel?"

There was a knock at the bedroom door that I ignored.

"Do you know what's happened to my child? You haven't even fucking cared to ask what I found out. You're just worried about whether I'm fucking Antonio! I saw video of my child being raped! I don't give a damn how you feel about me not calling you. I am hurting. I am in pain. I don't know where my child is and all you fucking care about is why I haven't called?"

Isaac got quiet for a moment as if he was thinking about what I was saying. It was as if I was having an out-of-body experience. I was floating somewhere above the room watching myself pace back and forth as I yelled into my cell phone. I had no idea what Isaac said in return. For moments, he was quiet. All I could hear was him breathing on the other end of the phone.

After a while he said, "I told you about yelling at me. Don't yell at me," he snarled. "I told you over and over again to not raise your voice to me. You speak to me harshly when you're angry and sometimes even worse when you're not. You're abusive, verbally so. Is that what you're used to? Is that what that nigger, Antonio, taught you?"

I frowned, pulled the phone back, and stared at it like it had offended me. Isaac had called Tone "nigger" as if his kind of black were better than Tone's. As if Tone weren't a renowned surgeon. As if him being a scientist trumped Tone's smarts and status as a doctor. That angered me. The way he spoke of Tone, my missing daughter's father, made me want to fight him. If he had been in front of me, I would have tried to.

There was another rapid knock at the door. Tone yelled, "Kenya, get dressed. We need to meet the old man on the veranda."

I didn't know why I hadn't seen it before now. Yes, Isaac was a true-to-form Southern gentleman but he was also possessive and he believed in gender roles. If I were to be honest, I hadn't liked it from the beginning, but because I'd been told I had the mouth of a sailor when angry and words that could cut deeper than a double-edged sword, I was trying to do things differently. I was trying to be more submissive, so to speak.

"Fuck you, Isaac, and I mean that," I said.

"Don't do that, Kenya. Stop talking to me like that."

"Fuck off. You called me, knowing that finding Jewel is my top priority, and all you can ask about is Antonio and why I haven't called. I'll never forgive you for that."

He made some kind of guttural sound in his throat. "Listen, you're right. I'm sorry. I shouldn't have come at you like that, but—"

Whatever he was about to say got lost in transmission. Tone pushed the room door open. He walked in dressed in all black like he was about to go on some kind of blackout mission.

Tone used the heel of his foot to kick the door closed behind him then he closed the gap between us. "You need to put some clothes on and come downstairs," he said. His face told me he didn't give a damn who I was on the phone with, and common sense told me he had been standing outside the door long enough to know it was Isaac on the other end of my phone.

"You're naked with him in your room?" Isaac asked.

"I have to go," I said.

Tone took my cell and pressed the end call button. I wasn't naked. The towel was still wrapped around me. He stepped back and gave me a look up and down before moving to the closet in the room. A few seconds later, he came out of the walk-in closet with black leggings and a black tank. I hadn't even bothered to shop for any clothes so I was thankful that some woman in Caltrone's harem had clothing that fit me. I took the clothes and quickly put them on.

I made a move to walk out the door, but Tone stopped me. I whipped my head around to look at him. "What?" I asked.

"What did I tell you about being around these people?" he asked. He'd said "these people," not "my family." That wasn't lost on me.

I shrugged.

He said, "Fix your face, Kenya. Whatever Isaac said to you, put it in the back of your mind for now. We're in a house full of predators. If they smell any kind of fear or emotions, they'll eat you alive."

"I'm hurting, Tone. I can't just turn my feelings on and off like that."

"You can and you will. I'm not giving you a choice. So fix your face or I'll have you shipped back to Miami. I'm here with my father. I can make it happen and there would be nothing you could do or say about it."

I squared my shoulders and took a deep breath while glaring up at him. *Did he just threaten to send me home without my child?* I got ready to rip him a new asshole too, until he cupped my chin and came closer to me.

"Before you get ready to cuss a nigga, know I'm not here to be an asshole. I say that out of love and concern for you. That's it. I don't want these people to latch on to you. And I don't want you to lose your mind. We've come too far. We're almost there. Like you told me earlier. We're close to her. I can feel that too. So take a few minutes, a'ight? Get rid of those tears. Forget Isaac right now. Focus on Jewel. Jewel is all who matters right now, okay?"

I didn't nod. I didn't say anything. I just looked at him through blurry vision. He was right. I knew that. But my emotional state was so fragile right now, I could barely think straight. He knew this. He knew me. We gazed at one another that way for a long time. Memories danced behind our eyes. I could see myself in his eyes and I was a mess.

"Take five. Get it together. Come downstairs," he said.

I thought he was going to kiss me. I needed it. Would have been all for it, but he walked out, leaving me to all my demons.

Ten minutes later, I walked downstairs, expecting to see a house full of Orlandos. However, on the veranda there were only Tone, Caltrone, Benita, who was sitting a few paces behind Caltrone, and that Lilith woman. Benita looked up at me when I walked down. She was as relaxed as I'd ever seen her: hair down and biker shorts and a black sports bra on with casual running shoes. There was no doubt in my mind that she was armed, though.

Lilith sat dressed like she was in a corporate business meeting. She wore a power suit, white, that framed her athletically curvy body, with red bottom pumps on her feet. Her hair was pulled back into a bun at the nape of her neck. She wore minimal makeup and watched Tone a little too closely for my liking.

Tone and Caltrone were in the middle of a conversation about Augusta when I took a seat next to Tone. He gave me a cursory look then continued talking to his father. "I want to move in on the area just before nightfall. I need to draw out any security he may have," Tone said.

Caltrone nodded. He looked stressed. I'd never seen Caltrone stressed. But something was bothering him. Maybe it was the fact that Knights had been spotted in the area. "I agree, *mijo*," Caltrone said.

"Draw them away from wherever he is then move in on him when he's not expecting it. Clearly, homeboy isn't that smart."

"So tomorrow then? We move out. Get this thing handled as quickly and as smoothly as possible." Caltrone's accent was thicker than normal. He had a glass of rum in his hand but he barely took a sip. "How are you, Kenya?" he asked.

I glanced over at the old man. "I'm going to be a lot better once Jewel is back with me, us."

"Understood," he said. "You need anything, ask Lilith. She is at your disposal."

Lilith's body stiffened and she put her wineglass down. Benita cracked a hint of a smile but kept her head down as if she were reading her book.

"You want me to be her handmaiden?" she asked Caltrone.

"If that is what I asked of you, that is what you're to be," he responded. There was no nonsense in his voice.

Lilith looked at him head-on. "You're serious?"

Caltrone tilted his head and gave the woman a look that dared her to challenge him again. Lilith backed down.

"As you wish," she said.

I chimed in. "I don't need her to be or do anything for me."

I was about to say more until I saw Tiffany making a fast approach to Caltrone. She'd come from the house, dressed similarly to Benita. She stopped just inches away from Caltrone. He gave her a passing glance then turned back to Tone.

"It's been almost two weeks," Tiffany said.

Caltrone stopped whatever he was about to say to Tone. I thought he was about to say something to Tiffany, but he went back to his conversation with his son. Tiffany shifted her weight from one foot to the other. Benita laid her book down. There was concern etched on her features.

Tiffany looked as if she was about to cry. "You said for me to wait and I did. You said wait until Thursday and I did. It's Friday now."

Caltrone ran his tongue over his teeth and his brows furrowed. He turned to the girl. "Go to Marco or Frederick. I am in the middle of speaking to my son. Do not interrupt me again."

Tiffany shrank back a little. I thought the girl would have some sense and go on about her business, but no. Lilith was shooting daggers at her. Benita watched Lilith. I had the feeling that if Lilith did anything to Tiffany, Benita would have no problem blowing her brains out.

Caltrone continued talking to Tone. Tiffany looked as if she was fighting with what to say or do next. Part of me wanted to tell the girl to leave it be for now, whatever it was. But I knew trying to get her to let it go was futile, and I was right.

"I don't want to go to Frederick and I refuse to go to Marco," she blurted out.

The girl was wringing her hands and tears were in her eyes. I had the urge to get up and drag her away. I didn't want to see what Caltrone would do to her when he was angry. She had been nice to me and Tone. She always had a smile for me and she regarded Tone with much respect, not ass kissing, just simple human kindness.

"You said I just had to wait. I've been waiting and—"

Caltrone stood so fast, it scared me. I shrieked. Dishes fell from the table and a wine bottle spilled onto the floor. Tiffany screamed out and dropped to her knees like she was regretting her decision to speak up, like she knew she had fucked up. Benita toppled the chair she was sitting in and rushed to stand in front of Tiffany.

Benita threw her arm up to stop what I was sure was going to be a backhand from hell. I was certain that if Caltrone's hand had connected to Tiffany's face it would have broken a few bones.

"She didn't mean it," Benita yelled out.

Tiffany was cowering on her knees still. Lilith was laughing.

"She didn't mean it, *papi*. She's not in her right mind. Please," Benita pleaded. "I'll take her in the house and give her something to put her to sleep. I'll take whatever punishment meant for her. Just don't. *Por favor*."

The fear in that woman's face was real. It made me think about Jewel. Was she that scared of Keith? Had he instilled this kind of fear in her? I'd kill him if he had.

Caltrone dropped his hand and looked at the mess that had been made. "Get her away from me," he said coolly. "Then get back out here to clean this mess. *Vamanos*."

Benita quickly helped Tiffany from her knees and ushered her into the house.

"Silly-ass little girl," Lilith quipped.

I'd no idea what Tiffany wanted or needed that badly to risk the wrath of Caltrone Orlando, but I didn't like the vibe Lilith was putting off. Clearly, she was getting off on the young woman's misery and that didn't sit well with me. I could have been a bit biased. Maybe every young woman I saw put me in the mind of Jewel, but I wanted to tell Lilith to go take a hot bath in a tub of molten lava.

I asked, "What's wrong with her?"

"Little nympho," Lilith chortled.

I'd asked Caltrone, but she'd answered.

Caltrone grunted.

"Should probably get the little bitch some help, get her fixed," she continued.

"She would need no more help than you. Have you been fixed?" Tone cut in.

I quirked a brow then looked at him, wondering what he knew of the woman.

Caltrone had leaned to the side in his chair. His thumb and pointer finger resting against his face, reminding me of the photo of Malcolm X doing the same. I turned to look back at Lilith, who now had a scowl on her face while studying Tone.

With a look that said something stank, Lilith regarded Tone. "You don't know me," she said to him.

Tone sat back and, like a mirror, leaned over and propped his thumb and pointer finger against his face. Same as his father. He looked resolved, as if he was tired and had no desire to trifle with pettiness. "All bitches are the same when it comes to my father," Tone answered, coolly.

"Would that include—" Lilith started.

Both Tone and Caltrone turned their heads to look at her so slowly that the air chilled. The wind picked up as if even it knew that Lilith had almost signed her death warrant. Trees on the land rocked and swayed as if even they had become angry. I knew what she was about to say before she even thought it. She seemed to be a petty immature woman as such. She was also Caltrone's right-hand woman. A woman who could stand next to Caltrone had to be petty and a bit devilish, hence the name Lilith.

When both Caltrone and Tone said, "Say it," in unison, I knew Lilith backtracked to where she had them fucked up and decided to go in the other direction. Her face reddened and she took several deep breaths before turning her head toward Benita, who had cleaning supplies in her hand.

Benita rushed over and was set to clean until Caltrone touched her arm and told her to step back. She did as she was told.

"Erica, clean it," Caltrone said.

I looked around, wondering if there was a woman there I hadn't seen, but when Benita's eyes widened and Lilith looked as if her soul had just been snatched from her body, I figured that her real name was Erica. That smug look and arrogant demeanor went from simmering to lukewarm. She swallowed, pushed her chair back, and then stood.

I watched as Lilith knelt, in her power suit, on her knees like a servant, and started to clean the broken glass and wine from the veranda.

Caltrone said, "Knights are on the grounds in Atlanta. And they want me to know they're here. They're not hiding."

"I thought Uncle Rueben was handling that," Tone queried.

"I've placed calls to him. He told me he would get back to me once he had done what he needed to do."

"And until then?"

"We continue as if we don't know they're here."

I cut in. "Will this hinder us from getting Jewel?"

"Depending on why the Knights are here, it could slow us down a bit," Caltrone said.

My nerves started jumping. "But we're so close," I damn near whispered. I was afraid that we wouldn't be able to get to my child in time. Panic took up residence within me.

"We only know of what his henchmen told us. That information can go either way. Once we scout the area tomorrow, we'll know more."

"But didn't your men tell you the same thing? Damien's people also?" I asked, a bit of desperation now in my voice.

Caltrone gazed at me. For a moment, I saw pity in his eyes. He could hear my desperation and it seemed to burden him. There was a look on his face that said he was afraid of something. If I didn't know Caltrone the way I did and if I weren't paying enough attention, I would have missed it. It was a look a man got just before he went into a battle he knew there was a strong possibility he could lose. I wasn't able to readily recognize it at that very moment, but later I would. After the shit hit the fan, I would.

"Kenya," Tone called me. His voice was stern with just a bit of worry and concern.

I snapped my head around to look at him. Whatever he saw in me, looking at him from behind my eyes, it gave him pause. He got ready to say something, then he stopped.

"We'll get her back," he said.

I knew that Tone believed that with everything in him. I could sense it, feel it in his words and the way he looked at me. But something was crawling up my spine. Something in the back of my mind told me we may have been running out of time.

"Stay," Caltrone said, bringing me back to what was going on in front of me.

Lilith had been about to get up. She had cleaned up the mess that had been made, but Caltrone's order kept her down on her knees. I looked up at Benita, who was clearly pleased. Lilith, even being ordered around, still tried to hold on to that air of arrogance.

Caltrone knocked his plate off the table, intentionally. "Clean it," he ordered her.

Benita damn near smirked. Lilith's eyes watered, but she did as she was told.

"Never forget your place, Lilith. To fix your mouth to even utter an insult at a woman you have no idea of means I've allowed you to lick my face one too many times. And, like with any good dog owner, it must be addressed. No woman who has borne me a son is a bitch, especially not Carmen Ortiz."

I would have felt sorry for Lilith, but I didn't give a damn at that point. I picked up my wine and downed the whole glass in what seemed to be one swallow. I grew tired of Tone and Caltrone's strategizing. I needed to get to my phone just in case Jewel had tried to reach out. No, she hadn't after all this time, but still. Just in case, I needed to be there to answer. Just in case.

Chapter 21

Father Rueben

Time was of the essence. After Emmanuel Knight made his grand stand, I put boots to the ground to see what his possible next plan of execution would be. I had a feeling that while he was showboating with me, he was keeping me from noticing something else. I made a call to Miami and told Carmen to get on a private flight to a safe place that only she and I knew of. Not even her son, Antonio, knew of this place. I couldn't take any chances of her being hurt because of whatever Carlos had going on.

My niece had flown in. She was exactly what her father had trained her to be: a killer. She, in turn, had trained my grandniece, Maria-Rosa, to be the same. That would be a story for a different time. However, she would be a great asset if there was a need to defend ourselves.

"Father Rueben, I have some information for you."

I looked at Father Benoit and nodded for him to tell me what he knew.

"Queen Yasmine Knight has left the area. Sources tell us she's heading south to Georgia."

"Do we know the reason?"

"It appears that their youngest daughter, Caitlyn, is missing as well."

That made little sense to me. If the Knights' youngest daughter had been missing, then why had Emmanuel only mentioned the missing niece? Something was fishy about all of it. I had to wonder if Carlos had thought this whole thing through before jumping in headfirst. Yes, we all knew he loved Antonio, probably more than he loved any of his sons. More than likely because of the way he had loved Carmen, his mother. However, my baby brother should have turned over every rock and stone before charging ahead. He should have looked into this thing.

But I understood Tone was desperate. I could see it and feel it in his eyes, the way he moved, and even the way he spoke. I could even see it in the way he regarded his father, a man we all knew he detested.

"Also, Father Rueben, we have information that would lead us to believe that the boy who masterminded Jewel's kidnapping is, indeed, a Knight himself," Father Benoit reported.

My eyes widened and my soul sank. For as much as I hated what Carlos had become, for as much as I detested his presence anywhere near me at times, I didn't want him to be led to what could be his death. It didn't take a genius to figure out that some things just weren't right. Why would a Knight knowingly kidnap an Orlando? Or did the boy even know she was an Orlando? With the old beef between the two factions, I found it hard to believe that Jewel's kidnapper didn't at least know who her father was or that he was an Orlando.

My heartrate skipped a beat and sped up as I realized my brother and nephew were about to walk into a trap.

Chapter 22

Antonio

Kenya wasn't here. Immediately, it put me on edge. More than likely it was due to the fact that we were close to Jewel. Damn, I felt so drained and anxious that I felt lifted from my body. The old me watched as a spectrum, while the darker me sat in the chair and nodded at whatever my father was saying. I knew what he was saying but a brotha wasn't clocking. The longer we sat around the longer my child would be held against her will, harmed, assaulted. I couldn't just sit and let this go on any longer, not being as close as we were to her. My stomach felt nauseated from it all and I was ready to end this now.

My ex was breaking and changing. I could see it in her mannerisms and body language. Now that we weren't focused on our past, meaning fighting about it, and our attention was about our daughter, strangely it'd brought us close enough to get in sync about each other's stress points. And Kenya was reaching a point of no return.

"Father, might I make this suggestion?" I glanced to the right of me. I really didn't need Kenya to be breaking down, not when we were so close.

"*Sí*, my son."

"I believe that if we wait any longer, there could be more damage to your granddaughter. The fact that his trail led us here makes me believe that he's been planning for this moment, don't you think?"

Caltrone, in his typical regal manner, reached for his glass. It was filled with amber liquid and perfectly carved ice. One slow sip, and he gave me a look of appraisal. "But of course he is. His usage of Jewel has been like dangling meat to piranhas."

"The outcome isn't to bait us; it's to strike by inflicting fear, then effectively feeding us to the fish."

"*Sí*. Very good, son."

Subtle anger had my temples throbbing. The fact that this was all a ploy bothered me. Had I not been an Orlando, my daughter would have been safe from that monster. Her life would have continued as any other teenager's; her desire to learn about intimate relationships hopefully would have been shaped by healthier means. However, none of that was possible for her. My baby girl's life was practically mapped out for her because of my blood, and now she was nothing but a tool against my family.

If I could, I'd go back in time and change everything.

Exhaling, I rubbed my temple. "Once word comes back to us on the exact location of where he's at, I wish to go in sniper style. Covert. Darkness. No backup."

"And if he is sitting, waiting, in a trap for you?"

"Father, I'm an Orlando." I shifted in my seat, focusing my eyes directly on my father.

This was a moment of seriousness. I wasn't here to prove my worth to the man before me. I was here for my daughter and I needed him to understand that even though that was the truth of the matter, I understood that his blood ran through me. I had this.

"The training is such that, even so, I'll kill him before being killed."

Our jaws clenched and locked in a similar manner. Both of our minds were more than likely processing and calculating the outcome of the plan. I knew mine was. There was nothing

more to say in my request to him. This was
my right as a father. I really didn't need any
approval.

The sound of soft classical music filled the
silence between us. My father kept his gaze on
me and it reminded me of when I was but a child
staring up at him. I was taught to fear him. I was
also taught to admire him. Back then, he was but
a man who set himself up to be worshipped like
a god. I used to be one of those who worshipped
him because he was my father. A son always
craves the affection of a father, especially a
strong one such as Caltrone, regardless of how
insane the man was. Now, here I was falling
back into that old space of familiarity as he
watched me, probably checking for my weak-
nesses. Instead, now, I wasn't a scared child, but
a grown man. I didn't idolize him anymore, but I
did find myself having come to respect his ways
of doing things when it came to going after the
asshole who took my daughter.

After a moment of silence, my father leaned
back in his chair. His leg was already crossed
in a manner where his ankle lay upon the top
of his left knee. He placed his fingers together
to form a steeple in front of his chest. When his
cell phone went off, he dropped one hand and
picked up the small object resting on the arm of
his chair.

Listening, I watched his expression seem to change. It was as if he was proud of me as his son. I found that interesting. I also knew in the secret space in my being that I was afraid of that. Once Caltrone sees you as an interest, there was no shaking him. Ever. Even in death.

"Speak," was all he said in a commanding tone.

Before me was Satan himself. His face went blank. The nails of his left hand dug into the chair; then he scowled. Whatever he was being told wasn't good and, regardless of the outcome, I needed it not to be about my daughter.

When that evil scowl melted away into a sultry, insidious one, I knew that the conversation had switched.

"Keep the area clear. I want no one to know you all are there. Surround the house. Tone will be in charge, and you will listen to every command he says, understood? Good. Now hang up."

Leaning back in his chair, he smoothed a hand across the inside of his jacket. A cigar appeared between his fingers and he casually drew it out. Teeth on the butt, tearing into it then spitting it in a crystal ashtray on the small table with an inlay beside him, he watched me.

"Hmm." Slowly, he removed a lighter then lit up. I studied him as he took several puffs. The light haze of smoke curled against his lips, then his mouth. He gave me a grin then nodded.

"I agree. It's time that you took this in your control. You'll go in as you said; however, we never do anything completely alone. Our people will assess if the area is clear. Once in, you signal. I will be there, Kenya will be there, and then you and I will commence introducing ourselves to the *punta* who took my grandchild. Are we in agreement?"

That really wasn't a question, I noted. "*Sí*, Father. We are in agreement."

"Then good. We will commence and, after, I expect you to return to Miami and resume your life."

But at a cost, I thought, and soon found that thought answered.

"You will return to family, to me. Jewel is your daughter; and as it is your right to avenge every wrong placed upon her, such as it is my right to reclaim my prodigal son."

That sickness in my stomach had returned. It made my abs tighten and it almost made it difficult for me to keep a poker face. "But of course. I will return."

"Indeed. Your mastery skills as a surgeon are needed in this family and you will provide them. Your beautiful mother was always an intelligent woman, and still is. Her supporting you in your track through medical school was the best decision of hers and she garners my respect."

What do I say to that? I cleared my throat, then turned my hands upward on my knees and bowed my head slightly. "Thank you, Father. As long as I'm able to use my gift as a healer with these hands, then I will be able to take care of the family, as was my destiny."

Fuck, the politics of this crap.

"But of course." Tossing me his phone, Caltrone took a puff of his cigar. His pearly whites glinted as he held on to the cigar, pointed with a gesture toward the phone, then spoke. "There you go. Go through it. It is the address to the house. Prepare yourself. We'll be right behind you, *niño*."

This was it. First, let me say, I was stunned that he'd allow me to view his phone. I knew that this object held power. It was a part of him and I figured this was a gesture of something I wasn't in the mindset of computing as of yet. Immediately, my eyes went over the logistics of the map, the coordinates of what was around the area, and, last, the address.

"Will the team secure all exit locations, including roads going in and out, trails, et cetera?"

A deep, hardy laugh rumbled from my father. I immediately handed him back his phone, telling him thanks in the process.

"But of course, son. Who do you think I am? What you can't protect yourself from, I will." Regally standing like the king he made himself to be, my father stared down at me, that strange warmth back in his eyes. "Prepare yourself. By nightfall you will have your daughter back, my grandchild."

"Along with the head of that bastard." I stood with my father. He clapped a hand against my shoulder, squeezing, then backing away to leave. I waited, as was custom, my mind already calculating what to do. I now just needed to check on Kenya; then it was time to ride down to Augusta.

I wasn't surprised when I found her in her room. Actually, she was leaning against the balcony of her window with tears in her eyes and rage causing her body to tense. Quietly, I closed the door and locked it. I took my time walking up to her. What we were was complicated. I wasn't trying to purposely break up a damn thing she and her fiancé had going on. I just understood that, sometimes, shit happens. We still connected in the manner of sex, and it was helpful in keeping both of us from going completely insane; but, honestly, I knew it was short-lived. We weren't going to go there again; at least, so I thought.

"There're a couple of things that I need from you before we go," I quietly stated. My tone was low and even. I wasn't trying to make her feel ordered around. In this family, there was enough of that going on. I just needed her to understand that I was trying to protect her. If she could understand that, and understand how to play this endgame, then we'd be all right in saving our child.

"I called her cell phone."

Confused, I tilted my head to the side.

"I said, I called Jewel's cell phone. I . . . I just needed to hear her voice. Let her know that she's not alone. I just needed to hear her voice." Kenya's voice sharply cracked. Her emotions drowned in constrained tears that made her beautiful face contort in the pain of a parent who had lost a child.

That stabbed me right in the heart. Loyalty was a motherfucker. I walked up to Kenya, and carefully slid my arms around her. I pulled her to my chest. Allowed her cheek to press against my heart, as I cradled the back of her head.

"She's the one good thing that came from our marriage. Second. The second good thing. We were good for a while. Our love was good and Jewel made it better."

My cheek rested on top of Kenya's hair. I didn't close my eyes because I was already on edge being in this house. So, my focus stayed on the outside as I did my best in trying to comfort my wife; I mean, my ex.

"I remember when you first saw her, Tone. I never saw serenity until I saw you holding Jewel."

Kenya's soft sniffles broke me down. I hated for a woman, a good woman, to cry. It didn't help anything with the fact that we both were reminiscing about our little girl. This was not something we should have been going through. Our only worries should have been the mundane realities of teen life and soon-to-be empty nesters. I should have been worried about putting my foot up the ass of a good-spirited, little, young nigga who found himself adoring my daughter. The trafficking and kidnapping of my princess wasn't something any parent should go through. "So, why did I fail her? Where did I go wrong in raising her?"

"You didn't, Tone. I feel like I did, but I know we didn't fail in raising her," Kenya answered.

"That monster was just that good in finding her weakness."

Damn. She sounded like an Orlando there. "I'm sorry, Kenya." The thickness in my throat made it hard for me to swallow so I cleared my throat instead. "I hadn't realized that I spoke out loud."

The sensation of her shaking her head against my chest made me hold her closer. "It's okay. It's okay. I'm dying here, Tone. I'm literally dying."

"You have to stay strong. I came up here to tell you that—"

"Her phone picked up," Kenya interrupted.

I swore it was like a knife cutting across my throat at what Kenya said. My head tilted to the side. I leaned back, my body becoming rigid as my heart thumped hard against my chest. It hurt so much that I found myself rubbing it as I stupidly asked, "What did you say?"

"Jewel's cell picked up." Turning from me, Kenya walked back to the edge of the balcony. She fisted the railing then slammed a fist down against it.

A brother was frozen in place. All blood has rushed from my body. I was locked in my emotions and not able to will myself to breathe, to move, to think, to even blink. All I heard was, "Her phone picked up. Her phone picked up."

"He was hurting her, Tone. Making me listen to her screams." Kenya turned. The emotion in her voice was intense. It was frantic. It was shattering. It was hostile. It was furious. She pushed at my shoulder to stop my shock then clapped her hands under my face.

I will kill that motherfucker!

"Do you hear me? He was hurting her! Why are we still here?"

Several blinks and my mind seemed to reboot. Everything Kenya said made me snarl. If I had been a pit bull, I'd have growled. We were close to our daughter, and this shit was the last straw.

"I don't fucking know." Taking Kenya's wrist, I forced her to exit the room. I needed blood, and I needed it now! "It's time to go."

Chapter 23

Antonio

Leaving Kenya in the hands of my father didn't take but a second. Breaking down what she said happened when she called our daughter didn't take but a second. What did take long was getting to Augusta. I wanted to be there as soon as I stepped out of my father's home, but that isn't how traveling works. Each of us rode out in blacked-out Escalades. Each SUV left fifteen minutes after another, so not to appear suspicious. That meant that, because I was in the first car, I left first.

Kenya had explained that she'd called our daughter, only to get her voicemail. A secret part of her had done it in hopes that she'd pick up. Kenya was holding out faith, but that didn't happen. Therefore, because of that, she called back, this time just to hear our daughter's voicemail again. When she waited for it to click over, on the last ring her call was answered. She explained that she heard nothing for a long time. All she heard was dead air, then a whimper. Then the sound of springs creaking as if it were an old bed. Then screams and cries. Then our daughter calling for our help, followed by a loud, crashing bang. Then harsh laughter and silence.

It didn't take any coercion in getting Caltrone to leave. He was like me, already leaving before she could even form another sentence. By the time we made it, it was so dark not even shadows could be seen. We were parked hidden in the forest that blanketed the terrain. From what I saw from the map, the place was a dilapidated old farmhouse sitting on almost a full acre of land. Because it was near farmland and forest, the next home to it was maybe ten to twenty minutes away if walking.

That was perfect for us and clearly it was perfect for him. This meant that if anything loud popped off, no one would really hear it. The forest would swallow up the sound and provide cover in our battle. Rearing myself up for the main battle, I rolled my shoulders, then climbed out of the SUV. Grass and leaves crunched under my military-grade boots. I stood in all black from head to toe, full ski mask on, black functional jeans under which I had on armor leggings and a beater, Kevlar vest, and a ballistic jersey. I was ready for battle. Military-grade face paint added to the mix, camouflaging me into the dark.

It was dark. Not the typical darkness. Naw, this was the kind of inky blackness that always swallowed the swamps of Florida if you found yourself out too far from the city of Miami. I grew up in this type of darkness. As a kid, I used to watch the skies on the back patio, counting the stars and hanging Christmas lights as my only source of vision while *mi madre* left me to teach tourists how to salsa and merengue. *Mi madre* trusted no one but my aunt Mariposa. Whenever she was in town on tour with her band, she'd usually watch me. Other times, I'd sit in the back of the clubs studying my mother's dance moves and soaking up the music, or in the back staring at the skies.

Thinking about being a kid back then always put a smile on my face. It was the start of me, the start of my growth into the man I was today. Let me break this rehash of my past for a moment. There's a saying I grew up hearing the old heads back in Cuba saying: "A lie runs until it is over-taken by the truth." My life at that time had been nothing but truth until I had to embrace my bloodline. But back when I was an innocent kid, living a relaxed lifestyle was what gave me the tools I needed to survive in a world where the only light you sometimes can get came only from the stars.

Which was why I was able to move through the pitch-black darkness of my surroundings. I did it with ease. I was at peace in it because I controlled it. I manipulated my circumstances and, tonight, I was merging into a part of my bloodline I had chosen to avoid for years. If I hadn't asked for help, I wouldn't be where I was right now. Though I didn't like what I had to do to get here, I was grateful about it.

A sharp scrape then skittering noise drew my attention. Some feral cat was making its rounds and had run past my feet while I entered a room. Musty smells tried to irritate me but I kept my cool. I had been trained well and this was nothing but a cakewalk for a nigga like me. I kept moving, stepping over shoes, running into cobwebs, all while feeling my surroundings become tighter.

I was outside a dilapidated old farmhouse in the rural outskirts of Augusta, Georgia. Being in this state wasn't something I wanted, but circumstances occurred that pushed me to the brink of no return. My daughter willingly leaving, only to be kidnapped, was that push. No man in his right mind would allow another to take from him, no man, and I was no different. The problem for the person who took my baby girl was that he didn't know who the fuck I was, or maybe he did. Either way, he clearly didn't know that my bloodline was ruled by insanity. But, he was about to.

Painful, muffled cries drew my attention. I was getting closer. Ahead of me was a horizontal bar of glowing light indicating that I was approaching the front of a door.

"Keep calm and listen as I taught you, *mijo*," was muttered by my side.

A large part of me didn't want to just listen. My daughter was behind that door and I wanted to rip her from her captor's hold, but I couldn't. All I could do was nod and keep my calm as I was told, and listen.

"I want to go home," was shouted out and it made my gut clench in response. It also made my finger curl against the trigger of my long-range gun while I listened to a grown-ass man bark out his wrath.

"This is our home. Shut the fuck up and act like you're happy about it, Jewel!"

From my position, I dropped to a knee, and slid a mirror under the large gap under the door. I counted only my daughter and a bulky motherfucker. He appeared to be in his mid-twenties.

Rocking Tims and a black polo shirt, nigga had a rugged pretty-boy look that I knew was the reason he was able to lure my daughter in. I watched him pull off his shirt then throw it to the side.

The nigga kept walking around a bed where my daughter lay with only a large shirt covering her body. At seventeen, my baby girl was breathtaking as her genes dictated it. It was something that was always a problem for me being that I was a father who didn't take kindly to my only child being gawked at. See, her mother and I had her when we were sixteen and every day it was a battle for me to protect her from going through the same shit her mom and I went through at her age.

"Look, I didn't mean to hurt you like that, Jewel. I was just excited about us finally getting away from your pops and having you here with me," I heard while watching the mirror at my feet.

My daughter was tied up. She sat on her knees bound by several ropes linked to the headboard of the bed. Her face was untouched but her arms and, from what I could tell, the top of her thighs were cut and bruised. Fat tears fell down her caramel brown cheeks and she bit her lip while watching her kidnapper's every move.

"I know, but I just want to go home to get some stuff, Keith," I heard her say in a pleading voice.

"Why can't you be happy about what you got now, huh? I brought you here 'cause I thought you'd appreciate a spot like this. Used to belong to my grandmother. Thought you'd appreciate it but, no, all you do is bitch now. Shut the fuck up, damn! You stay nagging," he spat out. Keith took several steps toward the bed, reached out, and gripped her by her neck, squeezing as he did so.

My baby girl's neck was not that big, so considering that nigga was built like a basketball player and his hands were large as fuck, I knew that it wouldn't take much to snap her like a twig. When he pushed her down on the bed, straddled her, and kept choking her, I watched as he grabbed her breasts and forcefully squeezed them.

The sound of frogs croaking seemed to soothe me. Everyone on the team knew to wait for my signal. I needed to hunt alone. Stretching my arms out, I stood near my ride staring up at the skies mentally preparing myself. Nothing but the stars shined. I inhaled and caught the scent of dew, moss, grass, and other vegetation. It was then that I moved out, leaving my whip behind me. Midnight goggles adorned my eyes; my choice rifle was strapped to my back. Two blades were in my boots, some were on my wrists, then there were my pistols. I had them on my waist, at the small of my back, on my calf, and then some.

"No, *mijo*. We control the moment, not him," was said to me.

Realizing that was truth, I waited and, when I felt it was right, it was then that my shoulder met the side of the door and broke it down. Shrill screams mixed in with the pounding of my gun against that nigga's head. I became the light in that moment, and it became my duty to follow through on everything that had been planned.

Chapter 24

Antonio

"What will you do to protect family, *hijo?* Remember what you've learned about what it takes to be a true Orlando." A harsh zipping noise then a grunt filled the room while my father walked around me with revulsion marring his furrowed face whenever he looked around the room. "Good, you remembered your rope work," he said in pride, thumbing his wrinkling nose.

There was a loud clamoring that ended in a satisfying bang. I moved around to clear out a suitable space with my foot. Books were everywhere. Old pizza boxes with stale crust pieces were piled up under a crowded computer desk. Soda and water bottles mixed in the cluttered madness and I knew that my pops would not be entering this room under normal circumstances.

But because this involved my daughter, who sat in a ball on a bed in the farthest corner with her eyes peering over her bruised and bloodied knees, I understood that he'd be right by my side. Soiled bedsheets lay on the floor. The bed my daughter had been chained to, now unchained with the help of my pops, was the cleanest area in this fucked-up cesspool. Used condoms lay under the bed and staring at them only pissed me off.

Without missing a beat in assessing my surroundings, my fist slammed into the temple of my daughter's kidnapper. A second blow followed to land on his mouth and I hunkered low to stare in his face. Muffled grunting then clinking and repetitive scraping started. I watched in silence as this nigga bulked, tugged, and pulled against his bindings.

"Cable cord, my friend. The only thing you're doing is causing your own pain," I said in a low, even voice.

Around his waists were taut cable cords. His forearms were bare and on one was a crest branding of a knight chess piece, along with various other tattoos. Disposing of his body was going to take the lessons I learned from my father in my hunting of this nigga, along with some useful medical science.

The menacing baritone chuckle of my father began as I heard him say in Spanish, "Come with me, granddaughter. You do not want to be here for this, sweetheart."

"Daddy?" my daughter called out to me with fear lacing her voice.

"You can trust him." I paused in my words, resigned to what I had to say next. "He's your grandfather and he won't hurt you."

Jewel's pained whimpering started again. I looked up to see her sobbing but staying where she was. Fury simmered in my spirit. It made me punch her kidnapper in his throat. I then reached out to vise grip his Adam's apple.

"She's crying, you see that? You hear that? Huh?" I said through gritted teeth as I stared him in his beady eyes. "Jewel, go with your *abuleo*."

When my baby girl didn't budge, I got ready to bark at her until she shockingly said, "Daddy, I want to stay. Please."

There was a change in her, I knew that when I blasted through the door and she shouted my name and help. My baby wasn't the innocent seventeen-year-old she once was. Long gone were her carefree teenage years and now sat a young woman aged drastically by the trauma she had experienced. It broke me down and it had me focusing my attention back on her kidnapper.

"*Sí*, a'ight."

"Yes, this is good. It's time you learned the family way, granddaughter, and visually see what wrong choices can lead to," Caltrone said behind me in a cold yet coddling tone.

He casually moved through the cramped room, turning on lights with his latex-covered hands. I watched from the corner of my eye while he walked into the hallway only to come back later with Kenya behind him. In her hands were several containers I had asked her to bring up from the car prior to entering this place, and on her shoulder was a huge sports bag. She had spent her time in the car waiting for our signal to enter. Kenya had fought us tooth and nail about waiting, but I had to explain without yelling that we didn't know what we were walking into and we needed to scope the place out, which she eventually accepted. Now, she was here, ready to go into our next plan.

Hastily, Kenya sat everything down then rushed to our daughter, climbing onto the bed. "Jewel! My baby," she cried out.

Both Kenya and Jewel held each other tightly, sobbing against each other's shoulders. "I'm so sorry, Mommy. I thought . . ." Jewel's voice cracked in her emotion. "It wasn't supposed to go down like this. I'm sorry."

I had so much that I wanted to ask my daughter and yell at my daughter, but I had more important, pressing matters. Behind me, Caltrone pulled out everything I needed, and I helped while keeping my eye on our common target.

"Keith Taggard. No, your real name is Keith Anthony, right? Yeah. Pick your poison." Holding up two water jugs, I sloshed around one with yellowish liquid and another with clear liquid. A contemplative chuckle came from me; then I slammed them down, standing from my low crouch. Taking two long strides toward him, I gripped him by his face then pulled from his mouth his restraint: a dirty sock and shirt.

"Nah, I'll pick. See, I've changed a lot since you took my daughter. Never in my life would I have believed that I'd step into this type of mentality, but I learned something from my pops: treat the world as your enemy so you never are surprised when she fucks you over. Best believe, my friend, I'm learning that well."

Keith struggled, grunted, and then spit at my feet. "Fuck you! She's mine. I made her become exactly what I wanted and needed. Fuck you, Orlandos."

Nigga gave a sour laugh then tilted his head to glance at Jewel and Kenya. "Baby girl became my dirty bitch. Sucked me off, let me fuck her in every—"

"I hate you," Jewel screamed, shaking where she sat.

At that same time, Kenya aggressively pushed off the bed, rushed the chair, then wailed on Keith. I stepped back to let her do her. She sent her elbow into his face, hitting his nose; then she pulled his head back hard to the point that, if she had the strength, she could have snapped it as she glared at him.

"Stop playing with him; fuck this bastard up," she spat out at me in rage. "This motherfucker took our daughter. He hurt our baby. Do what the fuck you're going to do. Fair exchange is no robbery."

Funny enough, Kenya made my day. I smirked, studying her heated cocoa eyes, respecting the fire there and her anger. I then glanced at my father, who stood back with malice in his gaze. He said nothing and there was no need for him to do so. I knew the game. *Never let your target manipulate you. Take your kill how you want. Patience is an excellent battle tactic.*

"No doubt, mama. Fair exchange is no robbery."

And that's what I did. Yanking that bastard by his mouth, I widened his mouth, punched him again when he tried to fight me, and took one look at Kenya as she held the back of his head. A clear plastic tube was in my hand, along with a black PVC pipe fitting. With purposeful ease, I forced that fitting into his mouth then smiled.

"Do you know what we had to endure in finding you both, huh? Do you understand the mental breakdown we went through?"

Keith struggled while attempting to spit the tube out.

I chuckled as I put my black rubber gloves on then scowled. It was not a good thing for him, because when I did so, Kenya sent her elbow into his throat, which caused him to lunge, choking.

"Take it like a big boy, Keith," Kenya taunted, slapping his face.

Pleased with that, I continued. This time with slamming the clear tube into his mouth and happily forcing the tube down his throat and into his stomach. Tears slid from Keith's eyes, along with a thick trail of saliva from the corners of his mouth while he fought his bindings.

My baby girl's gasps then sobs mixed with Keith's and I spoke on. "Let me slowly break down what we exactly had to endure in hunting your lowlife ass down, a'ight? All while we enjoy this tender moment of, well, your throat game, nigga. Listen well because we have a long night and many more gifts to give you, my friend. Now, let's start with Mexico then Texas."

Patting his face, I turned my back and squatted, pulling out a mason jar of scorpions. I then stared at the jugs that would be a part of something I learned to do in medical school: forced ingestion or force feeding. In the jugs were two base liquids: one water, the other a natural body-absorbing acid and other foul, corroding shit that I knew would kill him slowly but also would disappear without issue. By the time I was done with my plan, Keith would no longer be a threat to my daughter, or anyone else. *Never ever fuck with an Orlando.* That was legacy.

An hour later, it stank. More like reeked of the foulest of scents. The potency of it was so profound that my eyes watered. Reaching behind me, my gloved hand gripped a red plastic cup. I dropped it into warm liquid then splashed it on the source of the stench: a young nigga who felt that he could get away with taking from another man, taking from a father. The insult of it made me suck my teeth out loud in disapproval as that gagging continued.

"You shit yourself, Keith," I said.

Slobber hung from my captive's lips. His head lolled around and he tried his best to stare at me from behind his right eyelid, swollen shut, to no avail.

Running my gaze over the droplets of water that skimmed, dripped, and splattered onto the plastic runner that was under his chair, I watched him in thought. In my mind, I was back in med school studying the cadavers and developing my surgical techniques, except now I was squatting with that red cup between my thighs.

"So you're awake now? Huh?" I asked in a cool, calm voice, still watching him with dark, seething hatred.

The amused baritone chuckle of my father filled the room. From my peripheral I made note of a man I never thought I'd seek out to ask for help. Because of this situation, I had stepped to the throne of the devil and accepted his counsel, and now I had to embrace the council seat he crafted for me at birth. As my father smoothly took several strides forward, his handsome face was twisted in disgust and similar anger. His disgust was not at what Keith said, but at the filth of the room and the shit that spilled to the floor from where he sat bound.

Holding a painter's mask against his nose and mouth, he stopped near me, then took the mask away. "I like your fire, but we don't want your fear."

Swiftly my hand clamped down on Keith's, and I angrily snapped his middle finger back and watched him scream.

"*Hijo,* I think we need to start back at the beginning, right?"

Looking up at my father's stone-cold expression, I nodded, then stood up, grabbing the clear tubing. This time, I dropped it purposely into this nigga's shit then picked it up, frowning.

"So unsanitary, son," I heard Caltrone say, flashing his pearly whites then stepping behind Keith to grab him by his mouth and force his lips apart. "Pick your poison, Keith."

"No. No. No," Keith sputtered.

Capping his mouth then jamming the shit-covered tube down his throat, I dropped low and picked up a pair of dice. Clicking them around in my fist, I dropped them then smiled. "Looks like your lucky day. Scorpion venom it is." Tapping the jars behind me, I watched as the liquid slowly crept up the tube.

Keith sputtered and jerked and tears ran down the side of his face.

Pressing my gloved hands on top of Keith's bound ones so they would cut into the wood of the chair, I leaned close to his face. "So, back to the beginning, as my father said. We found ourselves in Mexico, trailing your lowlife ass, and guess what we find out."

My gaze shifted to lock on my father as Keith's screams filled the room and he nodded in approval.

"Right. Death."

Chapter 25

Antonio

The sound of gagging and choking was now a comforting melody for me. I stood in front of Keith as his chair scraped and rocked. He was exhausted from being pumped with fluids and forced to swallow scorpions. The anti-venom shot I gave him was the only thing keeping him going. Which was purposeful because I wanted him to suffer for as long as he hurt my child. Darkness had eaten at my sanity and goodness because of this nigga and I was aiming to hear his excuse why. Now, if he didn't give it, I really didn't give a damn. Having him suffer as he was right now was enough. It put a huge smile on my face and had me slapping him to get his attention.

"Now, how was that story, Keith? That was the day we learned your real name and the day I learned the extent of the pain you put on my daughter by your friends. Through your friend Fallon's death, I learned and saw what you did." The sound of straps harshly rubbing against each other as they zipped to snap and hold Keith's arms down behind him kept me in my zone.

Casually moving around the small room, I frowned as I kicked items out of the way and pressed my hands behind my back. It was then that I heard rustling on the bed and Kenya gently whispering to my daughter who spat out, "No!"

My attention went to her immediately as I stared at dark eyes that matched my own.

"That day . . . That day, Daddy . . ." The pain in her voice was broken and rimmed in agony and anger. Fury was apparent in the way her knuckles turned white from gripping the ends of her T-shirt on her thighs.

I saw blood seeping from her palms and the old part of me, the doctor, was ready to tend to her wounds, but my attention was on the man who had her here. Sadly, another part of me, a darkness that was angry at my daughter, was also tapping at the door in my mind, but I had to keep that back for both of our sanity.

"I thought we were going back home. He told me that we'd be going on a quick trip, a tiny getaway to just chill and have fun. Like a kind of spring break. That's why we were in Mexico. But when he got this strange call about picking up some package and I heard it, that's when he changed."

Keith grunted loud, struggling and shaking his head.

An amused chuckle came from me. "Ah, so you say she's a liar? Bet that's what you're trying to say. But, check it, you'll have your time to talk soon. Just relax, okay?" Patting his hand, I snapped another finger and nodded at my daughter to continue.

Wide-eyed, Jewel scooted to the edge of the bed. "I'm not lying though. We were checking out when he got that call. Before that, he was acting all normal; then, after, he told me that he was going to take me home but he wanted to have me meet some of his family. Because he said he loved me and wanted them to meet me. So, thinking that he was down for me, I gave him more money and we left for Houston."

The shame in Jewel's face ate at my spirit as she spoke on, "I didn't feel any type of way until we got there and they decided to throw some type of party. Then, I mean, by then it was too late. I'm so sorry. I felt sick and woozy and wanted to go, but I ended up in the back room and—"

"Pills and laced weed. We found evidence of
that at the apartment," I said cutting her off, not
wanting to hear more.

I stared at Keith and he locked his watery eyes
on me. When that nigga winked at me, I sent
my fist into his face. That chair rocked back and
forward. Rolling my shoulders, I turned to head
back to my table where Kenya now stood.

"Here," she said unfolding a bundle that had
various tools in it.

Caltrone had given her the instruments and
told her to learn to use them. However, it was
the duffle bag she picked up and handed to me as
she walked past Keith, where our daughter sat,
that was important in this moment.

The sound of Kenya grunting then sharp, muffled screaming had me noticing Kenya holding a
fingernail in her hand. She gave me a blank look,
then turned to where Caltrone stood holding a
bag.

"Drop it inside, *mami*," he said with a sinister
chuckle. "You are a prized treasure."

Sweat started beading at my temple. I wiped
it clean with my arm then smirked when Kenya
strolled back to where that nigga sat and wrapped
her arm around his neck in a choke hold.

"Now pay attention to what *papi* has to say.
It's only going to get better," she hissed in Keith's
ear.

It was funny to me because in my years of knowing Kenya, she never spoke Spanish, except here and there due to what she learned from me. The diction in her tone was all what she absorbed from me and our time around my mother and other Latinos, and it was a mixture of our black heritage as well. That blend and the way she occasionally threw specific phrases in there always made me smile and, at that moment, I was grinning wide.

Walking up to the chair, out of old habit, I smacked her ass then focused on the threat. "We brought you a present from Fallon," I said.

Leaning over to dig in it, I pulled out a plastic jar. It was one of those bulk-size mustard jars. Unscrewing the white top, I tilted it forward and let Keith peer inside. When he started screaming, I smirked.

"See, after letting Fallon relax on the Judas Cradle, it was my nephew who decided to collect several souvenirs. See, I'm not about harming children but since you decided to harm mine and he participated, I mean, what could a nigga like me do in that situation? I thought, I am a surgeon and these people sure do look like they need my help." Tapping my chin, I chuckled and then grinned. "What would Keith do?"

As I spoke, Kenya had let him go so that I could do my work.

I moved to stand back in front of him and glared. "I asked that a lot on my journey to find you and you know what? I tapped into my joy of dissecting. All thanks to you and my nephew, Mark. But back to Houston: taking Fallon's woman apart was difficult, but I say that it was when my nephew began to work on those children that everything changed. I blame you for it. Just to let you know. All that blood, these eyes in this jar, the teeth, the ears, and the tiny fingers: all your doing."

Stepping back, I sighed and stared at the ceiling in a long, drawn-out silence. I'd never betray my truth of how disgusted and torn apart I was in taking the children out and watching my nephew take out everyone associated with Fallon. Killing on this mass level wasn't something I had prepared myself for but, at the time, I was in it and there was no turning back. I knew I was going to burn for my actions but, at the same time, I didn't care. This was vengeance and I intended to dish it out to those who hurt my child.

Flexing my gloved fingers, I tilted my head somewhat to the side and saw from my peripheral Kenya reaching for Jewel. It was time for her to take care of our baby girl and move her out of this room. She gave me a slight glance and I knew that Jewel had seen enough of my madness. Kenya quietly escorted Jewel out of the room then closed the door behind her. I knew that she would be back shortly, because she too wasn't done flexing her wrath.

On the way out, Jewel turned to look at me as she weakly struggled to walk out and said, "He said the Orlandos killed his grandparents and raped his girl. That they took everything from them and he was going to do the same."

I gave a loud sigh after the door closed and I settled on what was said. When Caltrone laughed, I saw him crossing his arms over his chest and smirking.

"*Mierda!* Bullshit. Everybody says that and though you wouldn't be wrong, this time you are. I don't know of you or your family," he casually gloated as if he didn't give a damn, or as if that wasn't an effective excuse. I liked to believe that my father felt that Keith's reasoning wasn't an effective excuse, because the motherfucker was crazy and I had fallen down that pit with him.

Focusing my attention back on Keith I stared down at him, standing wide-legged and studying him. "My pops might be right in that, so guess what, homie? You know that this is your fault and all of this is only a taste of what you're going to feel. Now, let's move on to our next adventure. Going after your girl, Donna."

It was then that my father walked out of the room. He immediately came back with another bag then set it on Keith's lap. "We have another special gift for you. Something I took pride in hunting down personally," my father said.

"And something I had to pull apart," I added.

Unzipping the bag, my father walked to Keith like an old-school gangsta. No expression, just stoic blinks, and I stared at our enemy the same way. He widened the opening in the bag and an arm with a similar chess piece on the shoulder plopped out, along with a mane of black curly hair. When Keith let out a fierce roar from behind his mouth binding, I knew that we had hit home.

"On to the next phase, *hijo*," my father said while handing me my next torture device.

I gave my father a nod. He stood against a wall, making sure not to touch anything. Also keeping my movement to a minimum, I thumbed my nose while walking around the chair. "'Baby girl put up a fight and she gave it up so damn good.' Isn't that what you said on that tape with my daughter?" I asked, my voice turning to pure ice.

Pausing at Keith's shoulder I didn't miss a beat when I dropped a clear bag over his face, pulling hard. I watched the nigga shake and quake and try his best to pull at his restraints, including kicking while the plastic conformed to his face, vacuum-sealing itself to his face. Counting slowly, after watching his body and checking his pulse, I knew that he was close to passing out.

That was when I ripped off the bag, leaned close to him, and muttered, "It's not time for you to burn in hell. We're not done here and Satan is waiting his turn. So sit back and listen."

Chapter 26

Kenya

As I walked Jewel out to the van, I felt a mixture of elation and disappointment. I was happy as hell to have my child back, but disappointed that it had taken us so long to find her. There was no doubt in my mind that she was forever changed behind this. She had been missing for five months. For five months she had been in the hands of this monster. I prayed she didn't hold it against us. Even though she had left willingly, I prayed she knew and understood the lengths we had to go to find her.

Jewel walked like she was sore. Judging by the bruises on her body I was sure that she was. Her lips were dry and chapped. Dried blood caked one corner of her mouth. She looked like she had aged way beyond her seventeen years. She looked down at the ground and then at the trees like she hadn't seen outside in a long while.

She smelled, too, and I couldn't wait to get her somewhere so she could bathe and relax.

Then she, I, and her father would have a long conversation.

"I'm so tired, Mama," she said once I helped her into the van. She looked exhausted. Her hair had grown longer, but it was matted to her head. There was no need for me to ask what she had been through because I had long ago figured it out, not to mention the evidence of her ordeal that I'd laid eyes on.

"I know, baby," I said. "Keep the blanket wrapped around you until we leave. We can get you a hot bath and some food, and then we can all talk, okay?"

I didn't care that she was soiled and filthy. I ran a hand over her head and then caressed her face. We were quiet a moment after I slid into the van to sit next to her. I wrapped my arm around her as she laid her head on my shoulder. So much had changed in our lives over the past few months. More had changed over the last month to be exact. I'd been away from my home and away from my fiancé. I'd been on the road and locked away with my child's father for over four weeks. My relationship with Tone had changed, and more for the better actually. But that was another topic for another time. We'd found Jewel and that was the only thing that mattered to me in the moment.

Soon, her body started to shake and her tears returned. I let her cry as I did also. We shed tears for different reasons I was sure.

"Is that man really my grandfather?" she asked.

I sighed then nodded. Jewel had no idea that her father and I had signed over our lives to find her. "He is, baby. He is."

"Why didn't I know about him?" she asked.

"Your father was . . . He felt as if it was the right thing to do. I didn't even know he was your grandfather until a few weeks ago."

"He looks like that man you put in prison," she said. "The man who used to be on the news."

I knew she was referring to Lu Orlando. One day I would explain it to her, but now wasn't the time. Just as I was about to tell her that, gunshots rang out in the house. I jumped. Jewel screamed.

One shot.

Two shots.

Three shots.

Four.

My heart leapt into my throat. There were only three people in that room. One was tied down to a chair. That only left Caltrone and

Antonio. For as much as I appreciated the old man for helping us find Jewel, something in me still wouldn't allow myself to trust him.

Four shots.

I scrambled from the van, almost tripping over my own feet, rushing to get to Antonio. I rushed in to find Caltrone cursing in Spanish, Keith laughing hysterically, and Tone lying facedown on the floor.

"Antonio," I screamed. My heart had leapt into my throat. Tears clouded my eyes. He was lying facedown, blood pooled underneath him.

"*Por qué no Jewel decirnos alguien más estaba aquí?*" Caltrone spat out venomously.

I ran and dropped down near Tone trying to turn him over. The fact that Caltrone was angry and asking why Jewel hadn't told us someone else was there didn't register to me. I didn't even see that the cane Caltrone was carrying had been pulled apart and a long sword was dripping with blood. Didn't pay attention to the fact that the old man was sweating bullets and had started pacing the floor fussing and cussing in a mixture of Spanish and broken English.

Nor did I question the reason Keith had seemed to flourish with new life as he laughed and laughed. "I'm good now," he groaned out. "So good now. You killed her. Thought you

Orlandos were a smart bunch, especially you, Caltrone, but you did it. You really did it," Keith taunted then threw his head back and laughed. "You cut off the head of a daughter of Emmanuel and Yasmin Knight."

Keith was so tickled by the notion that he started to choke on his own blood as he sat like a rag doll in the chair. I didn't care in the moment. I flipped Tone over to see blood covering where his heart was.

"No, no, no," I moaned. "Antonio," I screamed as I shook him. "You better not leave me and Jewel here with this crazy-ass old man, Tone. I swear to God if you're dead, I'm going to kill you," I cried. "Tone," I yelled again, still shaking him.

Panic rippled through me. I never thought about what it would mean for Jewel and me if Tone died. I never thought about how that would affect our relationship with Caltrone and the rest of the Orlando family. If Tone were killed, it would kill his mother no doubt, but it would crush me. *To have done all of this to get Jewel only to lose Antonio . . .* The thought caused a blinding moment of grief to overtake me.

Before the reality of the moment could set in, Tone opened his eyes. "He had another girl in here," was all he said.

I breathed a sigh of relief and rushed in to hug him. He returned the hug then gently pushed me back. In his hand, I saw a gun. He slowly sat up and looked behind him. It was only then that I noticed the headless body of a girl. Near Caltrone's feet lay the head of Caitlyn Knight.

"She came out of nowhere," Caltrone barked. "Gun in hand, shooting to kill. She shot my son," he said.

I didn't know if he was talking to me or himself. If I didn't know any better, I'd say Caltrone had lost touch with reality a bit.

"She came from down the hall, yelling and screaming about something. I don't know. She shot me then shot at Father. I grabbed her; the gun went off. I took the gun from her and she picked up a broken piece of glass. Ran for me with it. I shot her and then Father took her head off. It happened too quick for me to think rationally. I had no choice but to kill her or she would have killed me," Tone said. He glanced up at his father. He too seemed to be at a loss for words.

"I didn't mean to shoot her," Tone said once he looked back at me; only, he wasn't looking at me. He was looking at our daughter who stood in the doorway of the house with a horrified expression on her face.

"Oh, my God. Caitlyn, no," Jewel cried. "No, no, no," she kept repeating. She slowly walked to where the girl's headless body was. Before kneeling beside it, she cradled Caitlyn's head in her arms. It was as if Jewel were trying to magically attach her head back to her body.

"Oh, Caitlyn," she cried. "Keith told me you were dead, bestie. Daddy, why?" she cried then looked back down at Caitlyn's lifeless body. "He did this to you. He did this," Jewel said so low we could barely hear her. "It's all his fault."

She rocked back and forth like she was rocking a baby in her arms. Jewel's eyes fell on her father and, for a moment, I assumed she was blaming him. Tone must have thought the same thing because his eyes seemed to gloss over with the kind of grief that couldn't be explained.

Jewel laid the head of her best friend down and then stood slowly. Keith started laughing again.

"You were always stupid, Jewel. Believed any- and everything I said, even after I brought your stupid ass here," Keith rambled.

"She's your blood, Keith. She was your cousin. Why? Why would you do it?" Jewel asked him.

"She wasn't shit to me. Always thinking she was better than me. They all did but, in the end, I won," he croaked out then laughed manically. "I won."

Jewel was trembling. She was facing her attacker, but she was trembling. Her emotions had the better of her. It was only then that Tone and I realized her anger wasn't directed at him, but at Keith, the man who'd stolen what was left of her youth. She closed her eyes briefly then she turned as if she was about to walk away. In hindsight, we'd all probably say it happened too fast to stop it, but while it was happening, it all seemed to play out in slow motion. Jewel jetted forward and yanked her grandfather's sword from his hand.

Tone was quicker than she was, though. He quickly grabbed the sword from her while wrapping her in a protective embrace.

This was the way of the Orlandos. There was a "one-drop rule" that applied to that bloodline: if you had even a drop of Orlando blood inside of you, you were tainted and could kill at a moment's notice. All it took was that one flicker of fate to ignite the switch and Jewel had just flipped her lid.

"Nah, baby girl. They don't get to turn you into a monster. You keep your soul. Your mother and I have done away with ours for you," he said to her.

Jewel broke down. She was inconsolable as her father held her. Tone passed her off to me.

He had the sword in his possession now. Keith never saw it coming. Antonio shoved the sword through his side and then petted the man on his head. Keith's yells rumbled through the small room as blood poured down his sides.

"You don't get off that easy, you piece of shit," Tone taunted. "Keep breathing, nigga. We ain't done yet."

Chapter 27

Antonio

"String this bastard up," Caltrone said with a tone so deadly it straightened my spine and chilled my bones. "I've reached my endgame."

Jewel stood trembling beside me. She had tried to kill the man who had kidnapped, raped, abused, and drugged her, all the while forcing her across the country while committing other foul acts against her. It seemed her best friend, who now lay dead and headless on the filthy floor, was also a victim of Keith's madness.

I pulled Jewel's trembling body backward. "Take her back to the van," I said, more like ordered. "I don't want her to see this."

Before Kenya could respond Jewel spoke up. "No. You have to, Daddy."

My head spun around with a frown. "Have to what?"

"You have to let me see you kill him," she cried. "I want to see him die. I want to see him suffer." There was a wild, panicked look in her eyes, one that told us she was no longer the innocent child we once thought she was.

"Jewel, I don't think so."

"Let her watch, Antonio. It's her right to see her torturer tortured. Turnabout is fair play," Caltrone dictated.

"Pops—"

"Let her watch, Antonio," Caltrone said again, this time sterner than he did before. The old man's eyes were glazed over and his evil had been unleashed.

I stared at my father as if I wanted to challenge him. The air in the room had grown colder. The tension between father and son rippled around the place like static electricity. Although Kenya knew there was a devil in me, the one in Caltrone was bigger at the moment. The old man took breaths so deep that every time he inhaled and exhaled it looked as if his body bulked.

The muscles in my jaw ticked and a scowl took over my features. I stormed around the mess of a room, kicking trash out of my way. Kneeling in front of the black duffle bag, I snatched out chains and ropes. "Daddy got this."

I didn't realize I said that out loud as I dragged Keith behind me through the house. I was in my own zone when we strung him up. My father's voice was in my mind and beside me, of course.

"Tie him intricately like I taught you as a boy, *mijo*," he ordered. And like the dutiful son I was, I complied.

Silence was my friend. My gloved hands moved with precision while I worked. I was told I was the Picasso of surgeons. Tilting my head to the side, I had to agree. My rope work was on point. With a tap of my hand against his rib cage, I grinned. There was nothing to be said. He was about to die.

Behind me was my baby girl. I felt her watching on in equal silence; however, there was this energy from her, a cocktail of rage, grief, and sadness. It saturated the air. It connected with my pain and Kenya's pain and it flowed back to her in a sense of support through this madness. Once we got her home, we for damn sure were going to work on her healing with us as a family.

"No worries," I heard my father say. He grabbed Keith by his nuts. His muscles bunched in constraint as he pulled that nigga apart in glee. "Death is your companion," he added then handed me the scalpel.

Flesh fell at my father's feet. I watched on as
if I were an intern. As I held that scalpel, I then
reached up to insert an IV that pumped fluid
in him. It was a cocktail that forced him to stay
awake and feel every pain we gave him. Now, it
was my turn.

"Damn, *vato,* do you feel that?" Gripping him
by his chin, I stared into his eyes. "I pray that
you do. Every time you touched my daughter,
this is what she felt."

Somewhere in my darkness I heard the gagging of my daughter and Kenya. There was
nothing but darkness in my soul while I gripped
the neck of that bastard shaking him awake.
Hate recognized hate, and a demon recognized
a bitch who was trying to live the life of a monster. Something insidious crept in my heart. It
made me laugh slowly. It made me assess that
bastard's face, memorizing every detail of him,
until . . .

Rippppp.

Pleasure in the sensation of a surgeon's forged
steel slicing into the ribcage of my daughter's
attacker made me smile with malice. The tiny
blade in my hand was cleaner than a motherfucker. I mean, that shit went in like butter with
no damn protest except by Keith who began
seizing when I cut into him. *Mmm, shit.* That

was delicious, that pain, that fleeting moment of fear, that realization that maybe, just maybe, he fucked with the wrong Orlando. And that, right there, had my dick ready to stand.

Rip. Rip. Rippppp.

Blood washed over my hand, mixing with the red substance that ran down Keith's face. His mouth formed an agonizing, huge O. That same ruddy essence tinted his teeth while he screamed. I almost told him, "Thank you. Thank you for making this moment so precious for me," but I didn't. Instead, I said in a slick taunt, "Baby girl, do you think he loves this pain, or does he need more?"

"He's fading. Give him more fluids, *niño*," Caltrone ordered. He held his chin with a clean glove, standing over my shoulder as if critiquing my work.

While I fed the boy the juice, Jewel inched a little closer. She seemed so tiny and malnourished, like Dobbie from *Harry Potter*. Her hair was unkempt, lacking luster, and she was swallowed by a dingy, tattered shirt. It pained me. It angered me. From the corner of my eye I could see her leaning in to look Keith square in the eyes. Her once-warm eyes were dark like a true Orlando, iced over with cold hatred for the bastard in front of her.

"Damn, Keith, you look so pretty," she spat out as if trying to cut him with her words. "You look so good, nigga." Her beautiful face contorted in a mask of hatred. "Damn, you want more, don't you, you dirty slut-bitch? That sound you're making says you want more. Give him more, Daddy."

Her words made a lion roar in me. He had to die. I gave her a nod, and focused back on Keith. He had a hanging flap of flesh from where I sliced his skin. I grabbed a handful and pulled.

"Oh, shit. I'm sorry. I'm sorry. Please! Stoppp," Keith screamed.

I looked at Jewel and she shook her head.

"Did you stop when she asked?" I paused legit waiting for him to answer. When he didn't, we continued our show.

Taking my daughter's pound of flesh from Keith, then working on mine and then Kenya's pounds of flesh, I could hear him laughing in between, in harsh drags.

"Just keep dragging this out. My guest will shut this shit all down—"

"Shut the hell up and die, boy," I heard Kenya interrupt in a harsh shout behind me. "Take your fucking like a big boy and swallow that fucking tongue of yours, or he'll rip it out."

I chuckled low. I took the bags that my father walked my way with, then set them out in front of Keith.

"It appears you haven't learned a thing, boy," Caltrone spat out. He walked up on Keith and showed him a sizzling branding post that he had made. That thing was made out of wire hangers and shaped in a crude manner. Without a blink, or a care, he shoved it up Keith's ass.

We all watched as he shouted, tears running down his face. It was then that he screamed, "Stop. Stop!"

But we didn't. This was all about the levels of torture he had put on our daughter and the next was mental warfare. Unzipping the bags, I dug a gloved hand in the bag and looked up. Kenya was there. She held out gloved hands, and I handed her what was inside of each bag. She arranged some, looked at Keith, grabbed him by the head, as she jammed a scalpel into his gut. I realized that this was her way to show her help in this. She then walked away, and I chuckled, finishing putting down my prizes, slapping each item out in a nice circle.

"Say hello to your little friends, ya? I mean family, cousins, friends, yes, that's better." I smiled with such glee.

I chuckled while he struggled against his restraint. "Oh shit, you didn't expect that I see. Interesting. Well, there she is. My beautiful partner helped with this one. Say hello."

He stared at me with such anger that I wanted to make it worse, which I did.

Pulling the scalpel out without a care, I slammed it down against his thigh, pulled up, then slammed it down onto his right thigh. Staring up at him, I made the sign of the Holy Cross and moved to walk around him.

"Fuck all of you. You all will burn just like me. I ain't scared," Keith roared out then sobbed, his body shaking from all the trauma we put on him. "I ain't scared. This shit was worth it."

He said that over and over and over until I snatched his throat. That fear pumped up quickly in his eyes with each digit dug into his trachea. With a flash of metal glinting in the light he knew what time it was, and strange panic flashed across his face when that blade scored his throat.

With a slight lean to the side, I whispered into his ear, "This house is next."

"No." He garbled his words. "All I got."

I figured that much from what I learned in finding him. This house was the last place he felt safe and it reminded him of the people who actually gave a shit about his ass. Too bad he shit on whatever legacy they had. Fingers digging into his scalp, I twisted his head back and forth watching his carotid vein give him a bloody apron until there was nothing but his gasping.

Patiently, I watched his slowly blinking eyes until the sound of a bullet whizzing into his skull sent me shifting backward. I turned to where it came from and was greeted by a five foot eight woman with almond brown skin, wing-tipped lined brown eyes, thick thighs covered in tight dark blue jeans, with hips for days. Long red-tipped locs with gold locs jewelry pulled to the side into a large bun and a face like that of a round-the-way girl turned model stoically stared at us. The elegantly manicured hand that held the Glock that took out Keith turned, and that was when my world fell apart.

With swift effectiveness, another bullet escaped then slammed into my baby girl's skull knocking her head back. I'd never, until the day I died, forget the frozen shock in my baby's eyes or her last words.

"Daddy. Momm—"

Shouts rained out as I stared, stunned. I heard my father shout out in a mixture of Spanish and English. He stood over Kenya and my baby girl, in shock.

"What grounds do you have to do this, Queen Yasmine? What fucking grounds?"

Kenya seemed to be sinking into the floor. Her tears mixed with the red that covered her. Her pain shattered our souls and synced with mine. She held Jewel's lifeless body against her chest, her words repeating over and over: "My baby. My baby. No."

"We came so far, only to lose our daughter to this . . . this . . . bitch."

I didn't realize I said that out loud until I felt myself roar, with my arms stretched out wide, "Why?"

"Knights' order of fair exchange," said the bitch. Staring me in my eyes, there was a note of sadness there, mixed with a subtle note of madness matching my own father's. She turned to look Caltrone in the eye without even a blink. She dropped a set of pictures with a note, along with a photo of Caitlyn's death. Just as silently as she'd arrived was how she left. She disappeared into the darkness of the hallway with a hulking brotha. I couldn't register who he was.

Her voice echoed to us, saying, "Now we're even."

We heard the sound of a screen door opening then closing. A menacing smile was frozen on Keith's face. It would be later when I realized that this was his plan all along: war.

Chapter 28

Kenya

No.

No.

No.

No.

This couldn't be happening. I knew what it was. It was all a dream. A nightmare. *Somebody wake me up. Please. Wake me up.* Antonio had to wake me up. In the nightmare, some woman had come from the blackness of the woods and shot my baby between the eyes. I sat, holding her in my arms. Her eyes were wide, fixated on me. Her blood and brain matter had been splattered on my hands, shirt, face.

Please, my mind screamed. *Antonio, wake me up!*

In my nightmare, Caltrone's voice roared like a lion as he bear-hugged Tone to keep him from going after the woman who had shot our child. Even in the chaos, we figured out that Caltrone's men had been taken down. We were out here alone. Caltrone knew that if Tone followed that woman out of the house and into the woods, he wouldn't come back out alive. Caltrone couldn't allow that to happen. He loved his son. Had just gotten him back. He couldn't lose him. Not now.

Tone's yells and cries matched mine. I screamed in my nightmare. Slobber hung from my lips. Rage filled my lungs threatening to drown me. I screamed. I yelled as I rocked her. I rocked Jewel like she was that seven-pound, six-ounce newborn again.

Yes, that was it. In my nightmare, she was but an infant. She was sleeping. She was going to wake up any minute now. She was always hungry when she woke up.

In my nightmare, I stood, struggled to pick up my baby. She was so heavy. Why was she so heavy? I needed help. I looked to my right to see Caltrone holding his son, still struggling to stop Tone from trying to go after that woman. Tone was angry. He was livid. Tears ran down his face in his madness. He let out a guttural roar that would make a jungle go silent in fear.

Caltrone had to let him go. I needed help. I needed to lay her down. She was tired. She was so tired that she had fallen asleep right there on the floor.

"Help me," I cried as I looked at Tone. "She's tired. She needs to lie down."

Why was Tone just letting Caltrone hold him? Why wouldn't he come to help me lay her down? She was so heavy for an infant. So heavy . . .

If I had been in my right mind, I would have realized it wasn't a nightmare. I would have realized that my child wasn't sleeping. It would have registered that she was dead, that some woman had come like a thief in the night and stolen her, again. We'd done so much, killed so many, set a blazing trail across parts of North America to find her, only to have her stolen once again.

Over the next week, my sanity would return. I'd realize my child was dead and that we needed to lay her to rest. My nightmare was real and it was never going to end. Jewel was dead and she wasn't coming back. I knew that part would break Tone and me down, but the way Caltrone had handled it surprised all of us, even his family. For weeks, Caltrone shut himself in the basement. He locked himself away from everything and every-one.

Father Rueben and Uncle Savoy had been flown in. Apparently, the Knights had prepared for a war. However, Caltrone hadn't set the detonator off yet. While every Orlando faction was ready for whatever, Caltrone remained silent. The only people he would allow in to see him were Antonio, Carmen, and Father Rueben. No one else was permitted.

"Are you ready?" Tone asked as he walked into the room.

We were preparing to leave Cuba to head back to Miami. We'd left Atlanta on the first thing smoking back to Cuba. Caltrone had ordered an extraction of sorts. We buried Jewel in a cemetery next to all her ancestors. She had a beautiful home going. One that I was barely there, mentally, for. It wasn't until they lowered her all-white and golden-trimmed casket into the ground that I completely lost it. Tone had to sedate me. He knew me so well that he'd known to bring what he needed to the burial.

"No. I have no desire to go back home. I don't want to leave her here," I said.

I looked out at the landscape. Cuba, this part of Cuba, the part Caltrone had carved out for himself, was beautiful. However, all I kept seeing was that farmhouse in Augusta. I kept seeing that woman come from the shadows like the grim reaper. As the trees rocked and swayed outside and the smell of rain penetrated the air, I was numb. Gray clouds took over the sky and thunder clapped in the distance.

"You have a life you left behind. You probably should get back to it. You can't stay holed up in this room like my father is in that basement," he said.

Tone's voice was low. Sadness emanated from him like it did from me and Carmen. Carmen had fainted at the news of her only grandchild being shot down like a rabid dog after all she had endured. The woman fainted and, once she awakened, she had to be told again that Jewel was gone and she wasn't coming back. I'd never seen the utter look of horror on that woman's face before and I never wanted to again.

However, nothing broke me down the way Tone's tears had. The way he had fallen to his knees when we were alone, laid his forehead to the floor, and sobbed. His wails and tears, the way he apologized to me for failing me, for failing our daughter, broke me down some more. He cried. I cried. We mourned together.

I turned to look at him. "I don't have a life anymore. My child lies in rest here."

Tone watched me. He watched me the way a man watches a woman he cares for but whose mental well-being he worries about. Dressed in all black, the only color he'd worn since Jewel's death, he gazed at me. His eyes were red. His shoulders were kind of slumped, but he tried to be strong for me and Carmen.

"What about Isaac? What about the bakery?"

"I don't care about Isaac or the bakery. I called Isaac and told him to go to hell. I told him to fuck off and never call me again. All he cared about was if I was screwing you. Once I get back to Miami, I'll tell him to his face. I'll sell the shop."

"Don't sell the shop. She, Jewel, loved that place. Don't sell the shop."

He was right. Jewel did love the shop. She loved when I thought of a new cupcake recipe. I would always remember her smile when she would come in after school with her friends. I wouldn't sell the shop. "I won't sell the shop," I said.

I walked over to Tone, not sure about life anymore. Not sure of almost anything. But what I was sure of was that Caltrone Orlando had been right. All his philosophies and the way he thought about life in general had been right. No matter how much good you do, none of it

mattered. Evil would find you and evil would
have its way with you.

So, now the chips would fall where they may.
I would do all the things Caltrone had asked of
me. I would be that criminal-minded attorney
at law. I wouldn't be a bad guy. I wouldn't be a
good guy. I would be what life had made me to
be: criminally insane.

So, I laid my head on Tone's chest. I wanted to
cry, but I couldn't cry anymore. I listened to him
tell me that his father was doing badly. Tone told
me he had seen the old man in a way he hadn't
ever seen him before. Caltrone had been played.
Caltrone had been bested. Caltrone had lost.

"The old man is broken," Tone had said.

"He didn't know her," I said.

"But I'm his son, his prodigal son. The son
who came back home because I needed his help
and he failed me like I failed you, like I failed
Jewel. Uncle Rueben told us some things. Said it
had all been a ploy. Said that Keith had planned
it all from the beginning. Keith was a Knight. He
had cameras set up in that house so that the bed
he kept Jewel on was in a blind spot. So, there
had been no way they could see what he had
done to Jewel. The feed was sent to the Knights'
headquarters. There was no sound. So it looked
as if Pops and I were torturing Keith for fun.

Looks as if we killed Caitlyn because she was trying to defend Keith. Keith did all of this because
he thought Caltrone killed his grandfather. It
wasn't Caltrone who killed him."

I shook my head. Couldn't listen to any more
of this. I didn't want to hear any more about how
the supposed sins of Tone's father had killed our
only child. "So, now what? We retaliate, right?"
I asked.

Tone nodded. "But not right now. We wait.
We plan. They're expecting a war right now."

"For how long do we wait?"

"Uncle Rueben said we wait until they least
expect us. It could be a month from now. Could
be a year from now. Could be years from now,
but we wait. We wait and we plan. That's two
families Pops will have to fend off sooner or
later. The Kulu Kings and the Knights. The Kings
have all right to come after Pops, but Uncle
Rueben and my aunt just revealed something
to me that will surely bring Pops and the Kings
back to the table to have peace talks. However,
that's another time and another story. We have
to worry about the Knights now. Now, we do
whatever Pops asks of us. We become those
people we didn't want to become."

So much had been said, almost too much to
process. I was about to say as much until my

stomach lurched. I tried to rush to the bathroom but ended up throwing up all over the floor on my way to the toilet. I'd been doing that a lot for the past two weeks. Thought it was because of the grief of losing my daughter, but when I looked at the pregnancy test on the counter everything changed. During our brief affair, Tone and I had created another child. I'd only taken the test a few minutes before. Had asked Tiffany to get it for me.

Tone followed me to the bathroom. "You okay? Need me to get you something?" he asked.

I pointed to the counter as I emptied my stomach.

Epilogue

Antonio

Three Years Later . . .

"Y é chate pa'ca ¡Guaya, guaya! Eso me gusta, eso me encanta como tú me lo haces, papi a mi me pone sata . . ."

My attention focused on the robin blue Caddy that carelessly drove by blasting reggaetón, clueless of the evils of the world. The sun was blazing bright. There was a breeze that caressed my nose with the scent of the fresh sea and palm trees. In that Caddy were four people. All young, all slick from what I assumed was beach fun. Each one was in a string bikini or board shorts, dancing and twerking in the Caddy. Their music trailed up to where I stood on the balcony of my high-rise security condo. A part of me would enjoy the energy they kicked off. But the new me

saw them as vain idiots who were clueless about
the evil realities of the world. If they crashed, I
wouldn't give a damn. I'd probably toast them
in a salute and continue watching from my view.

A light giggle stilled my darkening thoughts.

Jewel, Daddy misses you.

Clearly, our life had changed. Where I was
living with an open sore in my heart, the soul
that I once had was locked away, leaving only a
hanging shard in its place. That shard belonged
to the only lifeline I had now, Kenya and our
little girl. I turned to see my wife watching me
from the bed we now shared. Crinkled white
linen sheets framed her as if she were Venus
rising from the sea.

Her nut brown skin was golden from the sun.
Her bountiful, swollen breasts and her thighs,
legs, calves, and feet were lightly covered in the
sheen of our sex. She was emotionless, except
for the hand that caressed the swollen belly that
protected our growing children within: twins, a
boy and a girl. Both futures promised, like our
second child, to be protected by my and Kenya's
deal with my father to be full Orlandos.

I lied. When she connected her broken, dark
gaze at me, a spark of light was there. It matched
my own and in tandem they faded into the
solemn bleakness of our shared first loss. Since

the murder of our baby girl, everything changed in a way neither she nor I could have predicted. Kenya left behind almost everything she had with Isaac. I insisted that she stay with me, only because I knew that if either of us was alone for too long, we both would be swallowing the barrel of a gun.

That reality made the transition easier for us. In the beginning, we weren't focused upon rekindling our relationship, but we were together, so to speak. At that time, we were two people locked in similar pain and loss with old love and memories keeping us together. So, I guessed that made us a couple. We had no label. We weren't in that type of thought process to even go there, but now three years and a beautiful daughter named Serenity later, I openly called her my wife. She was mine.

Kenya kept the bakery open, having it run by family, then she opened another one, naming it after Jewel too. The bakeries were her homage to our daughter. Her other life as a criminal lawyer was her crossroads in the light and dark as an Orlando. Her award-winning skills were far-reaching. She had saved a group of children being trafficked to Atlanta in a semi truck while burying, literally, the men who had collected them.

As for myself, I became a sought-after surgeon, top in the nation. My skills led me to open
a clinic that helped not only the community and
incoming immigrants, but all Orlando fronts.
Because of our life in Miami, both of us stacked
legit and shifty money to the point that we were
multimillionaires. However, we didn't give a
damn about it. It was just something to pass on
to others, and our legacy.

"How long will you be gone?" she asked.

I turned Kenya's way then walked slowly
toward her with our daughter Serenity on my
hip. My head bowed and I kissed the top of
her soft, coiled 'fro, just like her mother's. I
loved this little girl with every inch of me. In
her big eyes, I saw Jewel, but I also saw the
unique spirit that was my baby girl Serenity.
She helped make that shard in my spirit bigger,
yet guarded. A cool breeze brushed around us,
caressing us, causing my pants to quake. Kenya
shifted and closed her eyes with the same caress
of that breeze. I couldn't help myself in thinking, in asking, *Jewel, is that you?*

The weight of my body caused the bed to
indent where I sat. I let go of Serenity and
watched her crawl then curl up against her
mother, seemingly relaxing peacefully. My wife
shifted to kiss the top of her head and inhale her

scent then hold her close while returning her attention to me. Only when Serenity was in her arms or when Kenya and I were making love did the old her surface.

Watching on, I took Kenya's small foot in my hands, allowing my palms to swallow it as I gently rubbed. "An hour. Two, stretching. You'll be able to see everything once I'm there."

"And you're sure they are there?"

I bowed my head, and lifted her foot to my lips to kiss the top. "Yes. Father gave out the order so Uncle Savoy is waiting."

"Then don't make him," she said.

"Of course." Slowly standing, I looked down at her and our now-sleeping daughter. "I won't."

It didn't take me long to meet with my legally insane uncle Savoy. I enjoyed the drive from Miami Beach to Flagler Beach. That same breeze seemed to stay with me, filling me with a comfort I hadn't had in a long time.

"Keep me covered in your grace, baby girl," I muttered as I parked my convertible drop top. "Because I don't deserve it."

Sun glinted against the surface of my sun-glasses. Music thumped: a mixture of African beats and Haitian hip hop. I gave a nod to the beautiful, smiling people around me walking toward outside plantation ruins. My hand dropped slowly from my hat, then slid into the pocket of my linen suit pants.

Women watched me in awe and I knew why: I had a clean face, my hair was cut low, and I was dressed in the style of a Miami businessman with the collar of my shirt open and buttoned down to show my smooth collarbone. My sepia-toned skin had that golden sun kiss that people envied. I trumped up that megawatt smile of mine, one that was a façade for the world, and I knew I smelled fuckable.

Everything was a ploy. Everything was a trap meant to draw people in, and keep me unassuming. This allowed me to take in the schematics of the area: four groups of security flanked the area, my Uncle Savoy and cousins in the mix. We didn't acknowledge each other and that was good.

I strolled through, grinned, held the hands and wrists of many flirting women, then found my seat in the back. I was cordially invited to the wedding of Tamika LeMont, niece to the queen herself, Yasmine Knight. Young Tamika was to be married to Jeffery Knight, nephew to King Emmanuel. Ain't love grand? Photographers flashed cameras. I happily posed in my seat for

393

a few, my hat tilted forward to shield my eyes.
I was here for a show and, look, it now was
beginning.

I checked my cell because it was kicking off its
vibration. The old man left me an encrypted text
telling me to fly back to Cuba with the family. I
had two long-lost nephews to meet. Two young
men who, I was told, reminded him of me. When
I read that, I couldn't help but think, *I pray not.*
Loss can change a person and I wouldn't have
wished that on them at all. If anything, they
needed to run and hide from this family or take
us down. But, that was the old me whispering in
my mind with that.

Music played, people danced, ate, waiting.
When the tune flipped to that standard wedding
jam, a beautiful cocoa sister stepped out to
sing in Haitian Creole. She had the look of the
woman who'd killed my Jewel. Everyone here
had the look of that bitch. Adjusting my jacket
with one hand, I quietly sat and observed. The
couple was beautiful walking down the aisle,
both in all white, matching the scheme of light
colors and white.

The bride was a gorgeous dark cocoa, where
her husband-to-be, standing and watching with
his Kappa brothers, was the typical color of shea
butter. The crowd was a nice, intimate medium

size. It had to be, considering where the wedding was, which allowed for the next part of the wedding.

The loud rat-a-tat-tat of a semiautomatic peppered the crowd. I sat back as everything went down like a *Scarface* film. Bodies quaked; others popped up then fell to the earth. A few tried to rush to see where the gunfire was coming from, but no one could see who was shooting. I sat with my fingers pressed against my mouth in a steeple. When a few eyes looked my way, I played the game and hunkered low trying to stay clear of the fire.

"Nooo," was screamed repeatedly in the crowd. "Please, stop," followed.

My hat low, I looked around waiting for the shots to stop. When they did, a slick smile spread across my face when I heard, "Help! Help. Please, someone, help!"

"We need a doctor. Someone call the police."

"Daddy."

"Mommy."

Those two screams made my body tense immediately. I was suddenly back in Augusta. My baby girl was shot backward into her mother's arms. Her face was forever frozen in shock. My baby girl, my world, Jewel . . .

I found myself gripping a folding chair hard as the smoke cleared. Sweat trickled down my back until a sharp scream reverberated in my skull and brought me back to the present.

"Help!"

Slowly, I looked around. I walked forward with my hands up. "I'm a doctor. I can help. Allow me to help."

There were several people still living, some crowded to the right and left, others standing around the bloodied bride, groom, singer, and wedding party. Everything looked like a Renaissance painting. Streamers fell, as did a podium stand. With each step, I moved with purpose. As I moved closer, Uncle Savoy stepped in behind me near the door. Screams made me look to the side and I saw him grinning with a cigar between his teeth. He chuckled, then again let off more rounds.

While Queen Yasmine and King Emmanuel Knight were not in attendance—something about their private flight being delayed, which was courtesy of my father, of course—this would let them know that we declared war.

My uncle finished off the sides of the wedding while I, well, I found myself with a scalpel in my hand. As I approached the group before me, I kept one gloved hand behind me and the other upward. They killed my daughter in cold blood. No care. No concern about the truth of their own who started this shit. Keith had won and he took my baby from me, along with my sanity. There was no more functional Tone. There was nothing but the son of Satan, an Orlando prince.

Eyes dark like those of my father, I took a knee, gave a deep, menacing chuckle, then swiftly connected my blade to the throats of everyone around me, including the bride, groom, and the singer.

"Shh, stay where you are. I can help. I'm a doctor."